FUGUE STATE

Fugue State

STORIES

BRIAN EVENSON

WITH ART BY ZAK SALLY

COFFEE HOUSE PRESS
MINNEAPOLIS
2009

Coffee House Press books are available to the trade through our primary distributor, Consortium Book Sales & Distribution, www.cbsd.com or (800) 283-3572. For personal orders, catalogs, or other information, write to: info@coffeehousepress.org.

Coffee House Press is a nonprofit literary publishing house. Support from private foundations, corporate giving programs, government programs, and generous individuals helps make the publication of our books possible. We gratefully acknowledge their support in detail in the back of this book.

Good books are brewing at coffeehousepress.org

LIBRARY OF CONGRESS CATALOGING-IN-PUBLICATION DATA
Evenson, Brian, 1966–
Fugue state : stories / Brian Evenson. — 1st ed.
p. cm.
ISBN-13: 978-1-56689-225-4 (alk. paper)
ISBN-10: 1-56689-206-6
1. Psychological fiction, American. I. Title.
PS3555.V326F84 2009
813'.54—DC22
2008052722

ACKNOWLEDGMENTS
I am grateful to the editors of the following publications for providing space for the stories collected in this volume: *Conjunctions* "Younger," "Desire with Digressions," and "Girls in Tents" • *The Ninth Letter* "A Pursuit" • *McSweeney's* "Mudder Tongue" • *Paraspheres* "An Accounting" • *Caketrain* "Dread" • *Mome* "Dread" (illustrated version) • *American Letters & Commentary* "Wander" • *New York Tyrant* "Ninety Over Ninety" • *Black Clock* "Invisible Box" • *Quarterly West* "The Third Factor" • *Fourteen Hills* "Bauer in the Tyrol" • *Bombay Gin* "Helpful" • *LIT* "Life Without Father" • *Columbia* "Alfons Kuylers" • *3rd bed* "Fugue State" • *The Brooklyn Rail* "Traub in the City" • "An Accounting" was reprinted in *Best American Fantasy* and in *The Apocalypse Reader*. "Fugue State" was reprinted in *Text: UR*. "Invisible Box" was reprinted in *Awake! A Reader for the Sleepless* and, in French translation, in *Inculte*. "Bauer in the Tyrol" was reprinted in the *New Standards* anthology, and "Traub in the City" in *The Brooklyn Rail Fiction Anthology*. "Mudder Tongue" was chosen for the *O. Henry Prize Stories 2007* and was read by David Straitharn for Symphony Place's *Selected Shorts* series.

I would also like to thank the Corporation of Yaddo, the MacDowell Colony, and the Camargo Foundation for providing me invaluable space and time to work, Gary Lutz for his meticulous reading of the manuscript, my editor Chris Fischbach, my agent Matt McGowan. Most of all, thanks to Joanna, Valerie, Sarah, and Ruby for their love and support.

Contents

FUGUE STATE

The scroll of the night sky seemed to roll back, showing
a huge blood-dusky presence looming enormous,
stooping, looking down, awaiting its moment.

—D. H. LAWRENCE, "The Border Line"

Younger

Years later, she was still calling her sister, trying to understand what exactly had happened. It still made no sense to her, but her sister, older, couldn't help. Her sister had completely forgotten—or would have if the younger sister wasn't always reminding her. The younger sister imagined, each time she talked to her sibling on the telephone, each time she brought the incident up, her older sister pressing her palm against her forehead as she waited for her to say what she had to say, so that she, the older sister, the only one of the sisters with a family of her own, could politely sidestep her inquiries and go back to living her life.

Her older sister had always managed to do that, to nimbly sidestep anything that came her way so as to simply go on with her life. For years, the younger sister had envied this, watching from farther and farther behind as her older sister sashayed past those events that an instant later struck the younger sister head-on and almost destroyed her. The younger sister was always being almost destroyed by events, and then had to spend months desperately piecing herself together enough so that when once again she was struck head-on, she would only be almost destroyed rather than utterly and completely destroyed.

As her mother had once suggested, the younger sister felt things more intensely than anyone else. At the time, very young, the younger sister had seen this as a mark of emotional superiority, but later she saw it for what it was: a serious defect that kept her from living her life. Indeed, as the younger sister reached first her teens and then her twenties, she came to realize that people who felt things as intensely as she were either institutionalized or dead.

This realization was at least in part due to her father having belonged to the first category (institutionalized) and her mother to the second (dead by suicide)—two more facts that her older sister, gliding effortlessly and, quite frankly, mercilessly, through life, had also sidestepped. Indeed, while the younger sister was realizing to a more and more horrifying degree how she was inescapably both her mother's and her father's child, her older sister had gone on to start a family of her own. It was like her older sister had been part of a different family. The younger sister could never start a family of her own—not because, as everyone claimed, she was irresponsible but because she knew it just brought her one step closer to ending up like her mother and father. It was not that she was irresponsible, but only that she was terrified of ending up mad or dead.

The incident had occurred when their parents were still around, before they were, in the case of the mother, dead and, in the case of the father, mad. There were, it had to be admitted in retrospect, signs that things had gone wrong with their parents, things her older sister must have absorbed and quietly processed over time but which the younger sister was forced to process too late and all at once. The incident, the younger sister felt, was the start of her losing her hold on her life. Even years later, she continued to feel that if only she could understand exactly what had happened, what it all meant, she would see what had gone wrong and could correct it, could, like the older sister, muffle her feelings, begin to feel things less and, in the end, perhaps not feel anything at all. Once she felt nothing, she thought, knowing full well how crazy it sounded, she could go on to have a happy life.

But her older sister couldn't understand. To her older sister, what the younger sister referred to as *the incident* was nothing—less than nothing, really. As always, her older sister listened patiently on the other end of the line as the younger sister posed the same questions over again. "Do you remember the time we were trapped in the house?" she might begin, and there would be a long pause as her older sister (so the younger sister believed) steeled herself to go through it once more.

"We weren't trapped exactly," her older sister almost always responded. "No need to exaggerate."

But that was not how the younger sister remembered it. How the younger sister remembered it was that they *were* trapped. Even the word

2

trapped did not strike her as forceful enough. But her older sister, as always, saw it as her role to calm the younger sister down. The younger sister would make a statement and then her older sister would qualify the statement, dampen it, smooth it over, nullify it. This, the younger sister had to admit, *did* calm her, *did* make her feel better momentarily, *did* made her think, *Maybe it isn't as bad as I remembered.* But the long-term effect was not to make her feel calmer but to make her feel insane, as if she were remembering things that hadn't actually happened. But if they hadn't happened the way she remembered, why was she still undone more than twenty years later? And as long as her sister was calming her, how was she ever to stop feeling undone?

No, what she needed was not for her sister to calm her, not for her sister, from the outset, to tell her there was no need to exaggerate. But she could not figure out how to tell her sister this—not because her older sister was unreasonable but because she was all too reasonable. She sorted the world out rationally and in a way that stripped it of all its power. Her older sister could not understand the effect of the incident on the younger sister because she, the older sister, had not let it have an effect on her.

For instance, her older sister could not even begin to conceive how the younger sister saw the incident as the single most important and most devastating moment of her life. For her older sister, the incident had been nothing. How was it possible, her older sister wanted to know, that the incident had been more damaging for her than their mother's suicide or their father's mental collapse? It didn't make any sense. Well, yes, the younger sister was willing to admit, it *didn't* make any sense, and yet she was still ruined by it, still undone. *If I can understand exactly what happened,* she would always tell her older sister, *I'll understand where I went wrong.*

"But nothing happened," her older sister said. "Nothing. That's just it."

And that was the whole problem. The sisters had played the same roles for so many years that they didn't know how to stop. Responding to each other in a different way was impossible. Every conversation had already been mapped out years in advance, at the moment the younger sister was first compelled to think of herself as the irresponsible one and the older sister was first made to be a calming force. They weren't getting anywhere, which meant that she, the younger sister, wasn't getting anywhere, was still wondering what, if anything, had happened, and what, if anything, she could do to free herself from it.

•

3

What she thought had happened—the way she remembered it when, alone, late at night, she lay in bed after another conversation with her sister—was this: their mother had vanished sometime during the night. Why exactly, the younger sister didn't know. Their father, she remembered, had seemed harried, had taken their mother somewhere during the night and left her there, but had been waiting for them, seated on the couch, when they woke up. He had neither slept nor bathed; his eyes were very red and he hadn't shaved. Somehow, she remembered, her sister hadn't seemed surprised. Whether this was because the sister wasn't really surprised or because, as the calm one, she was never supposed to appear surprised, the younger sister couldn't say.

She remembered the father insisting that nothing was wrong, but insisting almost simultaneously that he must leave right away. There was, the younger sister was certain, something very wrong: what exactly it had been, she was never quite certain. Something with the mother, certainly, perhaps her suicidal juggernaut just being set in motion—though her older sister claimed that no, it must have been something minor, a simple parental dispute that led to their mother going to stay temporarily with her own mother. And the only reason the father had to leave, the older sister insisted, was that he had to get to work. He had a meeting, and so had to leave them alone, even though they were perhaps too young—even the older sister had to admit this—to be left alone.

Her older sister claimed too that the father had bathed and looked refreshed and was in no way harried. But this, the younger sister was certain, was a lie, was just the older sister's attempt to calm her. No, the father had looked terrible, was harried and even panicked, the younger sister wasn't exaggerating, not really. *Do you love me?* the younger sister sometimes had to say into the phone. *Do you love me?* she would say. *Then stop making me feel crazy, and just listen.*

So there was her father, in her head, simultaneously sleepless and well-rested, clean and sticky with sweat. He had to leave, he had explained to them. He was sorry but he had to leave. But it was all right, he claimed. He set the stove timer to sound when it was time for them to go to school. When they heard the timer go off, he told them, they had to go to school. Did they understand?

Yes, both girls said, they understood.

"And one more thing," the father said, his hand already reaching for the knob. "Under no circumstances are you to answer the door. You are not to open the door to anyone."

•

4

And after that? According to the older sister, nothing much. The father left. The sisters played together until the timer rang, and then they opened the door and went to school.

But that was not how the younger sister remembered it. There was, first of all and above all, the strangeness of being alone in the house for the first time. There was a giddiness to that, a feeling they had stepped beyond the known world, a feeling the younger sister never for a moment forgot. A feeling which made it seem like not just minutes were going by, but hours.

"But it was just a few minutes," her older sister insisted.

"*Like* hours," said the younger sister. "Not actually hours but *like* hours." All right, she conceded, not actual hours—though she knew that when it came down to it, there was no such thing as *actual* hours. But for all intents and purposes she had already lost her sister, once again had rapidly reached a point where she could no longer rely on her sister to help her understand what exactly had happened. But she kept talking anyway, because once she had started talking what could she do but keep on?

The point was, time slowed down for the younger sister and never really sped back up again. There was a giddiness and a sense that anything could happen, anything at all. There were only two rules: the world would end when the timer rang, and under no circumstances were they to answer the door. But within those constraints, anything could happen.

What did they play? They played the same things they had always played, but the games were different too, just as the girls, alone, had become different. Her older sister, as always, went along with what the younger sister wanted to play, playing down to her level, but this time anything could happen. The small toy mustangs they played with dared do things they had never done before, cantering all the way across the parents' bedroom, where they gathered and conferred and at last decided on a stratagem for defeating the plastic bear, which, once bested, was flushed down the toilet and was gone forever. The two girls watched with sweaty faces and flushed cheeks as the bear disappeared: anything could happen. The younger sister pulled herself up on the bathroom counter and opened the cabinet and used the mother's lipstick on her own lips, something she was never allowed to do, and then used the lipstick to paint red streaks on the horses' sides, bloodied from where they had been gashed by the bear in battle. The most injured mustang limped slowly away and found a cave to hide in. He lay down inside it and hoped that the cool and the dark either would help him get better or would kill him. At first the cave was just the space under the couch, but the mustang wasn't getting better, so the younger sister stuck him in her armpit and called that a cave and held her arm clamped to her side. When, later, she reached him back out, the blood had smeared off all over inside the cave, and the horse was miraculously healed and allowed to return to the pack.

"It's not called a pack," her older sister told her over the telephone. "It's a herd."

But the younger sister knew they had called it a pack, that anything could happen and that *pack* was part of it too. They had known at the time it was a herd but they had called it a pack, and they had said it wrong on purpose. They were building a whole world up around them, full of things more vivid and slippery than anything the real world could offer. Just because her older sister couldn't remember didn't mean it hadn't happened.

And the sisters had become mustangs as well, had joined the *pack* as well—couldn't she remember? They took the two biggest rubber bands they could find and stretched them from their mouths over the back of their heads like bridles. They took old plastic bread bags their mother had saved, and filled the bottoms with paper napkins and rubber-banded them to their legs and then slipped shoes over their hands. And suddenly it wasn't just pretend but something was happening that had never happened before. Couldn't she remember? It was ecstatic and crazed and like they were fleeing their bodies—it was the only thing like a religious experience the younger sister had ever had, and she had had it when she was six.

And then suddenly it all went wrong.

They heard the timer go off and ran to turn it off but they were still wearing shoes on their hands and neither of them wanted to take the shoes off, so they tried to stop the timer by trapping its stem between two shoes and turning it, but the timer stem was old and too smooth to turn like that. So while the timer buzzed on, the younger sister had neighed at her older sister and together they had cantered to the dining-room table and taken a chair, supporting it between them with their hooves, and brought it to the stove. The younger sister stood on it and leaned over the burner, feeling the enamel warm in one spot from the pilot light, and turned the timer off with her teeth, by twisting her head.

That was, the younger sister knew, the sign that the world had come to an end, that it was over, that now they had to go to school. Only it wasn't the end, for as soon as the timer was turned off, the doorbell rang. It froze both of them and they stood there, bread bags on their feet and shoes on their hands, and kept very still and very quiet. They were not to answer the door, their father had been very clear about that. But they were also supposed to go to school. How could you go to school when someone was at the door, ringing the doorbell, trying to come in?

My older sister, the younger sister thought, *will know what to do.*

But her older sister was standing there not doing anything. The doorbell rang again, and still they waited, the younger sister nervously rubbing her hooves together.

They waited awhile for the doorbell to ring a third time. When it did not, her older sister leaned close to her and whispered *Come on*. But they had taken only a few steps when they heard not ringing but a hard, loud knock: four sharp, equally spaced blows right in a row. And that stopped them just as much as if someone had yanked back on their bridles.

It was like that for hours—for what, anyway, seemed like hours. Her hands were getting sweaty in the shoes. Her feet in the bread bags were much, much worse, the napkins at the bottom of each bag grown damp. Her mouth, too, hurt in the corners because of the rubber band. Her older sister took a few steps and the younger sister, not knowing what else to do, followed. Her older sister, she saw, had taken the shoes off her hands without the younger sister noticing and had gotten the rubber band out of her mouth and was now creeping very slowly past the door. The younger sister followed, trying not to look at the curtain-covered window beside the door, trying not to see the shadow of whatever was on the other side, but seeing enough to know that, whatever it was, it was big, and seeing too, when the knocking started once again, the door shiver in its frame.

In their bedroom, her sister helped her get the shoes off. They had been on long enough that they felt like they were still on even once they had come off. The rubber-band bridle got caught in her hair so that her sister had to snip it out with a scissor, which made the bridle snap and raised a red stripe of flesh across her cheekbone and almost made her cry. The rubber bands holding the plastic bags to her legs had left purple grooves on her calves, and her feet were hot and wet and itchy. She dried them off on a hand towel and put her shoes on while her older sister stood on a stool by the bedroom window and tried to see out.

"He's still there," she said.

"What is it?" asked the younger sister.

"I don't know," said her older sister. "Who, you mean."

But the younger sister had meant not who, but what. She wanted to climb on the stool beside her sister and look out as well, but was too scared.

"What do we do?" she asked.

"Do?" said her sister. "Let's play until he's gone."

So they had begun again, with the plastic horses again, only this time it was a slow negation of everything that had happened before. Before, it had seemed like anything could happen; now all the younger sister could think about was about how they were trapped in the house, how they couldn't leave, how they were supposed to leave but couldn't. The mustangs were just ordinary horses now and could no longer move their plastic legs but simply stayed motionless as they were propelled meaninglessly across the floor. The bear was gone for good and she and her sister weren't horses anymore, just two trapped girls. Everything was wrong. They were trapped in the house and she knew they would always be trapped. The younger sister kept trying to play, but all she could do was cry.

Her older sister was comforting her, telling her everything was fine, but the way she said it, it was clear nothing was fine. Everything was hell.

"What is it?" she asked again.

"He's probably not even there anymore," said her older sister. "I bet we can leave soon."

And, to be truthful, it probably was soon after that, though it didn't feel that way to the younger sister, that her older sister went back into the bedroom and climbed up on the stool again and looked out and said that it was safe now and everything was fine and this time seemed to mean it. They gathered their books and their lunches and opened the front door and darted out. The whole street seemed deserted. The older sister, who hated to be late, made them both run to school, and the younger sister reached her class even before Mrs. Clark had finished calling roll. When you looked at it that way, almost no time had actually passed. When you looked at it that way, as her older sister in fact had, really nothing at all had happened.

But for the younger sister there was less of her from there on out. Part of her was still wearing shoes on her hands and a rubber band in her mouth and was somewhere, sides bloody, looking for her pack. And part of her was still there, motionless, trapped in the house, waiting for the door to shiver in its frame.

She was still, years later, trying to figure out how to get back those parts of her. And what was left of her she could hardly manage to do anything with at all.

"So what do you want me to do?" her sister finally one day asked, her voice tinny through the telephone. "Play mustangs with you again?" And then she laughed nervously.

And yes, in fact, that was exactly what the younger sister wanted. Maybe it would do something, it was worth a try, yes. If her sister would only do that, perhaps something—anything—could happen.

But after so many years, so many telephone conversations burning and reburning the same paths through their minds, so many years of playing the same roles, how could she ask this of her older sister? She knew her role enough to know she could never bring herself to ask this of her older sister. Not in what seemed like a million years.

A Pursuit

For some days now, I have felt myself to be pursued by my second ex-wife. At first I believed the pursuer to be my third ex-wife, and perhaps for a time the two of them were working together—for all I know, they may still be. Indeed, though recent evidence has suggested the pursuer is my second ex-wife, evidence just a few days ago pointed to my third ex-wife.

Perhaps the two of them spell each other so as to stay fresh and alert, while I, alone, a solitary ex-husband, have only myself to rely on. Perhaps the second ex-wife drives while the third ex-wife sleeps, and vice versa. But is it always the same car that pursues me? I can no longer say. I try not to think too obsessively about my pursuers, but what else am I to think about?

They are behind me, watching me, waiting for me to make a mistake.

So far I have made no mistakes.

What, one might well ask, has become of my first ex-wife? Why, if the other two choose to pursue me, doesn't she? Is it simply that, time having passed, she neither cares for me nor despises me as do my two more recent wives? Perhaps she is merely indifferent?

Until a few weeks ago, it had been years since I had word from a single one of my trinity of ex-wives. I was living, alone and isolated, in peace near the sea—white stone, blinding sun—when I received a letter from my first ex-wife. This letter was written in a hand that, although admittedly familiar, did not seem her hand. Had my first ex-wife not burnt all my possessions upon leaving me—believing as she did for no sane reason that I was having an affair with the woman who would become my second wife (and, later still, my second ex-wife)—I could have compared her handwriting to that found in the letter, which struck me as the work of a decidedly male hand. My first ex-wife had many faults, but she was by no stretch of the imagination manly in either person or voice. To see her name signed in a masculine script surprised me. No, to find an ex-wife who could be described, in the mildest of ways, as masculine, one would have to look to my third and most recent ex-wife, but even she wrote in only a marginally masculine hand, what one might call a hermaphroditic hand. But no, as to my first ex-wife, no. True, it was her name scrawled at the letter's end. True, many of the letter's turns of phrase were, if not definitively her own, not outside her habits of speech as I remembered them, but no, the hand, no: either this was not a letter from my first ex-wife or this was a letter dictated by her to an amanuensis.

As to the contents of the letter, those are hardly important. In any case now, having driven for so long, I can recall only a smattering of details: expressions of affection (perhaps mere formalities) slowly decaying into veiled insults and accusations. This was perhaps not so surprising a combination to find in a letter from one ex-spouse to another. What surprised me was that she had chosen to write at all. For a decade, I had had only silence from her. At the divorce proceedings—held with her manacled and wearing prison garb because of her *incendiary spirit* and the jail time it had earned her—she had voiced not a solitary word, nor had a word for me escaped her during the entire course of her prison sentence, nor indeed after her release. But now, suddenly, ten wordless years later, she posts an epistolary outpouring crammed with affection and hatred? And not in her own hand but in the hand of another, a hand decidedly male?

There was, as well, wedged between blandishments and attacks, a puzzling request; viz., that I stop persecuting her. *Persecuting her?* I wondered. I had had no contact with her for more than a decade. And, despite its conflagratory difficulties, I looked back on our time together, our marriage together, with a certain melancholy fondness. I had nothing but the kindest of feelings toward her, had no desire to cause her any pain or discomfort whatsoever. Just the opposite. Yet here was a letter whose deep, low voice told me, *Stop persecuting me and leave me alone.* It was such a baffling accusation, considering the facts, that I could read her words only against themselves, as a statement of an unconscious desire to *be* persecuted by me, as an appeal to see me again. This, coupled with the maleness of the handwriting, was enough to propel me immediately in search of her.

Yet now, pursued by my second ex-wife, unless it be my third ex-wife after all, I wonder if I read her veiled request correctly. True, were it only a question of one ex-wife operating in a vacuum, I would have been, undoubtedly, correct, but when you add a second and then a third ex-wife into the equation, particularly when one or both of the latter pair seem to be pursuing you, the psychology at work becomes a decidedly murky affair. People clustered in twos or threes or fours, I have come to believe, both constitute creatures in and of themselves and, together as tandems or triunes or packs, form another sort of myriad-minded creature whose actions are far from predictable. Thus, I find myself exponentially more shaken thinking that I might be simultaneously pursued by a pair of ex-wives than I would knowing myself pursued by either one alone, and much more shaken by the combination of my first ex-wife with the male hand in which her letter is inscribed—which suggests a second, shadowy presence—than I would be by the same letter inscribed in her own feminine hand.

But I am losing myself. I intended merely to say that once I had realized I was being pursued, I began to realize the situation was perhaps more complicated than I had initially supposed. Initially, I merely thought that perhaps my first ex-wife was being persecuted in my name but by some other party, or else that she had simply gone insane.

I set out to find my ex-wife, planning to question her face-to-face about the letter and to determine if it had actually been from her and, if so, to discover either who had transcribed the letter for her or how it was that her hand had become so masculine since I had last seen her. My intentions were, it should be clear, innocent. I simply wanted to verify, clarify, confirm.

I had no expectation of a long journey. I packed only a small overnight bag, which I placed on the seat beside me, where it still remains. I drove the car along a winding road up from the sea and into a series of rocky hills described in the better guidebooks as picturesque, twisting and turning through them until they gave way to mountains. I slid from one nation into another, and from there soon passed into a third. I passed through a squalid metropolis, made a steep ascent to the alpine town inscribed as the return address on my first ex-wife's envelope. I spent the night there, in a strangely dreamless sleep at a small makeshift guesthouse, with no guest register and a shared bathroom, and woke up refreshed. From there it was easy work, after deploying a few well-placed questions gleaned from a pocket Berlitz, to follow a narrow gravel road edging across the mountainside perhaps thirty meters above the town itself, a road that dead-ended at my first ex-wife's residence.

In the town I had bought, I will admit, flowers—but not from any intention to renew our intimacy. No, these were simply a peace offering, a device to render her more tractable, to forestall any burning. I climbed out of the car, carrying the flowers in their cone of paper, and approached the front door. There was no bell. I knocked, received no response. I knocked again. Still receiving no reply, I depressed the poignet. It levered down gently and the door slid open. I saw no reason not to enter.

Inside, the house was brightly lit, a generator slowly humming just behind a rear wall. Beside the sink was a bucket of silty water and into this I placed the flowers. The cone of paper I removed and smoothed flat, intending to use it to write a note, and this I would have done had I not noticed, just then, the line of blood trailing from the fireplace grate to the bedroom door. I approached it and prodded it with the tip of my shoe. It was mostly dry, but somehow that did not reassure me.

At times one wants to assert one's connection to one's ex-wives, at other times one reminds oneself they are ex-wives for good reason.

I am by inclination a curious man but have learned through the years, plagued by three wives in turn, to squelch this curiosity. Perhaps my first ex-wife was lying dying on the other side of the door, or perhaps she was already dead. Perhaps this was not her blood at all but the blood of another and she was there beside the cold corpse of the man (assuming it was a man) she had killed. Perhaps it was the same man who had written the letter. To find out, all I had to do was step across the room, perhaps four modest strides in all, and open the bedroom door.

But I could think of no scenario whereby I stood to gain anything by opening the door. I had read in my impressionable youth too many crime novels not to know that these things always go awry, that certain doors one should never open. So I left, stuffing the paper cone into my pocket, wiping the poignet free of my fingerprints on the way out, leaving my first ex-wife, dead or living, to her fate.

In subsequent days, driving, I have had a great deal of time to consider my actions. In one respect I was correct to remain in ignorance, to avoid precipitating myself into a difficult situation. Yet in another respect, had I opened that door, I would at least know what was on the other side, might at least have some vague sense of why I am now being pursued. As it stands, my first ex-wife, like Schrödinger's famous and long-suffering cat, seems a creature flickering between life and death, neither alive nor dead—which is to say at once both alive and dead. She is the worst kind of ghost. I would be lying if I did not confess to feeling haunted by her, feeling her presence close to me, almost just over my shoulder sometimes, as I drive. Taking that into account, you might say that, yes, perhaps, in a manner of speaking, I am being pursued by all three of my ex-wives.

I did not open the door. Instead, I fled. I would, I thought, just clamber into my car and regain my seaside town as quickly as possible. The sooner I fled, the less chance I would have, so my reasoning went, of being implicated in whatever had happened behind the door. There were, admittedly, the several villagers to whom I had spoken in order to get directions, but there was nothing I could do about them. And I should explain—and would in fact have explained at the outset were it not that the strain and exhaustion of being subject to pursuit have made me less methodical than I habitually am—that I had taken steps upon my initial contact with these villagers to misdirect them: a slightly altered appearance, a bit of mud smeared to obscure the license number and throw into doubt the car's nation of origin.

Perhaps you, sitting beside me as I drive, feel you deserve an explanation. But no, wait, I look beside me and see not a flesh-and-blood human but only my overnight bag: no one sits beside me. I am, as the French say, *parlant tout seul*, speaking all alone. No explanation is needed. Suffice it to say that after three wives I have become a careful man. Knowing my first ex-wife capable, quite frankly, of virtually *anything*, and my other two ex-wives cut of equally ruthless cloth, I would have been a fool not to take every precaution. Though I shall be the first to admit that these actions may strike others, at least those not privy to my life-experience, as an indication of culpability. But culpable of having done what? What, in fact, actually happened? And isn't anything, cast in the wrong light, an indication of culpability?

Would it help if I were to swear to you, by the deceased individual of your choice, that I had nothing to do with my first ex-wife's demise, assuming she is in fact dead?

No, it would not help, because you do not exist. I am speaking only to myself. I am speaking all alone.

One becomes so easily distracted. A part of oneself must watch the road, follow its twists and turns. What is left of one's mind, stripped of sleep, half-taken
with paying attention to the car behind, the pursuing car, when there is a
pursuing car, is prone to follow its own path. I have smoked a cigarette, a
Dunhill, a favorite of my second wife, one of six cigarettes remaining to me,
and feel now slightly light-headed but a little better, a little more focused.
This feeling, surely, will not last for long.

But for the moment here we are in the past again, leaving my first ex-wife's
house for the first time, driving as quickly as we can without drawing attention to ourselves—same muddied license plate, same altered appearance, perhaps just a bit of panic, perhaps even the vague desire to turn around and go
back, to open the bedroom door, consequences be damned. We have left, or
rather *I* have left, the alpine town, am beginning to wend my way homeward,
when I catch a brief glister in my rearview mirror. At first I pay no attention,
then it comes again, flashing across my eye, and then yet again, until at last,
forced to take a closer look, I see sunlight glinting off the hood of a car. I
adjust my mirror and think no more of it—I am after all on a road, cars are
to be expected. Yet when after a number of divagations and turnings and
accelerations it is still with me, I begin to pay it more heed. Can it be that I
am being followed? I slow to allow the car to pass and it does so, barreling per-
ilously around me on a curve, the sun slung upon its side window in such
fashion that I cannot catch a glimpse of its driver. And then it is gone.

Enough of the present tense. The car was gone. I relaxed. I crossed the
border. Anything to declare? No, nothing to declare. I continued my route
down toward the next border, the next country.

I had been driving for some time when I realized, of a sudden, that a car
was behind me and that it had in fact been behind me for quite some time.
Was this the same car? Perhaps. Or perhaps the same color but a slightly
different model. What had the other car been? I had already forgotten—
once it had passed me, there seemed no reason to keep it in mind. Was the
color really the same after all or merely similar? Or was it the same color but
simply cast slightly differently in the declining sun? Perhaps, I told myself,
I should take a circuitous route, just to be safe.

I turned down a smaller road, followed it. The other car followed me at
first, but as my route became increasingly convoluted, it disappeared. So,
not followed after all. I was relieved, but also, as it turned out, lost.

At first I thought it would be easy to get back to something I would recognize. Indeed, though I had engaged in more and more erratic maneuvers to

shake my imagined (so I believed at the time) pursuers, I had also carefully noted landmarks—a fountain, a hotel sign, the name of a restaurant reminiscent of my second wife's pet name, and so forth. Yet as I tried to make my way free of a drab little neighborhood without streetlights that bordered on what appeared to be an industrial wasteland, I had difficulty sorting the landmarks back into a coherent pattern. Thus I knew that, yes, somewhere I had passed that hotel with a stylized goose upon its sign, but not what to look for next nor where to go to find it. The darkness, too, impeded me, and by the time I decided it would be better to stop at the goose inn and spend the night, begin again by morning light, I could not find it. In the end, nearly out of fuel, I pulled up beside a well-manicured hedge, turned off the car, and slept.

Shall I tell you my dreams? Surely they had some effect on me, perhaps at the very least can account for the fact that I awoke more exhausted than I had been when I went to sleep, my back and neck sore, my eyes feeling as if someone had attempted to dig them out with a rusty spoon. There were dreams, of course, of pursuit, the activities of the day simply continuing into my sleep, dreams of constantly staring into the rearview mirror, depressing the gas pedal, turning, turning. There were dreams, too, in which I watched a hand, clearly male, compose the letter putatively from my wife—again no surprise there, and nothing extraordinary: hardly worth mentioning. The third dream, too, I realize now, is of the same sort, but since I have begun and since it was both the least recurrent and the most vivid of the three, I shall share it with you.

Here I am back in my wife's cabin once again, but this time I obey my curiosity and move toward the door, pursuing the line of nearly dried blood. My hand moves out to open the door, I push down the poignet, the door swings back, and what do I see inside but myself?

I awoke to the sun beryling off the windshield, a round, gouged circle of light. I felt a little shaken, tired, ready to return home. Clambering out, I urinated into the hedge, then washed my hands and face with water from a bottle taken from my overnight bag. I stretched and only then did I notice the car parked several dozen meters behind me, a car identical, more or less, to the car I thought had been following me the day before. There seemed a figure in the driver's seat, or if not a figure perhaps only a raised headrest, the sun glinting off the dirty windshield making it difficult to see anything with certainty.

I climb into the car and begin to drive. The other car at first is not with me and then it is, unless it is another, similar car. It is there, then it is gone, then it is there again. I stop for fuel and see no car but then, once I am driving again, there it is, behind me. From time to time it becomes easy to believe I am not being followed, the pursuit being, I have now come to believe, extremely subtle, invisible more often than visible. The car sometimes freshly washed, sometimes covered with mud, the paint such that it catches the light differently at different times of the day, making me always think, *Could that possibly be the car? Aren't I mistaken?* I keep changing my route, doubling back, the result being that by the time darkness falls I find myself farther from home than I was before.

I stop at a service station, fill the tank, buy a half-dozen bottles of water, bags of so-called crisps, foreign candy bars consisting of an unidentifiable sugary chewable drenched in chocolate, and, as an afterthought, a packet of cigarettes. These for the next several days will be my only nourishment. I drive that evening until I can barely stay awake. Sometimes there are headlights behind me, sometimes not. Sometimes the hair on the back of my neck tingles and stands up, like an animal, as if I am being pursued; sometimes the same hair lies still, like a dead animal. I stop finally on a small road, wheels edged against a ditch, and sleep.

Awake again. Is the car behind me? No, there is no car behind me. I drive for a few hours, beginning at last to relax. Is the car behind me? Yes, the car is behind me. Twist, turn, evade. Is there a car behind me? No. But yes, later, a few minutes, a few hours, who knows, there it is again. What is it waiting for? Perhaps for me to reveal where I am now living. Solution: do not return home until you are certain you are no longer being followed.

But how, I begin to wonder after a few days of this constant circling, traveling from country to country, never stopping except to sleep briefly in the car before going on again, my mind increasingly distracted, nerves increasingly unstrung, how can one ever be certain of anything? Once you start driving, how can you ever stop?

This accursed present tense. It keeps squirming into my discourse until I feel that everything that has already happened is happening all over again and all at once. Each turn I have already made I am about to make again, each moment of looking up to see the car following me again has both occurred and is about to occur. The car is weighted down with all these past selves threatening to push their way into the present, with the myriad tribe of selves plaguing me like ghosts until I do not know if it is me turning off this wide modern street and onto that narrow cobbled one or if it is one of them. And as I sit here *parlant tout seul*, I wonder if I really am speaking only to myself or if I am speaking to the ghost of someone who has been or will be in the seat beside. So there is perhaps hope for you after all. And perhaps, too, the self who speaks and the self who drives are not the same, and I myself serve as my own ghost.

I have smoked all my remaining cigarettes, lighting each off its predecessor, a chronologically arranged progression of tiny lives. I no longer feel so in flux, but am instead slightly giddy and nervous, but more focused as well.

Not much remains. I kept driving, but each time I thought I'd effected an escape, each time I felt I could risk returning home, each time I began to relax, the hair on the back of my neck would stand up again. The pursuing car would reappear. I slept only when I had to, and only in fits and starts, and by day became more and more haggard, less and less human. My back, from my having sat for hours in the same position, vacillated between experiencing a dull ache and feeling shooting, sharp pains. Once, it became so painful that I had to pull the car over onto the shoulder and lie flat in the gravel as one hundred meters behind and just out of sight my pursuer surely idled, waited. I lived on bags of artificially preserved bonbons and tins of anchovies and whatever else I could find without getting far from my car: bottles of water, sticks or rounds of bread.

In what must have been only a few days, I had lost any sense of how long I had been driving. The date slipped away from me, as did the proper day of the week. Days shaded into weeks at some point, but I could not say when. Nor can I say how many days had passed before I gathered the identity of my pursuer. One day, early afternoon, I crossed lanes rather abruptly and watched my pursuer make the same maneuver but with a certain fillip: she turned on the turn signal in the wrong direction, and before darting left drifted right, as if the driver had cocked the wheel slightly before forcing it left. Both of these were characteristic of my third wife's ineptitude. A few hours later, I executed a similar change of lanes and watched the same pattern repeated behind me. Perhaps the car had been doing the same thing all along and I, thinking only to avoid it, had simply paid it no mind.

Such ephemerae hardly amount to an identity, yet once I had noticed them I could not ignore them. And indeed the car itself seemed to respond to my gaze, giving me as time wore on more and more proofs that my pursuer was my third ex-wife. Never one to accept the evidence of my senses, I tested these proofs, engaged my own car in certain gestures intended to solicit certain reactions from her, and indeed these reactions were consistently provoked. I became more certain and also more confident. Now that I had assigned a name to my pursuer, I could develop a scheme to shake her.

My third ex-wife must have sensed my growing awareness, for she raised her pursuit to another level. She began, somehow, to employ different cars. At first I thought, not having seen her car for the course of an entire day, that I had shaken her. I became so confident as to direct my car in the direction I thought must be home, but when I noticed that another car—deep burgundy and of what I presumed must be Eastern European make—had stayed quite near to me for some time, I became suspicious. I engaged in a few tentative maneuvers and was not surprised to find the car reacting as if it were driven by my third ex-wife. Which, in fact, I concluded, it must be.

But, not content, she ratcheted the game up another notch. Or I should say *they*. For there came a moment when I was driving and there appeared a car behind me and I thought, somewhat smugly, *here she is, here is my third ex-wife*, and downshifted and pursued a maneuver intended to make her reveal herself, but no, she was not revealed. Not her, I thought, nor her car, and thus, I thought, not my pursuer. Yet this car stayed with me. Hours later, it was with me still, I wriggled around back roads through sleepy and aimless towns, and lost it. Several hours later, it found me again. So I tried to draw her out again, with another maneuver, another enticement, and this time too there was nothing to suggest my third ex-wife, though the car did something that disturbed me—a jerky movement as if the driver had pressed too hard on the brakes and then quickly stepped on the accelerator. A gesture characteristic of my second ex-wife, and one of the multitude of irritations that had precipitated the collapse of our marriage.

Can I be wrong? I wondered. *Is my pursuer in fact not my third ex-wife but my second?*

The next hours were spent testing this theory to my satisfaction, putting the car behind me through a series of proofs that slowly dissolved the image of my third ex-wife in my mind and replaced it with an image of my second ex-wife. *How*, I wondered, *could I ever have thought the pursuer was my third ex-wife?* For now everything suggested ex-wife number two.

Only slowly did another possibility creep over me. Perhaps it wasn't so simple as my having been mistaken. Perhaps, indeed, I had been correct then and yet was still correct now. Perhaps I was being pursued by two of my ex-wives at once.

A man might be capable of standing up to one ex-wife, but two ex-wives is something no ex-husband wants to consider, and if the ex-husband is exhausted, slightly deranged from driving, unshaven, unwashed, it is too much for him. Indeed it was too much for me. I had to pull over and switch off the car and press my forehead against the leather-wrapped steering wheel and breathe deeply.

And was there not, I wondered, a possibility—nay, even a likelihood— that my first ex-wife was involved as well? Indeed, the fact that the beginning of the pursuit coincided with my visit to her house suggested as much. An individual ex-wife could be outflanked, backed into a corner, subdued, dismissed. But against a triad of ex-wives, a solitary ex-husband has no hope.

I tried to calm myself. I tried to focus. After a moment I lifted my forehead from the steering wheel and turned and looked out the rear window. Was there a car behind me? Were two of my ex-wives gloating in tandem a few hundred yards behind me? No, there was no car there. Then why did I still feel their presence? And what did I smell?

But no, surely, I thought, I was imagining things, the smell was only my own unwashed body, the sweat had dried and then grown damp and sour, and then dried again and so on. I was calm, there was no reason not to be calm, no reason at all.

I regarded myself in the rearview mirror, the red-rimmed eyes, the matted hair, the ratty beard. Where in all of this, I asked myself, was the man who had beaten three marriages in turn and gone on to live solitary and content only a stone's throw from the sea? How had I become the ghost of that man, hardly alive, living an existence that consisted of nothing but shuttling back and forth in a car, subject to the whims of ex-wives? *You*, I told myself, *have allowed them to make you neither alive nor dead, a half-living thing.*

It would not go on, I vowed to myself. I would stop at the first hotel. I would purchase a room and shower and sleep and shave. I would open my overnight bag and remove the clean garments that, days ago, weeks ago perhaps, I had tucked into it, and put them on. And then, refreshed, and with dignity, I would face defeat at the hands of my ex-wives.

And had circumstances been only slightly different, it might well have happened in that way. I did stop at the first hotel and, with my overnight bag slung over my shoulder, went in. The concierge was, admittedly, a little reluctant to sign me in, thinking me a vagrant perhaps, but a generous remuneration finally persuaded him. I was assigned a room. All that remained, as it was a hotel that took pride in old traditions, nestled in a country imbued with a similar pride, was to sign the guest register.

And here, my dear, nonexistent friend, is where I betrayed myself. I had been so careful with myself, I had made no mistakes, and might very well have entered the hotel room and emerged a new man. Perhaps even, after awaiting the confrontation with my ex-wives, a confrontation that could never come, I might even have abandoned my car and climbed aboard a train. I might even have convinced myself that the reason for my action was that they could not follow me without revealing themselves, the cost of a car being very little compared to my own peace of mind.

But no, as I was handed the pen, a part of me wondered, as if innocently, *Wouldn't it be better to sign the register in another name?* Yes, I thought, why not, better to be cautious, I had always believed as much—having faced three wives in turn, I had learned to be cautious. *And wouldn't it*, suggested this same part of me, *be better to disguise one's handwriting?* Having accepted the first premise, I could not but accept the second, and so, as I was given the pen, I shifted it to my left hand.

Awkwardly, I wrote a false name, a false town of origin, a false destination. When the register asked me to define the purpose of my trip, I wrote, *For my own pleasure*, which was certainly a lie. Then, after recapping the pen, I handed it back and made the mistake of appraising the results to see how well I had hidden myself.

Would it surprise you, my dear, nonexistent friend, were I to tell you that what I saw inscribed there filled me with fear? For I recognized the hand, a decidedly male hand, decidedly familiar: the same hand that had written the letter putatively from my first ex-wife.

What would you have done? Would you have had the sangfroid to shower and sleep and then, refreshed, bring yourself to look deep into yourself and sort out who you were and what exactly you had done? Or would you, like me, filled with confusion, unable to face what you had seen, have simply turned and climbed back into the car and once again driven away?

And this perhaps is where the story truly begins, for despite how quickly I fled the hotel, despite all the miles I have traveled since, I am filled with the unsettling feeling that had I at any moment stopped and stepped out of my car and walked back to the car pursuing me, if there had ever been in fact a car pursuing me, I would find slumped over its wheel the rotting carcass of my second ex-wife, the corpse of my third ex-wife, perhaps slightly fresher, lying curled on the seat beside her. And then, were I to leave their car behind and walk back to my own, were I to open my trunk, I would find them there again, my first wife having joined them now, all three corpses carefully tucked in around one another like the pieces of a puzzle.

But no, for now, I simply, as perhaps I did earlier, perhaps almost without knowing what I had done, climb back into the car and continue to drive. How long can I keep this up, my ex-wives neither alive nor dead, both alive and dead, and myself perhaps in the same state? How long can I keep driving?

With a little luck, a part of me, as if innocently, wants to suggest, *perhaps forever.*

Mudder Tongue

I.

There came a certain point, in his speech, in his confrontation with others, in his smattering with the world, that Hecker realized something was wrong. Language was starting to slip in his mouth, words substituting themselves for each other, and while his own thoughts remained as lucid as ever, sometimes they could be made manifest on his tongue only if they were wrung out or twisted or set with false eyes. False eyes? Something like that. His sense of language had always been slightly fluid; it had always been easy for him, when distracted, to substitute one word for another based on sound or rhythm or association or analogy, which was why people thought him absentminded. But this was different. Then, when distracted, he hadn't known when he misspoke, had been cued only by the expression on the faces of those around him to backtrack and correct. Now, he *heard* himself say the wrong word, knew it to be wrong even while he was saying it, but was powerless to correct it. There was something seriously wrong with him, something broken. He could grasp that, but could not understand where it was taking him.

The first time it happened, the look on his face had been one of appalled wonder—or so he guessed from the look of glee his daughter offered in return.

"Oh, Daddy," she said, for even though she was mostly grown she still called him Daddy for reasons he neither understood nor encouraged. "It's not gravy you mean, but fishing."

Gravy? he thought. *Fishing?* There was too far a gap between the two terms to leap from one to another by any logic available to him. He had heard his voice say *gravy* while his mind was busy transmitting *fishing* to his tongue. He was amazed by what he heard coming out of his mouth, didn't understand why it didn't have some relation to his thoughts. But to his daughter he was merely the same old father: absentminded, distracted.

"Oh," he said. "Of course. Termite." And was amazed again. But to his daughter he was only playing a game, taunting her. And then, a moment later, he was fine. He could say *fishing* again when he meant fishing. He alone knew something was seriously wrong. When would his daughter realize? he wondered. What, he wondered, was happening?

There were days. They kept coming and going. He opened his mouth and he closed his mouth. Mostly what he heard form on his tongue would make sense, but sometimes not. When not, he entered into an elaborate and oblique process of trying to convey what he had in fact intended. In the best of circumstances the person or persons came up with the words themselves and offered them to him. Nodding, not speaking, he accepted them, hoping that when he next opened his mouth, his brain and tongue would have realigned.

He quickly acquired a dread of meetings, of speaking in front of his colleagues. Once, his language collapsed in the middle of articulating a complaint against his chairman, colleagues touching their glasses or faces and staring at him and waiting for him to go on. Fear-stricken enough to improvise, he stood, speechless and shaking his head, and walked out. Some of them later congratulated him on his courageous gesture, but others shied away.

His daughter began to notice a tentativeness to him, though that was not how she would have phrased it. But he could see her watching him, slightly puzzled. His past personal behavior had been eccentric enough, he discovered, that she was willing to give him an alibi for almost anything. And yet, she still sensed something was wrong. At night, after she claimed to have gone to bed, he would sometimes hear her sliding through the halls. He would shift in his cushion on the sofa to find her behind him, in the doorway, staring at the back of his head.

"Why do you melba?" he said to her. "Pronto."

She looked at him seriously, as if she understood, and then nodded, returned to bed.

The dog began acting strangely, panting heavily around him, keeping a distance when he tried to approach, creeping slowly off with its tail flattened out. *Am I the same person?* he wondered. Perhaps that was it, he thought, perhaps he was not. Or perhaps he was only part of himself, and whoever else it also was had never learned to speak properly.

He tried to make friends with the dog again, offering it treats, which sometimes it took gingerly with its teeth, careful not to touch his hand.

In the classroom, where before he had been sure of himself, aggressive even, he became jittery, always waiting for the moment when the smooth surface of his language would be perforated. He took to dividing his students into small groups, speaking to them as little as possible. He tried, mornings before a class, to practice what he was going to say to thrust them into their groups as quickly as possible, how to deflect or quickly answer any potential questions. But no matter how many times he uttered his spiel perfectly beforehand, the actual moment of recitation was always up for grabs.

He instead began practicing alternatives for each sentence: on the first moment of collapse he would switch, attempting to get the same thing across with a different sentence pattern, entirely different words. But if a sentence crumbled, which it did once or twice per class—often enough in any case that the students, like his dog, like his daughter, like his colleagues, seemed now always to be looking at him oddly—the alternative usually crumbled away as well. But if a third variant did not hold, the fourth usually did, if there had to be a fourth, for by that time his mind had cycled around to a track that allowed it direct contact with his tongue again.

And thus it took a number of weeks before he found himself standing at the front of the class with all his options exhausted in the gravest misspeakings, each more outrageous than the last, so much so that he was afraid to say another word. The class, a carefully wrapped part of him noted, were more uniformly attentive than they had been at any other time in the semester, peculiarly primed to receive knowledge. But he had nothing to offer them. So instead he turned, wrote something banal on the board. *Nature of evil. Consider and discuss.* And then, suddenly, he could speak again.

For a time it seemed that writing would be his salvation. In the classroom, whenever his words started to come out maddened or stippled or gargled, he would turn to the board and write what he had actually meant. This worked fine up to a point, though he had to admit it sometimes looked odd when he suddenly stopped speaking and began to write. But still it could be dismissed by students as mere eccentricity, or as an attempt to avoid having to repeat something.

At home, such a strategy was more fraught, fraughter. Any time he tried it with his daughter, he found her turning away before he could find a pen, she perhaps believing that he had decided to ignore her. Elsewhere, too, it didn't seem to work. At a restaurant, one could point at an item on the menu, but this wasn't well received, and the one time he tried this in a social situation, it was thought he was making fun of the deaf.

But there were other places it did work. He could talk to his colleagues by note or by e-mail as long as he wasn't physically present. He also tried leaving his daughter scrawled messages, but she chose to ignore them or pretended she hadn't seen them. Once, when he asked her about one, whether she had seen it, she looked at him fixedly for some time before finally rolling her eyes and saying, *Yes, Daddy.*

"Well?" he said.

"Well, what?"

"What's your answer?"

She shook her head. "No answer."

"But," he said. "Corfu?"

"Corfu?" she said. "In Greece? What are you talking about? Don't play games with me, Daddy."

"Sandwich," he said, and covered his mouth.

"Here I am, Daddy," she said, angry. "Right here. I'm usually right here. I'm not going to let you mess with me. If you want to ask me something, you can just open your mouth and ask me."

But he couldn't just open his mouth, he realized. He didn't dare. *Sandwich?* he thought. He sat staring at her, hand over mouth, trying to gather the courage to speak, to misspeak, until, fuming, she gave a little cry and marched out of the room.

II.

As his condition worsened, he stayed silent for hours. His daughter rallied, sometimes referring to him railingly as "the recluse," as in *How's the old recluse this morning?*, at other times merely accusing him of becoming *pensive in his dotage*. Where, he wondered, had she picked up the word *dotage?*

The frequency of his mispeakings grew until finally he felt he could no longer meet his classes; the last few weeks of the term he phoned in sick nearly every day, or rather had his daughter phone in for him. He sent his lesson plans in by e-mail, got a colleague to fill in for him, finally wrote a letter to the department chairman requesting early retirement.

"You're lonely," his daughter said to him one evening. "You need to get out more."

He shook his head no.

"You need to date," she said. "Do you want me to set you up with some-one?"

He shook his head emphatically no.

"All right," she said. "A date it is. I'll see what I can do."

She began to bring home brochures from dating services, and left the *Women Seeking Men* page of the city's weekly out with a few choice ads circled. Was he *adventuresome?* No, he thought, reading the ads, he was not. Did he like long walks and a romantic dinner for two on the beach? No, he did not care for sand in his food. *Bookish?* Well, yes, but this woman's idea of high lit, as it turned out later in the ad, was John Irving. Unless the Irving referred to was Washington Irving of Sleepy Hollow fame. Was that any better?

And what would he put in his own ad? *SWM, well past prime, losing ability to speak, looks for special companionship that goes beyond words?* He groaned, and arranged everything in a neat little stack at the back of his desk.

A few days later, e-mail messages began showing up addressed to "Silver Fox" or "the silver fox" or, in one case, "Mr. F. Silver." They were all from women who claimed to have seen his "posting" and who were "interested." They wanted, they all said in different but equally banal ways, to *get to know him better.*

He dragged his daughter in and pointed at the screen.

"Already?" she said.

He nodded. He had begun to write something admonitory down for her to read but she was ignoring him, had taken over his chair, was scrolling through each woman's message.

"No," he said. "I don't—"

"And this one," she was saying, "what's wrong with this one?"

"But I don't," he said. "Any of them, no."

"No?" she said. "But why not? Daddy, you *said* you wanted to go on a date. I asked you, Daddy, and you said yes."

No, he thought, that was not what he had said. He had said nothing. He opened his mouth. "Doctorate," he said.

"Doctor?" she said, and looked at him sharply, her eyes narrowing. "Are you all right?"

That was not what he had meant his mouth to say, not that at all.

"You prefer the one that's a doctor?" his daughter said, clicking open each message in turn as she talked, "but I don't think any of them are."

But what was he to do? he wondered. First of all, nobody would listen, and second of all, even if they did listen, he himself did not know, from moment to moment, what, if anything, he was actually going to say.

She was there, chattering away in front of him, hardly even hearing what she herself was saying. Why not tell her, he wondered, that something was seriously wrong with him? What was there to be afraid of?

But no, he thought, the way people looked at him already, it was almost more than he could bear, and if it came tinged with pity, he would no longer feel human. Better to keep it to himself, hold it to himself as long as possible. And then he would still be, at least in part, human.

In the end he took her by the shoulders and, while she protested, silently pushed her out of the room. His head had started to ache, the pain pooling in his right eye. He closed his door and then returned to the computer, deleting the messages one after another. They were all, he saw, carefully constructed, with each woman trying to present herself as unique or original or witty but each doing so by employing the same syntactical gestures, the same rhetorical strategies, sometimes even the exact same phrase, as the others. *This is what it means to be immersed in language*, he thought, *to lose one's ability to think. To speak other people's words. But the only alternative is not to speak at all. Or was it? Nature of evil*, he thought. *Define and discuss.*

Depressed, he glanced through the last three messages. God, his head hurt. The first message was addressed to "silver fox," with three exclamation points following "fox." It was from someone who had adopted the moniker "2hot2handel." Music lover or bad speller? he wondered. He deleted it. The second-to-the-last one was to "F. Silver," from "OldiebutGoodie." Oh, God, he thought, and deleted it. The pain made his eye feel as though a knife were being pushed through it. The eye was beginning to water. He clenched it shut as tight as he could and covered it with his hand. He stood, tipping his chair over, and stumbled about the room, knocking into what must have been walls.

Someone was knocking on the door. "Daddy," someone was calling, "are you all right?" Somewhere a dog was growling. He looked up through his good eye and saw, framed in the doorway, a girl.

"Tights," he said, "cardboard boxes," and collapsed.

III.

He awoke to a buzzing noise, saw it was coming from an electric light, fluorescent, inset in the ceiling directly above his head. His daughter was there beside him, looking at his face.

He opened his mouth, then closed it again.

"No," she said. "Just rest."

He nodded. He was in a bed, he saw, but not his bed. There was rail to either side of him, to hold him in.

"I'm going to get the doctor," she claimed. "Don't move."

Then she was gone. He closed his eyes, swallowed. The pain in his head was still there, but subdued now and no longer sharpened into a hard point. He rolled his head to one side and back again, pleased that he could still do so.

His daughter returned, the doctor beside her, a smallish tanned man hardly bigger than she.

"Mr. Hecker?" said the doctor, who set down a folder to snap on latex gloves. "How are we feeling?"

"Groin," he said. *Goddamn*, he thought.

"Your groin hurts? It's your head we're concerned about, but I'll look at the groin too if you'd like."

Hecker shook his head. "No? Well, then," said the doctor. "No to the groin, then." He clicked on a penlight, peered into first one eye, then the other. "Any headaches, Mr. Hecker?"

He hesitated, nodded.

"Head operations in your youth? Surgeries of the head? Cortisone treatments? Bad motorcycle wrecks? Untreated skull injuries?"

Hecker shook his head.

"And how are we feeling now?" the doctor asked.

Hecker nodded. *Good*, he thought, *good enough*. He opened his mouth. The word *good* came out.

The doctor nodded. He stripped the gloves off his hands and dropped them into the trash. He came back and sat on the bed.

"I've looked at your x-rays," he said.

Hecker nodded.

"We should chat," the doctor said. "Would you like your daughter to stay for this?"

"Of course I can be here for this," his daughter said. "I'm legally an adult. Be here for what?" she asked.

Hecker shook his head.

"No?" said the doctor. He turned to Hecker's daughter. "Please wait in the hall," he said.

His daughter looked at the doctor and then opened her mouth to speak, and then gave a little inarticulate cry and went out. The doctor came closer, sat on the edge of the bed.

"Your x-rays," said the doctor. "I don't mean to frighten you, but, well, I'd like to run some tests." He took the folder from the bedside table and took the x-rays out, held them above Hecker, in the light. "This cloudiness," he said. "Do you see it? I'm concerned."

Hecker looked. The dark area, as far as he could tell, ran all the way from one side of his skull to the other.

"We'll have to run some tests," said the doctor. "Do you want to let your daughter know?"

Hecker hesitated. Did he want to tell her? No, he thought, but he wasn't certain why. Did he want to shield her or simply shield himself from her reaction? Or was it simply that he didn't trust words anymore, at least not when they came out of his own mouth? Maybe someone else could tell her. Maybe he would figure out what to do when he had to.

"Perhaps no need to frighten her until the results are back," said the doctor, watching him closely. "There's no reason to panic yet," he said. He turned and began to write on his chart. "Any difficulties? Loss of motor skills? Speech problems? Anything out of the ordinary?"

Hecker hesitated. Was there any point trying to explain? "Speech," he finally tried to say, but nothing came out. Why nothing? he wondered. Before, there at least had always been something, even if it was the wrong thing. Frustrated, he shook his head.

The doctor must have taken it to mean something. He smiled. "That's good, then," he said. "Very good indeed."

A few days later, waiting for the results of the tests, he began to panic. *First, he thought, I will lose all language, then I will lose control of my body, then I will die.*

He tried to push them out of his head, such thoughts, with little success. Now, having resigned from teaching, he didn't know what to do with himself. He sat around the house, read, watched his daughter out of the corner of his eye. He had a hard time getting himself to do anything productive. He felt more and more useless, furtive. She was oblivious, he thought, she had no idea that she would watch him first lose the remainder of his speech, then slowly fall apart, waste away. Having to live through that, she would probably pray for his death long before it actually arrived.

And so will I, he thought.

Better to die quickly, he told himself, *smoothly, and save both yourself and those close to you. More dignified.*

He pushed the thought down. It kept rising.

His daughter was trying to hand him the telephone. It was the doctor calling with the test results. "Standish," Hecker said into the receiver. But the doctor was apparently too worried about what he had to say, about saying it right, in the kindest way possible, in the most neutral words imaginable, to notice.

The tests, the doctor claimed, had *amplified his concern*. What he wanted to do was to recommend a specialist to Hecker, a brain surgeon, a good one, one of the best. He would open Mr. Hecker's skull at a certain, optimal spot, take a look at what was really going on in there, and make an assessment of whether it could be cut out, if there was any point in-

"I didn't mean that," said the doctor nervously. "There's always a point. I'm saying it wrong." The proper terminology to describe this was *exploratory surgery*. Did Hecker understand?

"Yes," Hecker managed. "Was fish guillotine sedentary?"

"Hmmm? Necessary? I'm afraid so, Mr. Hecker."

How soon, he wanted to know, could Mr. Hecker put his affairs in order? Not that there was any serious immediate risk, but better safe than sorry. When, he wanted to know, was Mr. Hecker able to schedule the exploratory surgery? Did he have any concerns? Were there any questions that remained to be answered?

Hecker opened his mouth to speak but felt already that anything he said would be wrong, perhaps in several ways at once. So he hung up.

"What did he say?" his daughter was asking him.

"Nobody," he said. "Wrong finger."

IV.

First, he thought over and over, *I will lose all language, then I will not be able to control my body. Then I will die.*

All he could clearly picture when he thought about this was his daughter, her life crippled for months, perhaps years, by his slow, gradual death. He owed it to her to die quickly. But perhaps, he thought, his daughter's suffering was all he could think about because his own was harder to face. Even as he was now, stripped only partly of language, life was nearly unbearable.

First, he thought. *And then. And then.*

He remembered, he hadn't thought about it for years, his own father's death, a gradual move into paralysis, until the man was little more than rattling windpipe in a hospital bed, and a pair of eyes that were seldom open and, when they were, were thick with fear.

Like father, like son, he thought.

First, he thought. *Then. Then.*

He lay in bed, staring up at the ceiling. When it was very late and his daughter was asleep, he got out of bed and climbed up to the attic and took his shotgun out of its case and cleaned it and loaded it. He carried it back downstairs and slid it under his bed.

No, he thought, *No* first, *no* thens.

He was in bed again, staring, thinking. The character of the room seemed to have changed. He could not bear to kill himself with his daughter in the house, he realized. That would be terrible for her, much more terrible than watching him die slowly. And too horrible for him to think about. No, that wouldn't do. He had to get her out.

But ever since he had been to the hospital, she had been sticking near him, never far away, observing him. She kept asking him what exactly was wrong with him, what had the doctor told him, why hadn't she been allowed to hear? And then, what had the doctor said on the telephone? She was always giving him cups of soup which he took a few sips from and then left to scum over on the bookshelves, the fireplace mantel, the windowsills. It wasn't fair, she said, she had only him, they had only each other, but the way he was acting now, she didn't even feel like she had him. What had the doctor said? What exactly was wrong with him? Why wouldn't he tell her? Why wouldn't he speak? All he had to do, she told him, was open his mouth.

But no, that wasn't all. No, it wasn't as simple as that. And yes, he knew he should tell her, but he didn't know what to say or if he *could* say it. And he didn't want her pity—he wanted only to be what he had always been for her, her father, not an old, dying man.

But she wouldn't let up. She was making him insane. If she wanted a fight, he would fight. He turned on her and said, utterly fluent, "Don't you have someplace to be?"

"Yes," she said fiercely. "Here."

"Fat cats," he misspoke, and, suddenly helpless again, turned away.

He made a grocery list, a long one, and offered it to her. She glanced at it.

"Groceries, Daddy?" she said. "Since when did you have anything to do with groceries?"

He shrugged.

"Besides," she said. "We have half this stuff already. Did you even open the cupboards?"

He was beginning to have trouble with one of his fingers. It kept curling and uncurling of its own accord, as if no longer part of his body. He hid it under his thigh when he was seated, felt it wriggling there like a half-dead worm. He and his daughter glared at each other from sofa and armchair respectively, she continuing to hector him with her questions, he remaining silent, sullen.

He ate holding his utensils awkwardly, to hide the rogue finger from her. She took this as an act of provocation, accused him of acting like a child.

It went on for three or four days, both of them at an impasse, until finally she screamed at him and, when he refused to scream back, left the house. He watched the door clack shut behind her. How long would she be gone? Long enough, he hoped.

He got the shotgun out from under the bed and leaned it against the sofa. He dialed 911.

"What's your emergency?" a woman's voice responded.

"I've just killed myself," he told her. "Hurry, please. Cover the body before my daughter gets home."

But it didn't come out like that. This had only been what his mind was saying, his tongue uttering something else entirely.

"Excuse me?" said the operator.

He tried again, his voice straining with urgency.

"Is this a prank call?" the operator said. "This isn't funny."

He fell silent, tried to gather himself.

"Sir?" said the operator. "Hello?"

He looked desperately around the room. The dog was now regarding him intently, ears perked. He picked up the shotgun, held it one-handed near the receiver, and fired it into the wall behind the sofa. The kickback hurt his wrist and made him drop the weapon. The dog skittered out of the room, yelping.

He put the receiver to his ear again. The operator was talking more urgently now. He hung up the telephone.

After picking up the gun, he sat down on the sofa. He hoped that they would come soon, and that it would be soon enough, before his daughter's return. He leaned back and closed his eyes, trying to gather himself.

When he was calm again, he braced the stock of the shotgun between the insoles of his feet and brought the barrels to his face. Carefully, he slipped the ends of the barrels into his mouth.

It was then that his daughter chose to return. He heard her open the front door and then she came into the room, her face pale. It was clear she had been crying. She came in and saw him and stopped dead, then stood there, her face draining of blood. They stayed there like that, staring, neither caring to be the first to look away.

He waited, wondering what words he could use, what he could possibly say to her. How could he ever talk his way out of this one?

"Daddy?" she said finally. "What are you doing?"

And then the words came to him.

He lifted his mouth off the barrels and licked his lips. "Insect," he explained as tenderly as he possibly could. "Grunion. Tent-pole motioning."

An Accounting

I have been ordered to write an honest accounting of how I became a Midwestern Jesus and the subsequent disastrous events thereby accruing, events for which, I am willing to admit, I am at least partly to blame. I know of no simpler way than to simply begin.

In August it was determined that our stores were depleted and not likely to outlast the winter. One of our number was to travel East and beg further provision from our compatriots on the coast, another was to move further inland, hold converse with the Midwestern sects as he encountered them, bartering for supplies as he could. Lots were drawn and this latter role fell to me.

I was provided a dog and a dogcart, a knife, a revolver with twelve rounds, rations, food for the dog, a flint and steel, and a rucksack stuffed with objects for trade. I named the dog Finger for reasons obscure even to myself. I received as well a small packet of our currency, though it was suspected that, since the rupture, our currency, with its Masonic imagery, would be considered by the pious Midwesterners anathema. It was not known if I would be met with hostility, but this was considered not unlikely, considering no recent adventurer into the territory had returned.

I was given as well some hasty training by a former Midwesterner turned heretic named Barton. According to him, I was to make frequent reference to God—though not to use the word *goddamn*, as in the phrase "Where are my goddamn eggs?" "What eggs are these?" I asked Barton, only to discover that the eggs themselves were apparently of no consequence. He ticked off a list of other words considered profane and to be avoided. I was told to frequently describe things as God's will. "There but for the grace of God go I" was also an acceptable phrase, as was "Praise God." Things were not to be called *godawful* though I was allowed to use, very rarely and with care, the phrase "God's aweful grace." If someone were to ask me if I were "saved," I was to claim that yes, indeed, I was saved, and that I had "accepted Jesus Christ as my personal Savior." I made notes of all these locutions, silently vowing to memorize them along the route.

"Another thing," said Barton. "If in dire straits, you should Jesus them and claim revelation from God."

So as you see, it was not I myself who produced the idea of "Jesusing" them, but Barton. Am I to be blamed if I interpreted the verb in a way other than he intended? Perhaps he is to blame for his insufficiencies as an instructor.

But I am outstripping myself. Each story must be told in some order, and mine, having begun at the beginning, has no reason not to take each bit and piece according to its proper chronology, so as to let each reader of this accounting arrive at his own conclusions.

I was driven a certain way, on the bed of an old carrier converted now to steam power. The roads directly surrounding our encampment—what had been my former city in better days—were passable, having been repaired in the years following the rupture. After a few dozen miles, however, the going became more difficult, the carrier forced at times to edge its way forward through the underbrush to avoid a collapse or an eruption of the road. Nevertheless, I had a excellent driver, Marchent, and we had nearly broached the border of the former Pennsylvania before we encountered a portion of road so destroyed by a large mortar or some other such engine of devastation that we could discover no way around. Marchent, one of the finest, blamed himself, though to my mind there was no blame to be taken.

I was unloaded. Marchent and his sturdy second, Bates, carried Finger and his dogcart through the trees to deposit them on the far side of the crater. I myself simply scrambled down hand over foot and then scrambled up the other side.

To this point, my journey could not be called irregular. Indeed, it was nothing but routine, with little interest. As I stood on the far side of the crater, watching Marchent and his second depart in the carrier, I found myself almost relishing the adventure that lay before me.

This was before the days I spent trudging alone down a broken and mangled road through a pale rain. This was before I found myself sometimes delayed for half a day, trying to figure how to get dog and dogcart around an obstacle. They had provided me a simple harness for the dog, but had foreseen nothing by way of rope or tether to secure the fellow. If I tried to skirt, say, a shell crater while carrying the bulky dogcart, Finger, feeling himself on the verge of abandonment, was anxious to accompany me. He would be there, darting between my legs and nearly stumbling me into the abyss itself, and if I did not fall, he did, so that once I had crossed I had to figure some way of extricating him. Often had I shouted at him the command "Finger! Heel!" or the command "Finger! Sit!" but it was soon clear that I, despite pursuing the more dangerous of the two missions, had been disbursed the less adequate canine.

Nevertheless, I grew to love Finger and it was for this I was sorry and even wept when later I had to eat him.

But I fear I have let my digression on Finger, which in honesty began not as a digression but as a simple description of a traveler's difficulty, get the better of my narrative. Imagine me, then, attempting now to carry Finger around a gap in the road in the dogcart itself, with Finger awaiting his moment to effect an escape by clawing his way up my chest and onto my head, and myself shouting "Finger! Stay!" in my most authoritative tone as I feel the ground beginning to slide out from under my feet. Or imagine Finger and me crammed into the dogcart together, the hound clawing my hands to ribbons as we rattle down a slope, not knowing what obstacle we shall encounter at the bottom. That should render sufficient picture of the travails of my journey as regards Finger, and the reason as well—after splicing the harness and refashioning it as a short leash for Finger—for abandoning the dogcart, the which, I am willing to admit, as communal property, I had no right to forsake.

Needless to say, the journey was longer than our experts had predicted. I was uncertain if I had crossed into the Midwest and, in any case, had seen no signs of inhabitants or habitation. The weather had commenced to turn cold and I was wracked with fits of ague. My provisions, being insufficiently calculated, had run low. The resourceful Finger managed to provide for himself by sniffling out and devouring dead creatures when he was released from his makeshift leash—though he was at least as prone to simply roll in said creature and return to me stinking and panting. I myself tried to eat one of these, scraping it up and roasting it first on a spit, but the pain that subsequently assaulted my bowels made me prefer to eat instead what remained of Finger's dog food and, thereafter, to go hungry.

I had begun to despair when the landscape suffered through a transformation in character and I became convinced that I had entered the Midwest at last. The ground sloped ever downward, leveling into a flat and gray expanse. The trees gave way to scrub and brush and a strange crippled grass which, if one was not careful, cut one quite badly. Whereas the mountains and hills had at least had occasional berries or fruit to forage, here the vegetation was not such as to bear fruit. Whereas before one had seen only the occasional crater, here the road seemed to have been systematically uprooted so that almost no trace of it remained. I saw, as well, in the distance as I left the slopes for the flat expanse, a devastated city, now little more than a smear on the landscape. Yet, I reasoned, perhaps this city, like my own city, had become a site for encampment; surely there was someone to be found therein, or at least nearby.

Our progress over this prairie was much more rapid, and Finger did manage to scare up a hare, which, in its confusion, made a run at me and was shot dead with one of my twelve bullets, the noise of its demise echoing forth like an envoy. I made a fire from scrub brush and roasted the hare over it. I had been long without food, and though the creature was stringy and had taken on the stink of the scrub, it was no less a feast for that.

It was this fire that made my presence known, the white smoke rising high through the daylight like a beacon. In retrospect, cooking the rabbit can be considered a tactical error, but you must recall that it had been several days since I had eaten and I was perhaps in a state of confusion.

In any case, long before I had consumed the hare to its end, Finger made a mournful noise and his hackles arose. I captured, from the corner of an eye, a movement through the grass, the which I divined to be human. I rose to my feet. Wrapping Finger's leash around one hand, with the other I lifted my revolver from beside him and cocked it.

I hallooed the man and, brandishing my revolver, encouraged him to come forth of his own accord. Else, I claimed, I would send my dog into the brush to flush him and then would shoot him dead. Finger, too, entered wonderfully into the spirit of the thing, though I knew he would not harm anybody but only sniff them and, were they already dead, roll in their remains. There was no response for a long moment and then the fellow arose like a ghost from the quaking grass and tottered out, as did his compatriots.

There were perhaps a dozen of them, a pitiful crew, each largely unclothed and unkempt, their skin discolored and lesioned as well. They were thin, arms and legs just slightly more than pale sticks, bellies swollen with hunger.

"Who is your leader?" I asked the man who had come first.

"God is our leader," the fellow claimed.

"Praise God," I said, "God's will be done, the Lord be praised," rattling off their phrases as if I had been giving utterance to them all my life. "But who is your leader in this world?"

They looked at one another dumbly, as if my question lay beyond comprehension. It was quickly determined that they had no leader but were *waiting for a sign*, viz., were waiting for God to inform them as to how to proceed.

"I am that sign," I told them, thinking such authority might help better effect my purposes. There was a certain pleased rumbling at this. "I have come to beg you for provisions."

But food they claimed not to have, and by testimony of their own sorry condition, I was apt to believe them. Indeed, they were hungrily eyeing the sorry remains of my hare.

I gestured to it with my revolver. "I would invite you to share my humble meal," I said, and at those words one of them stumbled forward and took up the spit.

It was only by my leveling the revolver at each of them in turn as he ate that each was assured a share of the little that remained. Indeed, by force of the revolver alone was established what later they referred to as "the miracle of the everlasting hare," where, it was said, the food was allowed to pass from hand to hand and yet there remained enough for all.

If this be in fact a miracle, it is attributable not to me but to the revolver. It would have been better to designate said revolver as their Messiah instead of myself. Perhaps you will argue that, though this be true, without my hand to hold said weapon it could not have become a Jesus, that both of us together did a Jesus make, and I must admit that such an argument is hard to counter. Though if I were a Jesus, or a portion of a Jesus, I was an unwitting one at this stage, and must plead for understanding.

When the hare was consumed, I allowed Finger what remained of the bones. The fellows whom I had fed squatted about the fire and asked me if I had else to provide them by way of nourishment. I confessed I had not.

"We understand," one of them said, "from your teachings, that mankind cannot live by bread alone. But must not mankind have bread to live?"

"My teachings?" I said. I was not familiar at that time with the verse, was unsure what this rustic seer intended by attributing this statement to me.

"You are that sign," he said. "You have said so yourself."

Would you believe that I was unfamiliar enough at that moment with the teachings of the Holy Bible so as not to understand the mistake being made? I was like a gentleman in a foreign country, reader, armed with just enough of the language to promote serious misunderstanding. So that when I stated, in return, "I am that sign," and heard the rumble of approval around me, I thought merely that I was returning a formula, a manner of speech devoid of content. Realizing that because of the lateness of the season I might well have to remain in the Midwest through the worst of winter, I concluded it was in my interest to be on good terms with those likely to be of use to me.

Indeed, it was not until perhaps a week later, as their discourse and their continued demands for "further light and knowledge" became more specific, that I realized that by saying "I am that sign," I was saying to them, "I am your Jesus." By that time, even had I effected a denial of my Jesushood, it would not have been believed, would have been seen merely as a paradoxical sort of teaching, a parable.

But I digress. Suffice to say that I had become their Jesus by ignorance and remained in that ignorance for some little time, and remain to some extent puzzled even today by the society I have unwittingly created. Would I have returned from the Midwest if I were in accord with them? True, it may be argued that I did not return of my own, yet when I was captured, it is beyond dispute, I was on the road toward my original encampment. I had no other purpose or intention but to report to my superiors. What other purpose could have brought me back?

In those first days, I stayed encamped on that crippled, pestilent prairie, surrounded by a group of Midwesterners who would not leave me and who posed increasingly esoteric questions: Did I come bearing an olive branch or a sword? (Neither, in fact, but a revolver.) What money changers would I overturn in this epoch? (But currency is of no use here, I protested.) What was the state of an unborn child? (Dead, I suggested, before realizing that by unborn they did not mean stillborn, but by then it was too late to retrace my steps.) They refused to leave my side, seemed starved to talk to someone like myself—perhaps, I reasoned, the novelty of a foreigner. They were already mythologizing the "miracle of the everlasting hare"—which I told them they were making too much of: were it truly everlasting, the hare would still be here and we could commence to eat it over again. They looked thoughtful at this. There was, they felt, some lesson to be had in my words.

The day following the partaking of the hare, serious questions began to develop as to what we would eat next. I set snares and taught the others to do the same, but it seemed that the hare had been an anomaly and the snares remained unsprung. It was clear that the others expected me to feed them, as if by sharing my hare with them I had entered into an obligation to provide for them. I tried at times to shoo them away from me and even pointed the revolver once or twice, but though I could drive them off a little distance they were never out of sight and would soon return.

But I am neglecting Finger. The men sat near me or, if I were walking, dogged my footsteps. I found my hunger filling my mind with a darkness and had no desire so strong as to abandon their company immediately. Soon they began to beseech me in plaintive tones, using phrases such as these:

Master, call down manna from heaven.

Master, strike that rock with your stave [n.b., I had no stave] *and cause a fountain to spring forth.*

Master, transfigure our bodies so that they have no need of food but are nourished on the word alone.

Being a heretic, I did not grasp the antecedent of this harangue (i.e., my Jesushood), but only its broader sense. Soon they were all crying out, and I, already maddened from hunger, did not know how to proceed. A fever overcame me. Perhaps, I thought, I could slip away from them. But no, it was clear they thought they belonged with me and would not let me go. If I was to rid myself of them, there seemed no choice but to kill them.

It was here that my eyes fell upon Finger, he who had shared in my travails for many days, the cause of both much frustration and much joy. Here, I thought, is the inevitable first step, though I wept to think this. Divining no other choice, I drew my revolver and shot Finger through the head, then flensed him and trussed him and broiled him over the flames. He tasted, I must reluctantly admit, not unlike chicken. *Poor Finger*, I told myself, *perhaps we shall meet in a better world.*

Their response to this act was to declare I had come not with an olive branch but with a sword, and to use the phrase *He smiteth*, a phrase which haunts me to this day.

•

It is by little sinful steps that grander evils come to pass. I am sorry to say that Finger was only a temporary solution, quickly consumed. I had hoped that, once sated, they would allow me to depart in peace, but they seemed bound to me more than ever now, and even offered me tributes: strange woven creations of no use nor any mimetic value, which they assembled from the tortured grass: crippled and faceless half-creatures that came apart in my hands.

I thought and pondered and saw no way out but to sneak away from them by night. At first, I thought to have effected an escape, yet before I was even a hundred yards from the campsite, one of them had raised a hue and cry, and they were all there with me, begging me not to go.

"I must go," I claimed. "Others await me."

"Then we shall accompany you," they said.

"I must go alone."

This they would not accept. *I cannot stop them from coming with me,* I thought, *but at least I may move them in the proper direction to facilitate my eventual return to my camp.* And in any case, I thought, if we are to survive, we must leave this accursed plain where nothing grows but dust and scrub and misery. We must gain the hills.

So gain the hills we did. My plan was to instruct them in self-sufficiency, in how to trap their own prey and how to grow their own foodstuffs, how to scavenge and forage and make do with what was at hand and thereby avoid starvation. This done, I hoped to persuade them to allow me to depart.

We had arrived in the hills too late for crops, and animals and matter for foraging had grown scarce as well. We employed our first days gleaning what little food we could, gathering firewood and making for ourselves shelter prone to withstand the winter. But by the time winter set in with earnestness, we discovered our food all but gone and our straits dire indeed. I, as their Jesus, was looked to for a solution.

We have reached that unfortunate chapter which I assume to be the reason for my having been asked to compose this accounting. Might I say, before I begin, that I regret everything, but that, at the time, I felt there to be no better choice? Were my inquest (assuming there is to be an inquest) to take place before a group of starved men, I might at least accrue some sympathy. But to the well-fed, necessity must surely appear barbarity. And now, again well-fed myself, I regret everything. Would I do it again? Of course not. Unless I were very hungry indeed.

In the midst of our suffering, I explained to them that one of us must sacrifice himself for the others. I explained how I, as I had not yet finished my work, was unable to serve. To this they nodded sagely. And which of you, I asked, dare sacrifice himself, by so doing to become a type and shadow of your Jesus? There was among them one willing to step forward, and he was instantly shot dead. *He smiteth*, I could hear the men mumbling. What followed? Reader, we ate him.

By winter's end we had consumed two of his fellows, each of whom stepped forward unprotesting, each as my apostle honored to become a type and shadow of his Jesus by a sacrifice of his own. Their bones we cracked open to suck the marrow, but the skulls of all three we preserved and enshrined, out of respect for their sacrifice—along with the skull of Finger, which I had preserved and continue to carry with me to this day. Early in spring I urged them farther into the hills until we had discovered a small valley whose soil seemed fertile and promising. In a cave we discovered an unrefined salt. I taught them to fish and how as well to smoke their fish to preserve it, and this they described as becoming fishers of men (though to my mind they were more properly described as fishers of fish). We again set snares along game trails and left them undisturbed and this time caught rabbits and birds, and sometimes a squirrel, and this meat we ate or smoked and preserved as well. The hides they learned to strip and tan, and they bound them about their feet. I taught them as well how to cultivate those plants as were available to them, and to make them fruitful. When they realized it was my will that they fend for themselves, they were quick to learn. And thus we were not long into summer when I called them together to inform them of my departure.

At first they would not hear of this, and could not understand why their Jesus would leave them. *Other sheep I have,* I told them, *that are not of this fold.* Having spent the winter in converse with them and reading an old tattered copy of their Bible, I had become conversant in matters of faith, and though I never did feel a temptation to give myself over to it, I did know how best to employ it for my purposes. When even this statement did not seem sufficient for the most stubborn among them, who still threatened to accompany me, I told them, *Go and spread my teachings.*

By this I meant what I had taught them of farming and clothing themselves and hunting but, just as with Barton, it would have served me well to be more specific. Indeed, this knowledge did spread, but with it came a ritual of the eating of human flesh throughout the winter months, a ritual I had not encouraged and had resorted to only in direst emergency. This they supported not only with glosses from the Bible, but with words from a new Holy Book they had written on birchbark, in which I recognized a twisted rendering of my own words.

It was not until I had been discovered by my former compatriots and imprisoned briefly under suspicion and then returned to my own campsite that I heard any hint of this lamentable practice. It was inquired of me whether I had seen any such thing in my travels in the Midwest. Perhaps it was wrong of me to feign ignorance. And I had long returned to my duties, despite the hard questions concerning dog and dogcart and provisions that I had been unable to answer, before there were rumors that the practice had begun, like a contagion, to spread, and had even crossed from the Midwest into our own territories. I had indeed lost nearly all sense of my days as a Midwestern Jesus before the authorities discovered my name circulating in Midwestern mouths, inscribed in their Holy Books. If when I was again apprehended I was indeed preparing to flee—and I do not admit to such—it is only because of a fear of becoming a scapegoat, a fear that is in the process of being realized.

If I had intended to create this cult around my own figure, why then would I have ever left the Midwest? What purpose would I have had in abandoning a world in which I could have been a god? The insinuations that I have been spreading my own cult in our own territories are spurious. There is absolutely no proof.

There is one other thing I shall say in my defense: what takes place beyond the borders of the known world is not to be judged against the standards of this world. Then, you may well inquire, what standard of judgment should be applied? I do not know the answer to this question. Unless the answer be no standard of judgment at all.

I was ordered to write an honest accounting of how I became a Midwestern Jesus, and to the best of my ability I have done so. I regret to say that at the conclusion of my task I now for the first time see my actions in a cold light. I have no faith in the clemency of my judges, nor faith that any regret for those events I unintentionally set in motion will lead to a pardon. I have no illusions: I shall be executed.

Yet I have one last request. After my death, I ask that my body be torn asunder and given in pieces to my followers. Though I remain a heretic, I see no way of bringing my cult to an end otherwise. Let those who want to partake of me partake, and then I will at least have rounded the circle, my skull joining a pile of skulls in the Midwest, my bones shattered and sucked free of marrow and left to bleach upon the plain. And then, if I do not arise from the dead, if I do not appear to them in a garment of white, Finger beside, then perhaps it all will end.

And if I do arise, stripping the lineaments of death away to reveal renewed the raiment of the living? Permit me to say, then, that it is already too late for all of you, for I come not with an olive branch but with a sword. *He smiteth*, and when he smiteth, ye shall surely die.

Desire with Digressions

In the end, suffering and not knowing what else to do, I left her abruptly and without warning, taking only the clothes on my back. She was out behind the isolated house, near the meadow, the creek just beginning to rise as it did every year, and I went out and looked at her a final time as she sat in the grass, looking at the creek, facing away from me.

Watching her, after all she had said to me, I felt that if her head were to turn toward me then I would see not her face but an unfeatured facelessness, as inhuman and smooth as a plate. And then, standing there, I realized I could not even imagine what her face looked like, nor recall ever having seen it at all, and this feeling grew until it became a form of panic. In the end, not knowing what else to do, not daring to risk seeing her face, I turned and walked back through the house and out the front door and was gone.

Do you love me? her voice was saying in my head as I walked up the dirt road and then up the gravel road and then down the paved road until I found a car I could steal. *Do you love me?* it was saying as I drove quickly away, not knowing where I was going. But even in my head I could not bring myself to answer her, and when, finally, to stop her voice from saying it, I finally said *Yes,* I could not even in imagination lift my eyes to meet her unimaginable face.

So began what proved to be days in orbit, with myself both afraid to go back and afraid to get too far away from her. I knew what I had felt about her face could not be natural, could not have anything to do with any reality connected to her. I could rationalize my fear away, and yet I still could not bring myself to return and look her in the face. I drove, I stole for food and gas, drove some more. Each time I seemed about to go far enough that I would no longer be able to think of going back, I found the car coaxed by my hands into a slow arc, an orbit with her at its center. *Why not simply go back?* I asked myself, at night, sleeping on the ground beside a guttering fire or sleeping curled in the car's backseat. And I would tell myself, *Yes, I will go back.* But when morning came, the sun a blank and burning round such as I feared her face to be, I could only continue my dim and erratic orbit.

Until at last I was forced to abandon the car, engine smoking and radiator stuttering, at the height of a mountain pass and to continue forward alone and on foot, shivering my way over the summit and plodding down the other side. I tried to thumb a ride, but cars were few and none stopped, and in the slow and beautiful descent from mountain to valley I began, ignored again and again, to think of myself as a ghost. What was it she had said to me, that day before she had abandoned me to sit beside the creek and grow strange? And how had I responded? Why could I not recall?

Midway downslope into the high valley was a graveled pullout and a small tavern, little more than a shack, fallen into poor repair. The door was sticky at first, and I thought for a moment in forcing it that it was locked, but then suddenly it gave way and I tumbled in. It was a dim place, lit by little more than the evening light streaming through its single window. It seemed nearly as cold inside as outside, the wind whistling through the walls. There was a small bar, nothing behind it but two bottles of cheap scotch and a weathered keg of beer. A grizzled and poorly toothed barmaid merely stared at me as I approached.

"What you want?" she finally asked.

Nothing, I claimed, only to get out of the cold for a moment and warm up before—

"We got beer, whiskey," she said. "Which suits?"

Both suited, I told her, but I was at the moment fallen in the cracks of life and a little short on funds.

"Got to drink to stay," she said, and so I dug around in one pocket and came up with a few coins. She looked at them and counted them and then poured me just enough whiskey to wet the bottom of a shot glass. "Get on with you," she said.

I carried the shot glass over to the table and sat down. The old woman at the bar kept her eyes on me. I tried to look at anything else but her.

Still, I had been there quite some time before my eyes adjusted sufficiently to make out, in one dark corner, another man. When he realized I had noticed him, he nodded slightly. I nodded back and lifted my shot glass to let the little that was in it trickle down my throat, licking the glass clean afterward. When I finally put it back down, I found him still watching me.

"What you want?" the barmaid barked, and it took me a moment to realize she was speaking to me.

I was fine, I told her, I didn't want anything.

"Got to drink or split," she said.

And so I stood up and made my way out. I moved down the road in the fading sunlight.

I had gone nearly a half-mile before I realized that I was not alone, that the man in the bar had followed me out and was now at a little distance behind. I stopped and turned to him. He stopped as well.

"What is it?" I asked.

He just shook his head and shyly smiled.

I turned and started down again. When I looked back he was still there, still following.

"What?" I said again, and this time took a few steps back, toward him.

"Nothing," he said.

"What do you mean, nothing?" I asked.

"I'm still trying to decide if you're the man."

"The man for what?"

"There's something," he said, "needs getting down. One man can't do it alone. It needs two. I'm trying to decide if you're the second."

"What's in it for me?" I asked.

He smiled. "Maybe you are the man," he said, and came closer.

I stayed as the light fell, and listened to him, watched the glints of his eyes, tried to read the dimming lines of his face. It would, he claimed, take only a day or so, a quick trip up into the mountains, and then we would come back down, our fortunes made. *And what is it?* I asked. But he merely shook his head. I would have to trust him, he said.

I shrugged. What, in fact, I wondered, did I have to lose? At the very least this was a distraction from my own life. And so I agreed.

48

He took me by the arm, began to tug me slowly off the road, into the slush and snow.

"Wait," I said. "Let's wait for the morning."

But no, was I not the man after all? I had to trust him, we had to go now, there was not a moment to lose. And what, finally, did I care? Another day of shivering and cold? I would have it sooner or later, so why not sooner? So I allowed myself to be led off the road and away.

We trudged through the night, my hands gone blue with cold, my feet so numb I could hardly feel them. When he saw how I was suffering, he drew from around his shoulders an old blanket, which I wrapped around myself, and then felt at least slightly less cold.

We stopped near dawn and he cleared a spot of snow and ice and with a solitary match and pine needles started a small fire, slowly feeding it into a blaze. My feet, out of my wet shoes now, at first stayed numb and then felt as if they were being repeatedly stabbed. It was almost more than I could bear.

"Just a little more," he said to himself. In the firelight I could see just how haggard his face really was. "Just a little more," he said again.

And I looked at him and saw in his eyes a look closer to death than to mere exhaustion. A shadow had settled into his face and it lay there, just beneath the skin, blurring his features.

"Perhaps," I said, "we should go back."

He gave a little start, and then his eyes settled on me and he slowly smiled. "Just a little more," he said again. "Just a little more."

And so, just a little more. A slow tramp up into the mountains, the snow no longer slush but deep and powdery now, sticky, and the two of us tramping forward, he pushing a path through the snow and I following, the going slower as the sun slipped lower in the sky.

Until at last, past exhaustion, he seemed to glimpse what he was looking for, and we made for it.

It was a small miner's shack. Inside, it was empty, not even wood for a fire. We were, both of us, too exhausted to trudge back out and go in search of dry timber, so instead we worked our way into a corner and huddled together, our bodies tight around each other, as the wind whistled around us.

I felt his face next to mine grow slowly cold, the heat draining out of him. And then I fell into a state between waking and sleeping and perhaps as well between death and life. In that state I saw myself again staring at her back, again afraid that she might turn around and reveal her face in a terrible way. But she did not turn around. It was as if she were frozen: she neither moved nor breathed. This made me even more afraid than if she were to turn around.

When the wind fell and morning light struck again, I opened my eyes to see my companion's lips gone blue, his face turning blue as well. He could open his eyes and move them, but hardly more than that.

And now what? I asked him. He was in no condition to go on, I argued. Now that we were here, would he not tell me what it was we had come in search of?

He regarded me torpidly through half-closed eyes. Slowly his mouth opened itself, his lips pulling apart only reluctantly, as if his face were being slowly torn, but then, instead of speech, a dim, wracked sound issued from his throat, and he died.

There is, in every event, whether lived or told, always a hole or a gap, often more than one. If we allow ourselves to get caught in it, we find it opening onto a void that, once we have slipped into it, we can never escape. The void here—only one of several in what, from the wandering of love, my life had become—was this notion of some vague treasure awaiting me, something waiting to be taken, if only I could figure out what it was. I searched my companion's pockets, my fingers trembling with cold, but found nothing to indicate what we had been looking for, nor anything to tell me who, exactly, my companion had been. I searched the shack itself, carefully, but found nothing to indicate the nature of what we had been searching for and no signs of a hiding place. I stripped him to see if he had any tattoos or hidden markings that might reconfigure my sense of the world, and found nothing. But rather than putting the clothes back on him, I put them on my own body, over my own clothing, so as to keep warm, so as to disguise myself.

Since I was in a miner's shack, perhaps whatever it was I was meant to find was in the mine. But coming out of the shack, I could see no sign of a mine. I could, I thought, search until I found something, but I had no food, did not know what I was looking for. This was, I convinced myself, the hole that was opening into a void for me: a desire for some unknown riches, which I might not even recognize were I to see them, was coaxing me forward and into my own oblivion, offering to make me not rich but dead.

And it was with this realization that her face sprang up before me at last. In my head I saw her turn away from the creek and turn toward me and smile—her stark blue eyes, her high cheekbones, her beautiful, full lips, her slightly skewed teeth: I could piece together little of her beyond that—whole regions of her face and head remaining unrendered and incomplete—but it was enough to fill me with a desire to see her again, a desire that pulled me out of the void and saved my life.

I kept her image before me as I moved back down the mountain again, along the trail we had blazed through the snow during our ascent. The journey seemed quicker this time, the crust of the snow already broken, the path already there to follow, the downward slope urging me quickly forward. I kept putting one foot in front of the other, not stopping even after darkness fell. I kept plodding down, hardly conscious of anything around me until, unsure of how many hours I had traveled, how many steps I had taken, I found myself at last on the road.

What immediately followed I have assembled after the fact and by inference. The few bits and pieces that I do remember feel less lived than observed from a distance. I was found delirious and shivering and nearly dead, by some car that had stopped. I was taken to what seemed at first to me an asylum but which I have allowed myself over time to be convinced was a hospital. There, doctors in pale-blue coats lopped off the toes on one foot and removed most of the other foot. A few fingers were cut free as well, while a few others still continued to itch and buzz with pain. I was asked who I was, without result: in my addled state I hardly knew the answer myself at first and then I chose to keep to myself the answers slowly coming to me. Eventually they stopped asking.

All the while I kept her image before me: the movement of her lips as she asked me, *Do you love me?* and myself still unsure how or if I had responded, but knowing that now I would answer, *Yes.* And when, finally, I was coherent again, I lay in bed with my bandaged hands and stared at the ceiling and plotted how I would make my way back to her.

And then one day, abruptly and without warning, I simply climbed out of bed, slipped into my clothes, and left. I walked out the front door of the hospital and climbed into the first likely car I saw and not without difficulty hot-wired it and then, gripping the steering wheel with my bandaged hands, drove away. I could imagine her there, still by the creek, still waiting for me. I imagined how she would turn and face me and smile. *Where have you been?* I imagined her asking, and imagined myself shrugging and responding, *Nowhere*, though there was no place in my imagining for how her face might change once she saw my mangled hands and feet.

I drove through the night and I drove through the dawn, coming in from the west with the sun in my eyes. I left the car on the side of the paved road in place of the first car I had stolen, then walked the rest of the way up the paved road, down the gravel road, down the dirt road. The house looked just as I had left it, and I banged my way through the screen door and inside, calling her name, receiving no response.

The house was still, the floors and furniture dim with dust, and I wandered from room to room, confused. Finally I went out the back door and into the meadow.

I could instantly see her there, sitting just as I had left her, and I started quickly toward her, calling her name again.

But once I came a little farther I found myself slowing, stopping. For I could see that what I had thought was her arm was only the bones that had once structured the arm, the flesh mostly gone. And I saw that a part of her on the other side, too, was in the process of grimly disarticulating itself with the aid of vermin and time, and I remembered what, out of love or hate, had happened, and why I had left in the first place.

And then what choice was there but to turn about in my dead man's clothes and leave, to go through the house and out the front door and get into the car again, to set off again, to fling myself free of her gravitation and, this time, never, never come back?

Dread

I'd read once, in what book I no longer recall,
a phrase that for no apparent reason came to
haunt me.

I hardly ever thought about it during the day, only late at night when I was just slipping into sleep, and in early morning when I was not yet quite awake.

The phrase would toll once, briefly, a distant bell.

I would fall asleep with a vague but growing sense of dread, and would awake to a slowly fading sense of dread, as if the entirety of my sleep was the brief stretch it took for the dread to gather and then dissipate.

The phrase itself was simple:

He no longer resembled me.

Its original context, what I could recall of it, was nothing to incite any particular feeling whatsoever.

There was no real textual significance to the phrase -- its narrator uttered it merely in passing.

And yet, there it came, again and again, at the moment of falling asleep and at the moment of awakening, marking the descent from and re-ascent to consciousness.

I no longer was dreaming:

sleep had become nothing but a movement

from the first word of this phrase to its last.

I increasingly dreaded falling asleep.

My wife, sleeping beside me, knew nothing.

I swallowed so-called sleep aids, but the phrase still haunted me.

I tried to train myself to jar my-self awake, without result.

When I consulted a doctor, he asked me if I felt rested.

Well, yes, I felt rested during the day, but increasingly anxious with the approach of darkness.

He shrugged, prescribed an antidepressant.

When I took it, I found it simply to muffle the phrase slightly, blunting it as though it were being voiced

by a drunk through a bathroom door.

This made it much worse.

Every morning I felt slightly foolish about the dread I had felt the night before;

every night, I felt the dread inexorably rise again.

This continued until I awoke in a hospital, my shirt cut away, an oxygen mask over my face, feeling incredible, intense, unlocatable pain.

A doctor holding two gleaming metal paddles stood over me, and I thought I could smell the faint odor of burning hair.

Other faces, muffled behind surgical masks, were gathered around me. When they realized I was awake, the bodies they were attached to began to busy themselves.

A hidden mouth asked my name;

I offered up a slurred sound that was apparently close enough.

A set of gloved hands began to wipe down my chest with something cool. A third hand injected a fluid into an i.v. bag whose tube, I realized, ran into the back of what must be my own hand.

The doctor holstered the paddles into a device strapped onto a wheeled cart.

When he came closer, it was to shine a small penlight into

First one of my eyes and then the other.

I had, he explained, been, technically speaking, dead.

He went on to explain to me, in great detail but through his surgical mask, the difference between *technically*

dead and *actually dead*, thinking it might be of some interest.

"Well," he said, once he was finished speaking, "how are we feeling now?"

It was all I could do to breathe.

A little later, in another room, a fleshy nurse decked out in novelty scrubs, asked me if I believed in God.

Since I once had, I nodded my head yes, hoping to make her sympathetic to me.

I was told I could not possibly still be feeling the pain I was feeling.

This would be insisted upon right up until the moment when, days later, after the pain had become so intense that I figured the only way to stop it was to try to systematically dismantle my house with a sledgehammer, I awoke again, this time in a different hospital.

This earlier time, though, in this earlier hospital,

I kept looking around for my wife.

Most of the time she was in a chair beside me, seemingly sympathetic but equally immune to the demands I was, admittedly, having difficulty voicing.

All I wanted was for her or the nurse or anyone at all to go fetch me a mirror, even though the way my mouth was trying to broken the request made me pretty certain this was a bad idea.

Nobody paid me any heed, but i kept wanting it, wanting it, despite a growing dread of what I actually would see.

And when I finally felt well enough to climb out of the bed myself and make my way, swaying, toward a reflective surface, by then it was already far too late. What frightened me was not how the man thrown back so little resembled me, but how he so greatly did.

There was no getting around him.

And here we still are, staring each other down, haggard and grim, bodies aching.

each of us hoping the other will be the first to go.

Girls in Tents

In the late afternoons, after school, in the days just after their father had left their mother, the two girls would strip all the blankets off their beds. Gathering them up as best they could, they carried them out of their rooms and down the narrow hall to drop them in a heap in the living room. They tucked blanket edges under couch cushions or put them on furniture with encyclopedias piled on them, and then stretched the blankets from couch to chair or from chair to window ledge. When done, they had a series of tents, all overlapping, the living room become a series of billows and dips under which they could crouch.

For several months they lived each afternoon under these tents, light coming mottled through the fabric. They felt good there. Sometimes they read or drew or talked there, other times just sat. When their mother came home from work, she often knelt down and asked how they were doing, and what. The youngest girl mostly half-shrugged and said *fine*, they were doing *fine*. The oldest girl never answered unless she had to, unless the mother addressed her directly and more than once. It was not that she disliked her mother, only that she thought it was none of the mother's business. The tents had been the oldest girl's idea; she had made them so as to have a substitute house within the larger house, for now that the father was gone the house no longer felt like it was her house. It was only in the tents that she began to feel at home again. In the tents it was the two of them, the two girls, alone but together, and nothing changing unless they wanted it to. So when the mother knelt down to ask what they were doing in the tents, the oldest girl didn't feel she should have to answer: the tents were not about the mother.

When the father had left, it was as if he had taken part of the house with him. It no longer felt like the oldest girl's house, but neither did it feel like her house at the apartment the father rented across town. Every other week the girls' father showed up, looking somewhat disoriented, to take them away to his apartment, where they stayed for almost two full days, the father trying to keep them entertained until the mother arrived on Sunday afternoon to take them to church. At the father's house, in his apartment, the girls slept on the front-room floor in sleeping bags. This practice the father sometimes referred to as *camping*, which made the oldest girl try to imagine she was out in the open, under the stars. But still she never felt at home in a sleeping bag like she did in the tents.

One problem with the father's new house was that there were not enough blankets to make a good tent. The father was what the mother called a *cold sleeper;* he had only one blanket in his apartment and usually slept (so the oldest girl had found sometimes late at night when she couldn't sleep and went to the father's bedroom to see if the father was asleep himself) on the edge of the bed, half his body uncovered, the blanket splitting him in two. During the day, the girls were allowed to take this single blanket from the bed and stretch it from the back of the couch to the bookshelves behind, then tuck it in tightly between the books, but one blanket was not enough; it made a tunnel but hardly a tent. They had tried, the two girls, unzipping the sleeping bags to use them as blankets to make tents, but the sleeping-bag fabric was heavy and thick—light didn't come through in the way it did with a good blanket. And in any case, the father didn't have enough furniture to make good tents. All he had was a couch and a chair. Now that he was out of the house, the father didn't have much of anything. In the kitchen, all he had of utensils were three of each: three knives, three forks, three spoons, all taken from the larger collection of wedding flatware that still resided with the mother. If he and the girls ate anything, the father would have to wash utensils before they could eat again.

The father, when he was feeling exuberant, when he was at his best, would claim that they were lucky girls, that most little girls did not have two houses like they did. But the oldest girl felt that no, they did not now have two houses: they were between houses and thus in a way had no house. And it was clear to the oldest girl that their father did not feel at home in his new house, that in a way he had no home of his own either. Unlike the father, the oldest girl at least had the tents to go to, and after school, each day, she and her sister would make the tents and lie beneath in the warm space, watching the mottled light filter through.

Near the end of his fourth month out of the house, the father began to let them down. He still showed up on Friday to take them to his house, to his apartment, but they never could count on when. Before, he had always been sitting on the porch when they came home from school, but now it was hard to say. Sometimes he was there, waiting, but most days he would not show up until the mother was long home from work and it had begun to grow dark outside. A few times the mother got tired of waiting and called him, and when he showed up ten minutes later he was shamefaced and apologetic.

The oldest girl knew something was going wrong with the father, but could not say what exactly. She knew he was distracted but could not say why. In a way, what or why did not matter. The youngest girl, too, felt something going wrong with the father, and the youngest girl was nervous about him. The youngest girl was, so the mother always said, *high-strung*, and thus needed from time to time to be soothed and calmed down. The oldest girl always tried to calm her down. She did not always notice things as quickly as the oldest girl did, but when she did notice them she seemed to feel them more, and since the father had left, it had somehow become the oldest girl's job to help calm her down. Because of that, the oldest girl had learned not to show when she knew something or felt it, so that sometimes she felt like she was just watching things happening but nothing really was ever happening to her. The oldest girl thus had learned to cope with everything alone and quickly, so that by the time the youngest girl began to catch wind of things she could be there, as calm and placid as glass, to comfort her.

So while it was true that the oldest girl knew something was wrong with the father well before the youngest girl, by the time the youngest girl began to notice and feel it the oldest girl had stopped worrying and already saw this wrongness now instead as a condition of life to be adapted to. The youngest girl worried about what was happening with the father, but the oldest girl, while calming the youngest girl and distracting her and making up games in the tent for her, was not so much worried as only curious about where it would all lead.

The father kept coming to get them, mostly late but occasionally on time. Sometimes he seemed so distracted that he could not even be talked to. They would ride back with him to his apartment in silence. Once there, he would sometimes notice them and smile, and sometimes they would even walk a few blocks together for ice cream and then figure out something else to do, but mostly they would just sit around the apartment in their inadequate blanket tunnel while the father lay on the blanketless bed reading a book or just staring up at the ceiling. Sometimes he would come out of the bedroom and sit at one end of the blanket tunnel and give them choices about what they could do. They could order a pizza or they could have pasta. They could go to a movie or they could go to the zoo. Which did they want to do? The oldest girl had developed a system of not putting any demands on the father, figuring that putting demands on him would make him even less dependable than he already was, so mostly she shrugged and said she didn't care. The youngest girl usually followed her lead. But somehow not caring put another sort of demand on the father, so that he just shook his head and often went back into the bedroom without deciding on any particular thing, and nothing was done. Something was happening to the father so that he was slowly disengaging himself from them, even when they were actually present and there. The oldest girl could guess where it was going, that they would see the father less and less and one day see him not at all. But all she could do while she comforted the youngest girl and kept her from the truth was steel herself for what would happen next.

On the day the father failed to arrive, the mother had made *other arrangements*. She would not be home after work, had an *engagement*, would not be back until the next day. She had in fact called the father the night before to let him know this, to stress that he must come on time. This, the youngest girl thought later, once night had fallen and she and her sister were alone in the tents, had been a mistake on the mother's part. The mother did not understand how the father worked, since she herself, the mother, worked so differently. She did not see that saying such things to the father made him not more dependable but less so.

So, when they left in the morning, the mother gave them their lunches and reminded them that she would not be home, that when they got back from school the father would be there waiting for them. She kissed them and drove them to school and left them there like she always did, and they went to their classes and ate lunch and went to their classes again. When school was over, the oldest girl went to the youngest girl's classroom and got her and together they walked home.

At the house, the father wasn't there yet. They took the key from under the doormat and cleaned it off and let themselves in. *Hello*, the youngest girl called out hopefully as they entered the house, but there was no answer.

They put their schoolbooks down on the couch and then went to get their already packed overnight bags out of their rooms and put them next to the front door, up against the wall right beside the door, so that when the father arrived they would be all ready to go. They sat on the couch, waiting. Usually, the oldest girl thought, the mother was there and would have them do something while she herself called the father, but they were alone, the oldest girl thought, that was fine, the oldest girl thought, they would manage. Or at least she would. The youngest girl, she could see, was beginning to fidget and get anxious. She was sitting on the couch and trying to figure out what was happening, or rather not happening, and soon she was going to start to panic.

"Let's go get a snack," said the oldest girl to her, poker-faced, as if getting a snack and their father's absence weren't actually connected. They went into the kitchen and the oldest girl boosted the youngest girl up onto the counter so that she could stand there and open the cabinet and get the snacks out. Getting up on the counter was a special treat for the youngest girl, the oldest girl knew. The youngest girl got down the sandwich cookies and sat on the edge of the counter while the oldest girl opened the packages and divided the cookies out. The way the girls liked to eat sandwich cookies was to break them open and scrape the cream out with their teeth and then eat the cookie part later, dipped in milk. But even when they were done, cream and cookie halves and milk gone, the father still hadn't arrived.

The sun was getting low in the sky outside, the oldest girl noticed. She wondered how long it would be before the youngest girl noticed. The oldest girl helped her sister off the counter and they went back into the living room and the oldest girl, trying to be casual about it, turned on the light.

"When is he coming?" asked the youngest girl.

"He's on his way," said the oldest girl. And then she said, "Time for tents."

They did it the way they always did. The oldest girl went into her room and pulled her blankets into a pile and carried them out all at once, then dumped them on the living room floor. The youngest girl carried out just one of her blankets and then waited for the oldest girl to come get the other one. Together, they pushed the armchair closer to the couch and brought in the kitchen chairs as well. They got the encyclopedias down from the shelf and then set about spreading the blankets out, tucking them into the couch cushions and anchoring them down with books.

When they were done, the tents overlapped and stretched from couch to fireplace, in some places as high as the girls sitting and in others almost touching the floor. The girls crawled under an edge and got in and moved into the middle, where, near the armchair, they could sit upright without the tents touching them, the overhead light coming differently through the different blankets around them, shining oddly on their flesh.

"I'm hungry," said the youngest girl.

"We had a snack," said her sister.

"When is he coming?"

"Soon."

"Did you call him?"

The oldest girl did not answer. She did not want to call the father, though she knew that was what the mother would do. She wanted him to come on his own. Instead, she crawled out of the tents and got some bread and a knife and a mostly empty jar of peanut butter and crawled with it back into the tents.

"We're not supposed to eat in the living room," said the youngest girl.

"We're not in the living room," said the oldest girl, "we're in the tents. Besides, mother isn't here."

When the bread was gone and they had scraped the rest of the peanut butter out of the jar, they sat and waited. The oldest girl watched the youngest girl's pale and anxious face, and wondered how her own face looked. And while she was sitting there, looking at her sister's face and wondering about her own, she saw the face begin to change and her sister begin to cry. The oldest girl reached out across the tent and put her hand on her sister's back and began to move her hand. It was like she was petting an animal—or rather, since she herself, concentrating on staying as calm as glass for the sake of her sister, felt distant not only from her sister's back but from her own hand, as if she were watching someone else pet an animal.

The youngest girl, she realized, was asking about the father. Where was he? Wasn't he coming? Where was he? Why wasn't he here? The oldest girl just kept patting her back. And where was the mother?, the youngest girl wanted to know. Not only where was the father but where was the mother?

"She's not here," said the oldest girl.

The youngest girl kept crying and asking questions, which made the oldest girl think that she didn't really want an answer, or at least didn't want the real answer. The oldest girl kept patting her sister on the back and waiting for it to be over, waiting for her to calm down. When she finally did, her face was blotched red and her eyes were puffy. She sat in the tents looking drained and not looking at anything at all.

"What do we do?" the youngest girl asked.

"We wait for him to come," said the oldest girl.

"But what if he doesn't come?"

"He'll come," said the oldest girl.

"But what if he doesn't?"

"He will," said the oldest girl firmly.

She crawled out of the tents and got some pillows from their bedrooms. She brought them back into the tents and coaxed her sister into lying down. *We'll just wait*, she told her. *We'll just lie down and relax and wait for him to come.*

Later, the oldest girl was not sure how long they had stayed there together, waiting, the oldest girl sitting, the youngest girl lying down. The oldest girl watched the youngest girl's eyes narrow and finally close. Then she kept sitting and watching, the blanket fabric brushing her head lightly. She waited.

When her own head began to nod, she shook it and got up, crawled out of the tents. In the kitchen she checked the clock; it was after eleven, much later than she was allowed to stay up. She looked out the window; there was no moon, the night thick and dark. She could see the dim shape of the porch supports, the ghost of the garage a dozen feet past them, but little more. It was as if the world had dissolved.

She locked the back door, left the front door unlocked so the father could get in. She went around the house, turning lights on. When she was done, she went back into the living room, sat just outside the tents.

She could hear her sister inside the tents, breathing softly. Otherwise the house was quiet. Why not telephone the father? she wondered. But that was the sort of thing the mother would do, the sort of thing, the oldest girl thought, that made the father less dependable. The father, she felt, had to come on his own.

She sat there cross-legged, just outside the tents, guarding her sister, waiting for the father to come. Eventually, he would come, she was sure of it. He would remember them. He would remember her.

And, she thought as her eyes grew heavy, when the father did burst through the door, wild-eyed and unshaven, wearing only his pajama bottoms, she would still be there, she was certain, sitting cross-legged just outside the tents. He would look at her and she would look back, and then she would turn and crawl back into the tents and lay her head down next to her sister's on the pillow, and sleep. If the father wanted to follow her in, that was fine—there was plenty of room in the tents, and for the mother, too, if she wanted to come. But they would have to understand that in the tents it was the two girls who made the rules. It would be up to the girls now to be in charge, she thought, yawning. It was up to them, not the parents, which meant it was mostly up to the oldest girl. The father would have to understand that.

But if he didn't come, she finally thought hours later, her legs tingling from being crossed so long, the sky beginning to grow light outside, if he didn't come, she could learn to live with that too.

Wander

And after many days of wandering—days of bitter cold, days in which we wore out what remained of our shoes and then lost toes and then wrapped our feet in rags, days in which we were hard-pressed to decide what wounded and floundering flesh was safe to consume and what must be passed over, days when we passed warily by other tribes of men such as ourselves, days when we were forced to decide whether to haul one another forward or abandon one another along what remained of the roadside—we came at last to a place not utterly undone by devastation. The snow and ice first acquired a different sheen, and then grew slick underfoot, and then began to give way to water and soon was entirely gone. God in his mercy had left it undiscovered and awaiting us, or so we believed at the time.

The feeling returned to our fingers for the first time in many months. There were a dozen dwellings intact and sufficient among the ruins, and we made our way into one to find there the dead huddled together dry and hollow now, their bodies like emptied sacks. We lay them with respect in one of the beds of the house and sealed the room because the living should not hold ground in common with the dead. Then we took, from cabinets and closets, dried goods and cans, and many of these proved still edible, and for the first time in many days we did not have to scrabble for food.

We chose a room and tore the planking from the floor and built just outside the house a fire and slept the sleep of the dead.

But in the morning, we began to recall the dead boarded into the room beside us and began to wonder if we had sinned in our actions against them. Our leader, Hroar, determined that we must show them our respect by aiding them on their way to heaven, and so with the smoldering remnants of our fire we made of their house a pyre and let it burn until the dead were nothing but smoke.

"We must," Hroar told us, "find a dwelling free of the dead and make of it a dwelling for the living."

We chose another of the still standing dwellings and entered therein and there too we found the dead, their bodies dry and hollowed out, like emptied sacks. There were nowhere signs of life, only a thin settling of dust over all things. We took from the house all goods and cans and stripped it of what lumber it could spare and still be a pyre, and then commended the dead to God's notice and set the house aflame.

It proved the same with each dwelling standing, each clotted with the dead. Quickly we learned to approach the window of each dwelling and, seeing the dead, leave them undisturbed. It was Hroar who would have it thus, for, he asked, *Why would God have left the town for us to discover if our only purpose was to destroy it?* No, he said, if they were not disturbed, the dead would be willing to await their reward.

Thus at the end of the second day we had not found a dwelling to call our own. And when we camped, it was not within a shelter but on open ground, and though the ground was free of ice and we now had food and fuel for fires, many grumbled against Hroar and even suggested that we should merely heap the dead together and burn them all and keep their dwellings for ourselves.

On the third day we awoke to find our faces and hands strangely tender with heat and Hroar himself missing. We huddled together and consulted one another as to what should be done, and might in fact have left that place had we known a place to go. As it was, we clung to each other and sometimes searched through the ruins around us. Here too we found bodies, but not nearly so many, and most of them little more than piles of ash. Here too we saw, on what remained of building walls, strange figures: human in size and shape, but with their limbs and bodies odd and misshapen, as if the shadows of monsters had been torn from them to become immobile and fixed, and this filled us with dread.

The place which at first had thus seemed so much a deliverance to us now seemed a warning or perhaps a punishment. There were even those of us who claimed to see in the shadowed figures a premonition of our own deaths.

Hroar returned late in the day, claiming to have found a dwelling free of the dead, a wide and sumptuous hall with room for all, our new home. *Let us rejoice*, he proclaimed, *for our wandering may cease at last.*

We rejoiced and then did follow him. He led us through the ruined settlement and to the heart of the rubble and there, buried and hidden, where before we had seen only destruction, was a strange dwelling, partially covered over but seemingly intact. Under his direction we cleared a path to the doorway as best we could and then clambered our way inside.

It was, as he had claimed, a great hall, sufficient to accommodate all our tribe and even more. It was, as he said, intact, though the small windows along three sides were blocked and filled with rubble. Indeed, we would have been vexed to see for darkness were there not a glow from one corner of the room. There, at the juncture of wall and floor, was a hole brimmed with water, and through that hole came a bluish light and heat, and looking closer one could see the shape of a blinking eye. The water was hot and, as one reached into it and toward the blue eye, became hotter still. There were, too, here and there on the walls, the same dark shadows that we had seen elsewhere, but with more frequency here. Yet Hroar, who had shared none of our speculations about these markings, was of the belief that they were merely the guardians of the place itself, there to protect the place and preserve it for ourselves.

"This place is a gift from the true and living God," he was quick to say. "He has prepared it for us." And though many of us had our misgivings, we quelled them, found a place for ourselves on the floor, and slept.

I slept soundly and without dreams until the deep of the night, when I awoke to a strange rushing and gurgling sound, and when I opened my eyes the blue glow was gone. I could see nothing, but could hear some of my comrades stirring and some crying out, and the room growing hot and strange until there was the same rushing and gurgling and the blue glow began to return and the room started to cool. Then I sat up and looked about me in the half-light and saw many of my comrades in similar posture, but all of us finally lay down one by one and returned to sleep.

And yet when we awoke, it was to find our two comrades closest to the watery hole both dead, one side of their bodies afflicted with deep and grievous wounds. Some of the men behind them had wounds on their faces and hands as well, and yet they claimed to have felt nothing, and then we knew we had been victim of the creature whose eye we had seen in the hole. Hroar, full of fury, plunged his hand deep into the water to try to pluck out the monster's blue eye, but brought back a hand boiled and stripped of much of its flesh.

We burnt the bodies of our comrades, and then we took counsel from Hroar and it was determined that as the creature had come at night it was a creature of darkness and would come again at night, at which time we would set upon it and lay it low. We prayed to God for strength and spent the day preparing our weapons.

The night again was peaceful until very late, when we heard the same rush and gurgle and the blue glow vanished. Immediately we were on our feet and striking about near the watery hole, the hall growing hotter until one of us managed to ignite a torch. But then we saw nothing except the water drained from the hole and the eye gone and terrible wounds on our hands and chest and arms—wounds that continued to grow without any tangible agent inflicting them, until one of our number, Hrafn, fell, and the remainder of us, sorely afflicted and knowing not where to strike, fled the hall.

The wounds continued to suppurate no matter how we tried to heal them. When several of us finally ventured back into the hall, we found the hole again filled with water, and the creature, eye staring balefully up at us, had returned to its lair. Hroar, heavy of heart and loath to lose more men, commanded us to leave the hall.

But we did not return to our wandering, instead circling day after day just outside the settlement that contained the hall we had thought offered unto us by God. Hroar, despite his boiled and dying hand, despite the wounds on his arms and face and chest, could not let go of the idea of the hall, of the end of wandering. And though we had been too sorely afflicted to venture a return to the hall itself, we had long followed Hroar and would not abandon him. So we stayed circling the town, while Hroar himself lost first his hand and then, from infection, his forearm. He grew gaunt and gray and ceased to speak. A few of us deserted him but the rest, stalwart, remained. There was, after all, food here for a time and wood to burn, and we were happier than we had been wandering—though the same could not be said for our Lord Hroar, who daily grew less of a man, more of a ghost.

Sometimes other wanderers would stumble into our midst. We would feed them and I would recount to them the tale of our lost hall and invite them to join us as we waited for God to relieve our suffering. To a man they declined, for who would swear fealty to a one-armed and maddened lord?

So we stayed and awaited God's will. We awaited Hroar's death, which would release us from our awful circling and allow a more aimless wandering. And yet he did not die. He was reduced to little more than a man of bone, eyes hollow in his sockets, but still did not die. Indeed, there were those among us who began to fear that he did not die because he was already dead, and these soon slipped away in the dead of night and were not seen or heard again. But the rest of us remained fatally bound to Hroar.

And then one day a man came who seemed unlike the others we had encountered, a man broad of face and of limb, a good head taller than even Hroar, and with teeth filed sharp. He hailed us from afar and asked to approach and we beckoned him to share our meal. He sat and ate silently with us and when he was done asked which was Hroar, the mighty lord of a people laid low? He had heard tales of the warrior who had been given by God a hall of ancient design only to lose it again and he was here to offer his fealty, to help Hroar recover his hall.

Hroar stood. He commended the stranger for his bravery and asked of him his name and the name of his father.

"I have no father," the man said. "As for my own name, I have none."

He would, he said, challenge our enemy and regain our hall, and thus make a name for himself. Our Lord Hroar swore to him that if he would do as he said, he Hroar would take him unto his bosom as his son and heir, and the name the man would have would be Hroar's own.

He stayed with us until the fall of darkness, and then several of us led him to the hall and prayed over him and let him enter therein to meet his fate. I shall admit that I for one was not sorry to be far from him. *For how, I wondered, can a man have no father?* So I further wondered if he were in fact a man such as you and me or another creature entirely.

All night we huddled together. We heard his cries and the bellowing of the beast, or told ourselves we did. We heard the rush and hiss of the creature as it slid, invisible, from its hole to the attack, or told ourselves we had. We huddled and awaited him until, at last, as the sky grew light, we spied him lurching through the ruins, looking as if he had been flayed alive. His arms were stripped of skin to the muscle, and his face, too, looked as though it had been burnt away so that one could see bone, and his eyes too had gone blind and had sizzled away in the sockets. His hand, like that of Hroar, was boiled away and he could no longer move its fingers, and when he breathed, blood pearled like sweat on the skinned surface of his chest. And again I could not help but wonder, *Is this in fact a man or another being entirely?*

He told the story of his battle with the creature and how when the water had rushed away he had seized its stony hide and not let go until it broke to pieces and the creature was dead. It was safe to return, he claimed, and then asked Hroar to give him a name. But before the mad lord could answer, the man turned his eyes back to examine the inside of his skull and died.

We built for him a pyre and laid his body upon it and burnt him, the few remnants of his skin charring and sizzling, his leg splitting from heat to reveal a strange and silky bone, quickly consumed. We prayed over him, and Hroar breathed a secret name into the flames for him to take with him and stop his wandering, and then he was gone.

As for us? We returned to the great hall to find it still thrall to the same eerie glow, to find ourselves still observed from the water by the same baleful blue eye. And yet Hroar claimed to be certain that the creature, if not yet dead, was dying, for had not the nameless stranger said as much? And did not the eye itself seem fractured now, less vivid, imbued with less light? *We must,* he told us, *stand fast. We must trust our God and then nothing shall touch us.*

We have followed him so long we do not know how to stop. And so we remain in the hall, lit by the monster's eye. Night has come and we are deep into it. I am writing by the glow of our enemy as he bides his time and awaits his chance to destroy us. I am writing in hopes of persuading myself to stay and face this death, I am writing in hopes of persuading myself to flee. Perhaps there is a third path for me, but as of this writing I have not discovered it. When the eye shuts and the monster forces itself upon us, I shall either be gone and wandering tribeless and alone, or be beside my brothers and wandering the paths of the dead. May God, if he exists, have mercy upon us all.

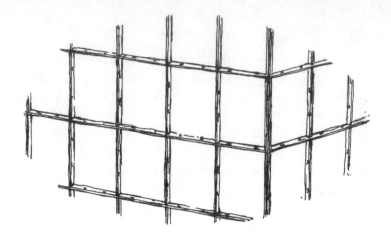

In The Greenhouse

After nearly ten months of struggling to write *Craven Words*, the introductory study of novelist Roger Craven that he had been commissioned to write by Craven himself, Sindt reached an impasse beyond which he was certain he could not progress. He destroyed the one hundred and seventy page manuscript, abandoning sheets to fire at measured intervals, and then promptly wrote Craven to inform him of what he had done. *I cannot*, Sindt wrote upon the back of a postcard, *complete the study I agreed to write. I fear I find myself inadequate to the task of circumscribing your prose.*

This note was not entirely truthful. Rather, Craven's work, which had initially intrigued Sindt because of its concern with dislocation and possession, its insistence on postulating all human relations as a form of torture, had upon further scrutiny fallen apart. Craven's oeuvre contained, Sindt felt, not a single original idea. During months of research and composition, he became increasingly convinced that Craven's work amounted to nothing.

He mailed the postcard and endeavored to force Craven from his mind. After boxing up Craven's books, he committed them to his basement. He was now Cravenless, he told himself, locking the basement door behind him.

It was thus with considerable chagrin that several weeks later Sindt discovered in the mailbox an envelope inscribed in a familiar hand. There was

Craven, in his mailbox, admittedly in condensed form, beckoning to him. When Sindt opened the envelope, the letter within invited Sindt to visit, asking *the favor of your company, forgiving all, asking only that you come spend a few weeks with me.*

Having failed to accomplish what Craven had asked of him, Sindt had no desire to visit the writer. The visit could be nothing but uncomfortable for both of them. He wrote to excuse himself, suggesting that he could not come *at that particular moment,* pleading *pressing business, urgent matters.* Craven wrote in return that he would ask only this single thing of Sindt, that Sindt come stay for a few days immediately, and that he would demand nothing further of him ever again. *As you failed to write the study you yourself repeatedly assured me you would write,* Craven claimed, *this is the least you can do.*

To reach the house, Craven had written, one left the train station and traveled west on foot half a mile until one arrived at a taxi stand. From there, one traveled by taxi on what was referred to as the *logging road,* following it upward to its terminus. There one would discover a footpath that led through a stand of trees—pines—and wound about until it issued into the clearing in which one would find at last the house.

As it turned out, the trip from train station to taxi stand was in fact several miles rather than half a mile, and what Craven had referred to in his letter as the *logging road* was, according to the taxi driver, properly called the *timber road.* As the taxi climbed said road, Sindt wondered if Craven had purposefully mangled these details or if he had simply underestimated the mileage, misremembered the road. Certainly Sindt could not blame Craven for having misled him in such fashion, considering his failure to write *Craven Words. But in that case,* he wondered, *why invite me to visit at all?*

He paid the driver and then set off through the pines (what was left, apparently, of the timber the road had been named after), coming at last upon the house itself. The house was made all of stone, the roof of slate, a squat tower jutting out. It rested on relatively flat land, with some sort of greenhouse beside it, the mountain rising behind. *Like something out of Craven's work,* Sindt thought, and felt a pressure start up in his head. Craven himself was waiting for him under the archway before the front door. He was wearing what could only be described as a Tyrolean walking costume, complete with lederhosen and a hunter's cap. He seemed pleased to see Sindt, and quickly led him into the house, where he prodded him into the room he referred to as the parlor. It was an uncarpeted and drafty chamber, floored with stone flags, empty save for the two of them and two wooden chairs set before an extinguished fire.

Craven took off his hunter's cap and scratched the crown of his head, then abandoned the hat on the mantel. He left the room, returned with drinks.

He was glad Sindt had come, he wanted Sindt to know. *Salud*, he said, and touched his glass to Sindt's own. He was pleased that they could let bygones be bygones and spend the next few weeks redeveloping their friendship. He admired Sindt's candor, the audacity of sending such a post-card, and though at first he had been, he had to admit, enraged, he soon came to realize that it would have been a mistake for Sindt to write about his work if he honestly did not feel he could master the prose. Sindt apologized again, more profusely than he had managed to do on the back of a postcard, and they both sat down, sipped their drinks. From time to time Craven would smile at him, perhaps to reassure him that all was well, that he had been sincere about his genuine forgiveness of Sindt, which made Sindt increasingly nervous.

There was, Craven said, just he and his chef in the house, just the two of them, and now, he said, there was Sindt as well. The chef would keep entirely to the kitchen, according to Craven, at most darting into the dining room to serve dinner but retreating as quickly as possible back to the kitchen. In point of fact, the chef kept his bed in the pantry—not because Craven had forced him to do so (for Craven had offered him any of the seven beds in the house) but by choice. The chef wanted his bed in the pantry—it was not a case of a master giving his servant short shrift, and one preferred not to use words such as *master* and *servant* in times such as these. It also had to be said that in the case of the chef, *bed* was the wrong word, as what he slept on was more of a pallet. Craven would show Sindt the chef's pallet as part of the tour, though it would not, Craven claimed, be the highlight of the tour. He too was not in the main body of the house often, *for as you can see by my garb*, he said, fondling the embroidered hem of his lederhosen, *I tend toward communion with nature*. It would not be too much, indeed, to call him an outdoorsman, for the majority of his waking hours he spent either in the remnants of the woods or out in the green-house. The greenhouse was admittedly not a greenhouse but rather a *modified greenhouse*, something he had converted into *an enclosure for the growth of the word*. In it, he had written not only his most recent book but several books prior to it. It paid to keep one's writing out of the house, at a certain distance, else the house itself become infected with the imaginative process. The imaginative process could ruin a good house in a matter of days. "This house," Craven said, gesturing around him, "consider it your own. Your home away from home."

The tower was nearly as bare as the parlor had been. There was a bed in the center. On the floor beside it was what Sindt judged to be an imitation Persian rug, grown discolored from sunlight, threadbare in its center. Pushed against a wall, just beside a window, was a small writing desk, a place for an inkpot cut into it. A chair sat next to it, the back of it cracked down the middle.

"Satisfactory?" asked Craven, and, when Sindt nodded slightly, he left.

The room was roughly circular. He found, when he went to the leftmost of the three windows, that the tower was high enough for him to see out over the remains of the forest and catch a glimpse of the town below. The rightmost window revealed only the mountain rising beyond the house. The center window looked down on the roof of the modified greenhouse. Sindt ran his finger against the wall and it came away filthy with ash. *There are ways, perhaps,* he thought, *to bow delicately out of this visit to Craven— perhaps by pleading a bleeding ulcer or some other dolorous yet difficult-to-verify condition.* Down below, the sun glinted off the greenhouse panels. He could see Craven, even smaller than usual, walking past the greenhouse and then out toward the trees, ridiculous in his alpine costume. Then he lay down on the bed, slept.

He was awoken by a jangling sound, which, as he soon discovered, was coming from outside his door. It was Craven. He had shucked his alpine costume in favor of a pair of slacks and a blazer a decade out of style. In his hand he held a battery of sleigh bells that struck Sindt as vaguely sinister.

"Dinner?" Craven asked.

Sindt rubbed his eyes, buttoned his shirt back up, followed Craven down the stairs. The house had come to him almost by accident, Craven informed him. A train he had been taking had broken down a few miles shy of the town below. Instead of waiting for it to be repaired, he climbed out of the train's window, hoping to travel on foot to the station. Once under way, however, he left the iron rails and quickly lost his sense of direction. Hoping that by climbing higher he might be able to see the station, he mounted the slope and stumbled onto the logging road—

"—timber road," Sindt suggested.

"Timber road." Craved nodded affably. "And here it was, unoccupied, but nearly in the condition you see it now."

He ushered Sindt toward his seat. The table was already laid, medallions of pork bleeding on their plates, greens in bowls beside, wine decanted, chef nowhere to be seen. They ate quickly, both sitting clumped at one end of the rather large but remarkably crude table. When finished, they repaired to the parlor and sat facing each other, brandy glasses in their hands.

"You don't mind living here alone?" Sindt asked.

"I'm not alone," Craven said. "You're here as well."

"Just for a day or two," Sindt said. "My back, the twenty-second verte-bra, tremendous pain—"

"No," said Craven. "I won't hear of you leaving so soon."

Not knowing what else to do, Sindt emptied his glass.

"In any case, there's the cook," Craven said. "Don't forget the cook."

He was oddly beaming as he said it. There was, Sindt realized, a certain resonance in the words. Sipping his brandy, staring into the cold fireplace grate, Sindt realized that somewhere in the middle of Craven's novel *Velvet Fury* a variation of the same phrase had appeared, uttered by the parodic detective and protagonist as a kind of obscure joke:

There's the crook. Don't forget the crook.

For an instant Sindt held himself perfectly still. He could feel a pressure in his head. The alpine garb Craven had been wearing earlier, he now realized, recalled that of a minor character in Craven's philosophical novel, *Melly & Tate*, a character mentioned briefly, passed over in the course of a paragraph. The meal they had had, bloody medallions of pork, greens without other veg-etables or side dishes, had appeared, if he was not mistaken, as a dinner eaten by the wife of the protagonist in *Knife Diet*. Perhaps Craven's simple outfit now, slacks and outdated sport coat, was an obscure reference to another of his texts. The house was apparently less a literal space than a literary space.

"I'll leave you in peace," said Craven. He stood and, after setting his glass on the mantel, picked up the hunter's cap discarded there earlier.

"And which room is yours?" Sindt asked, choosing a phrase he hoped was devoid of any literary referent whatsoever.

"My room?" Craven said, and frowned. "Hardly important."

Once Craven was gone, Sindt finished his drink, then set the glass beside Craven's own. And then, realizing that Craven's characters were always leaving drained glasses on fireplace mantels, he carried both glasses into the dining room, then set them on the table. He stayed there looking at them and then picked them up again, carried them into the kitchen.

The kitchen was dark. From under the pantry door he could detect a feeble light. Having set the glasses on the counter, he knocked softly. There was no reply. He knocked again, again heard nothing. When he opened the door, he saw that the room stretched back farther than he had imagined, parsed by tiers of shelves. Near the door was less a pallet than a pile of ragged blankets. He pushed at them with his toe. The chef was nowhere to be seen, perhaps hiding back behind the shelves.

He closed the pantry door and then methodically explored the house. There were six other bedrooms besides his tower, the dining room, the parlor, a library (filled only with multiple copies of Craven's works), a study. The house was sparsely decorated, the walls scorched in almost every room. Craven was nowhere to be seen.

He climbed the stairs to the tower, undressed. Yet when he turned off the light, he realized there was a glow coming through the center window. He watched light play on the ceiling and then, unable to sleep, got up, looked out. He could see, below, the greenhouse, the light from inside it illuminating the whole of the structure and shining up through the glass roof. Craven was inside, Sindt saw, sitting at a desk with his back to him, and Sindt could see that Craven was crouched over something, his right arm hidden before his body. There was a sheaf of papers to either side of him. Sindt watched, first leaning against the windowsill and then pulling the chair away from his own desk and putting it beside the window. Finally he saw Craven add a piece of paper to the rightmost sheaf, take a sheet from the leftmost sheaf. *There is Craven*, he thought with a certain amount of hatred, *desperately adding another insignificant work to an already insignificant body of work*, and with that thought, he found himself able to return to his bed and fall asleep.

He awoke several hours later, anxious. He was in a house, living out situations that seemed carefully constructed by Craven out of fragments of his novels. Where finally did that leave Sindt? He was not one of Craven's characters, was not a literary referent, had no intention of becoming one if he could help it. But perhaps even now Craven was writing about him. He could still see on the ceiling the wash of light from the greenhouse below, and when he stood, went to the window, could see Craven still hunched over his desk, a sheaf of paper to either side of him. He sat there watching Craven, the papers moving slowly from one sheaf to the other, until dawn broke and the transparent glass of the greenhouse turned sun-flecked and opaque.

He dressed, stumbled downstairs to the dining room. Craven was already at table, bright-eyed, a plate of eggs before him.

"Sleep well?" Craven asked, picking up his fork.

Yes, Sindt said, choosing his words with care, he had slept well, no interruptions, but his back—not his problem, the bed, you see, perhaps he would have to regretfully cut his visit short.

"Nonsense," said Craven. "We'll ask a chiropractor in from town."

As Craven ate, Sindt watched. Craven seemed fully awake, his face unlined, his eyes clear, as if he had slept soundly through the night rather than spending all night at a desk in a greenhouse, writing. Perhaps it had not been Craven, thought Sindt, but no, who else could it be? And even from the back he had been certain who the man was. Yet here Craven was, eager and visible despite everything, and well into his breakfast.

Was there anything planned for the day? Sindt wanted to know.

Planned? said Craven. No, nothing. As for himself, he would enjoy a day in the out-of-doors, wandering through the trees, perhaps climbing a little way up the side of the mountain. Sindt, of course, was welcome to join in.

Sindt declined. In the tower after breakfast, he watched from the window as Craven trudged around the greenhouse and set off through the trees. He spent his own day wandering the house, slept for a while in the tower. He wandered the clearing as well, catching glimpses of Craven from time to time. Approaching the greenhouse, he found it locked. Through the glass he could see rows of emptied clay pots along each wall, a dirt floor, the chair, the desk with sheaves of paper on both sides of it. He tried, by moving along the side of the greenhouse, to catch sight of the words on the top sheet, without success because of the angle of the pages, the waver of the glass. The lock on the door was simple, part of the latch, and he thought if he pushed on the door just right he might be able to spring it, though there was always the risk of the panes of glass breaking or slipping out. And what, in any case, would Craven think if he saw him? He couldn't have Craven thinking he remained interested in his writing. He certainly didn't care to give Craven material of that sort to use in constructing the Sindt of his novel.

That night, after a light dinner which again recalled Craven's work—the poached salmon found in the novella *Box of Sky*—Sindt climbed the circular staircase to the tower and again saw the light thrown on the ceiling. *He can't stay up all night,* he told himself. *This time I will watch until he falls asleep. I will watch all night. I will find him out.*

He stayed up, seated at the window, resting his arms on the sill, watching Craven's malfocused back, his slight and minute movements only partly available through the glass. *If only I had a pair of binoculars,* he thought, and wandered the house in search of those or some sort of spyglass, finding nothing save the thick bottom of a whiskey tumbler, which, while it admittedly magnified things, severely distorted them at the same time. This too, he realized, could have been an object from one of Craven's books, and though it was in none of the published books, perhaps it would be found in the book Craven was writing in the greenhouse now. When Sindt returned to the tower, Craven was still in the greenhouse, still at his desk, the papers in the pile on one side migrating slowly to the pile of paper on the other side. Sindt sat again at the window and for a time moved the tumbler from eye to eye to eye; through it, the greenhouse became a ghost of light, the light striking rings into the poorly ground glass base. After a while, he set the tumbler down on the floor, leaned again on his elbows. A little while more and his chin slipped onto the sill, and then he was waking up, morning having long arrived, his back sore, his body half-slid from the chair.

It was like that the next night and the next, and Craven each morning as bright and unblemished as if he had been freshly created instead of having spent all night at a desk, writing. Sindt, though, felt increasingly disoriented, hardly able to sleep either at night or during the day. It was as if there were more than one Craven: one who wrote, another who appeared in Tyrolean garb by daylight, perhaps others as well. He asked Craven, or one of the Cravens, if he had a pair of binoculars, and though Craven claimed that yes, he did, and that yes, Sindt could borrow them, he never produced them. Their relations seemed to Sindt to become more strained and he felt they *spent their days circling one another, excessively formal* (he realized this was a description as well of Jansen and Jensen's interactions in Craven's *Moody Mouths),* as Craven or Cravens waited for evening to come so they could write and Sindt awaited an evening of trying to make things out through glass. *How is your writing coming?* Sindt finally asked, and was surprised when Craven answered, *I'm not writing. I haven't written a word in weeks.* Yet there he was, below, scribbling away, night after night. Though Sindt could not, through the glass roof, make out the words—or even for that matter make out that there *were* words—he sat, peering out over the sill, trying by force of will to make his eyes see farther and farther. But he could never make out enough: only Craven, only the papers' slow flight from one sheaf to the other, a few sheets a night. He tried to imagine what was on each sheet, pieced together scenes from an imaginary novel, wondering where, if anywhere, he fit in.

By day he went through the house, searching for Craven's room, but there was no sign that any of the other rooms were occupied. Well over a week into the visit, he had still not caught even a glimpse of the cook. The pile of blankets on the pantry floor never seemed to have been slept in. There were, he thought, too many Cravens and too few chefs, and then he winced as he remembered another line from *Velvet Fury*

Too many ravens and too few corpses

for it seemed that the syntax of Craven's sentences was rewiring his head.

He would leave, he told himself, he would pack his things and depart that night. He even managed to fill and close his suitcase and sit in the chair awaiting darkness. But darkness was scarcely come when the light was there again, again cast upon the ceiling. He abandoned the suitcase to pull the chair again to the window, speculating on what Craven was writing, the imagined words swirling about within his head, settling briefly, then swirling off. The words would, he realized, continue to spin about, continue to batter the insides of his head even after he had left the house. Better, he thought, to see the actual words, to read what was there on paper, to allow the words to set and solidify and thus sink lower in his head and be forgotten. *The imaginative process can ruin a good head*, he thought, *and must be brought to a halt before it is too late*. The actual was the only way to stop the whirligig of the possible. There seemed no choice but to once again read Craven.

But when, and how, was one to go about it? It could not be done by night, for at night Craven was in the greenhouse himself, composing. Sindt could not simply ask Craven to show what he had written, for Craven had claimed not to to be writing at all. During the day, too, Craven came and went about the grounds and might well discover him as he forced his way into the greenhouse, particularly if there were more than one Craven. And where, too, was the chef? He had never seen the chef, but that did not mean that the chef had never seen him. Perhaps the chef was observing him even now.

He finally settled on early in the morning, thinking it possible, perhaps, to sneak down the stairs and out to the greenhouse after Craven had left it, while Craven waited for him at the breakfast table.

He slept, or tried to, through most of the night, finally jerking fully awake with the cold light of dawn. Having slipped on his socks, he slowly granched the door open. The stairway was empty. He made his way slowly down, turning around the narrow staircase, dragging his hand along the wall for balance. He crossed the hall carefully, eased the front door open, went out.

The air was sharp, crisp. He could feel the prick of gravel through his socks. He picked his way carefully along the side of the house, crossed to the greenhouse.

He peered in. The greenhouse was empty. Trying the handle, he found it locked, so he pressed his shoulder to the metal edging of the door and bore down. He could see the wall and door bulge, the metal grating against the glass, the lock slipping. And then the door burst open and he was in.

He approached the simple desk, the chair. On the desk: two sheaves of paper, the one on the left higher, a pen between. He approached the leftmost, found the paper empty, blank, but of course Craven had always moved the paper from left to right.

He approached the rightmost stack, found the top sheet blank. Turning it over, he found the reverse blank as well. He leafed down through the stack but there was nothing, no words, not a mark.

When he turned he could see, through the ceiling of the greenhouse, the window of the tower. Through that window, distorted by both the glass of the window and the roof of the greenhouse, he glimpsed a figure. *Perhaps Craven*, he thought, *Cravens, one of them. Or perhaps the cook. Don't forget the cook.* He had a feeling that everything had already occurred. The figure was looking down, he thought, looking at him.

Not knowing what else to do, he turned from the gaze, sat down at the desk. He could guess what was expected of him. Picking up the pen, he began to write.

After nearly ten months of struggling to write, he started. He continued writing uninterrupted until he again, both in prose and in life, found himself sitting in the greenhouse, pen in hand. He had, he realized, allowed himself to be used. *Yet, nevertheless, I have now approached some sort of conclusion*, he wrote. *All that remains is for me to destroy this manuscript as well.*

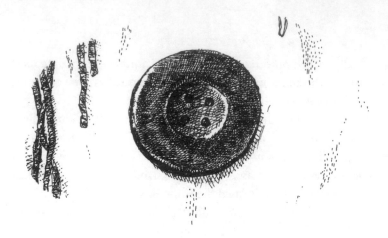

Ninety Over Ninety

I.

During his tenure at Entwinkle House, Philip Kossweiller had purchased fiction that received stunning acclaim but hadn't, to quote his boss, Vincenzo Darba, sold a good goddamn. Well, admitted the former publicity chief who insisted that everyone call him "Cinchy" and who enjoyed pronouncing himself "a boss of the people," sure they had sold, but they hadn't broken even. Well, sure they had broken even, but they hadn't made much. Not enough to sneeze at anyway.

"Think blockbuster," Cinchy told Kossweiller. "'Every book a blockbuster': that's your new motto."

"Blockbuster?"

"No," said Cinchy, jutting himself forward conspiratorily. "Wait a minute. Blockbuster isn't enough for us. You and me, we're not the sort satisfied with just blockbuster. Go for the three b's."

"The three b's?"

"Big-ass blockbuster."

"That's only two b's."

"Big-ass. Block. Buster. Three b's. No more of this literature crap. Sure, it's good, but literature's the icing on the cake. You don't spread icing all over an empty plate, do you? What have you got to do before you spread the icing, Karsewelder?"

"I'm afraid I don't know what you're talking about, Mr. Darba."

His boss gave him a look that seemed pained, slightly constipated. "Not Mr. Darba—Cinchy. You see," said Cinchy, throwing his hands up, "that's your problem. You have to bake the fucking cake first."

"What cake?"

"Go bake the fucker," said Cinchy, boss of the people, clapping Kossweiller hard on the back and pushing him out into the hall. "God help you, Karsewelder. Bring me something that sells for a change. Blockbuster!" he yelled after him.

Back in his office, Kossweiller examined his fingernails, then tried to clean underneath them with his lower incisor. He stared at the pile of manuscripts on his desk, then went back to reading the typescript for Robert Barney's *O Fickle God*, a "historical novel of the West" overladen with poorly veiled attacks on contemporary middle America. According to Barney's agent, it was written in a "fluid, beautiful prose," a stylistic strength that Kossweiller was having some difficulty locating. Perhaps this made it blockbuster material.

> Ole Zeke, like some poor misbegotten anthropophage, leaned a pace closer to the fire and spat, his spittlegob sizzling greedily in the cackling flame.
>
> "Seems to me," said the old-timer [Why not ole-timer? Kossweiller wondered], "that your so-called advert-iss-ments haen't more than a spit in the fire. Only yer middleminded are gone to 'tribute any importance to 'em."
>
> Big Jim nodded, half to himself. The old guy was making a curious heap of sense! Who'd have thunk he'd come to understand his own city slicker's world through the words of a stranger in the Savage West?
>
> He looked up to find Ole Zeke holding an open pouch toward him. "'Baccy?" the old-timer asked.

Bogged down, Kossweiller abandoned the manuscript and left his office.

Cinchy was at his desk, feet up, speaking loudly into the receiver to one of the stable of second-rate celebrities he published: an ex-president turned poet, a '50s film star who wrote an exposé on his '80s film-star daughter, a former TV evangelist's wife turned blandly pseudo-Buddhist.

Farther down, Tal Anders's door was open, Anders himself staring at his computer screen. Kossweiller went in without knocking, sat down.

"Who is it?" asked Anders, not turning.

"Me," said Kossweiller.

"Koss," said Anders. "I'm just on to something here. Absolutely the next big thing. Give me a minute."

"Want me to come back?"

"No, no," said Anders. "All I need's a minute."

Kossweiller stood. He went over to the nearest bookshelf, read along the spines, removed a slim handsome volume at random. *The Secret Lives of Housewives.* The back copy read: *Not just gossip and recipes for delicious cherry pie pass from one matronly hand to another. . . . Here, glimpsed through keyholes, the real hidden history of housewives in all its* chaleur: *high romance, lesbianism, bestiality, S&M, and every depravity imaginable, and yes, even a little tenderness. . . .*

"You actually published this?" asked Kossweiller.

"Published what?"

"This."

Anders turned slightly. "That?" he asked. "Sure. Eight printings in cloth, still going strong in paperback."

"Is it any good?"

"Define 'good.'"

"Is it worth reading?"

"People want it," said Anders. "They buy it. That's good enough for me."

"That doesn't answer my question."

Anders turned. "Koss, you're asking the wrong questions."

"That's what Cinchy thinks."

"Cinchy's absolutely right," said Anders. "You should listen to him. Remember: he may be a boss of the people, but he's still the boss." He turned his attention back to the computer screen. "Just a few seconds more."

Kossweiller sat down and stared at the back of Anders's head.

"I mean, why did you go into editing anyway?" Kossweiller asked.

Anders shrugged. "You have to be philosophical about these matters. It's not why you went in but how you stay in."

"That's cynical."

"Philosophical, you mean," said Anders. "Come on, Koss, lighten up." He shook his fingers out, pushed his chair back away from the computer. "There," he said. "Got him."

"Got who?"

"What?" said Anders. "Only the biggest ex-KKK memoir in publishing history."

"Off the computer?"

"From a chat room," he said. "Ran into this guy attacking the fascists on Nazichat.com and got him to agree to write his book for us before the supremacists blocked him from the chat room. Fortunately, I was the only editor monitoring that particular list."

"Doesn't it tell you something that you were the only editor logged on to Nazichat.com?"

"Sure it does," said Anders. "It tells me I'm the only one smart enough to sniff out the next big thing. Imagine this: you're a KKK member, happily living out your dreams of white supremacy, maybe even involved in a few lynchings—of course, you're not directly involved, or at least you won't be once a good editor gets through with you—when *Blammo!* it hits you like a ton of lead."

"What hits you? Did you actually say 'blammo'?"

"You find out your grandfather was a Jew. Yes, blammo. Why not? I'll say it again: blammo. So you give up the KKK, reform, and go to Israel to immerse yourself in your newly discovered heritage."

"Sounds like a bad TV movie."

"Exactly," said Anders. "It's sure to sell to TV. Cinchy'll eat it up."

"Cinchy wants me to bake him a cake."

"A cake? Is it his birthday? I didn't get him anything."

"'You can't spread frosting on an empty plate.'"

"What are you talking about?"

"It's a metaphor," said Kossweiller. "You still remember metaphors, don't you? It's the best Cinchy can do. He wants me to stop publishing literature and start publishing blockbusters."

"But you don't do blockbusters," said Anders. "You're the guy who does literature, who gives us respectability. You're the eye candy."

"I've got to do at least one."

"So, do one then."

"What do I know about blockbusters? I don't even know what sells."

"Look," said Anders, spreading his arms wide. "Don't think in terms of good or bad. Think accessibility. Think largest possible target audience. Knowing you, if you go against all your impulses, it'll work."

•

He called the agents he knew best, took them to lunch, told them that this time he was looking for something "really big." But his reputation as a literary editor meant they interpreted "big," no matter how he qualified it, as literary.

Their best varied drastically. Raymond Knoebler of Knoebler & Goebler sent him the aging Thomas Johnson's *As a Boy One Read Kipling: A Literary Life;* Jed Bunting passed along a copy of Sal Lazman's *The Slice*, a literary golf novel; Sally Johnson offered a new posthumous collection of occasional pieces and a few stories by minimalist Roland Pilcher, a collection that Kossweiller suspected had been largely ghostwritten by Pilcher's wife, a writer herself and a professional literary widow.

Carolyn Kiff, however, sent him Albert West's fourth book, *En Masse*, a novel of enormous scope and skill, so good that he knew it couldn't possibly sell. Not enough to sneeze at anyway. Cinchy would never sign off on it.

He sent the manuscripts back, except the West, which he couldn't bear to turn down. Perhaps if he could find one huge book, one real blockbuster, he thought, Cinchy would let him do the West as icing.

Once he'd run through the agents he knew best, he approached those he generally shied away from. There was Claudia Bart, who offered him a chance for an unauthorized biography of George Clooney, but by the time, three hours later, he'd gained Cinchy's approval, she regretted to inform him that she'd sold the book to a rival house. There was Robert J. Voss, who offered him a book about American one-hit-wonder bands, entitled *Where Are They Now?* Most of them were working at Wal-Mart, it turned out. Ducky Hawarth slid in wearing a spangly shirt to suggest *Follies*, a coffee-table book about dinner shows, musicals, and dancers, "done in three versions, one for each gender."

There were other books, some of which he made halfhearted offers on. But the day before the quarterly meeting, Kossweiller still had nothing in hand. There was only one lunch appointment left, with a somewhat frayed hustler named Ralph Bubber.

Bubber was fat and pale, his hair greased back. He had a way of lasciviously squeezing his interlocutor's arm, which made Kossweiller extremely uncomfortable. When he finally figured out that Kossweiller wasn't after literature and that he worked for Cinchy, he looked up toward the ceiling and, grabbing Kossweiller's arm, said:

"Picture this. *The History of Raggedy Ann*."

"The doll."

"Sure," said Bubber. "Kind of a picture book. Dolls galore. And there's a natural follow-up," he said, lifting his index fingers for quotations marks. "*The History of Raggedy Andy.*"

"Have they changed a lot over the years?"

"Have they changed?" Bubber shrugged. "Not really. It just depends on what your perspective is."

"And what's the book's perspective?"

"It can have any perspective you like," Bubber said. "It hasn't been written yet."

"It's not written?"

"Sure. But there's any number of great, really first-rate writers I have at my fingertips who could crank the sucker out in two weeks."

"Two weeks?"

"See," said Bubber, rubbing the back of his neck with one hand and leaning forward to take Kossweiller's arm again with the other. "A book like that has only three or four thousand words of text anyway. What you got is all pictures. Maybe ninety pictures over ninety pages. Dolls, dolls, dolls. Dolls on crackback chairs, dolls in barns, dolls on beds, dolls on swings, dolls with plants, maybe even dolls with dogs. Yes, definitely dolls with dogs. A natural."

"You think it will be a blockbuster?"

"Who doesn't like dolls?" asked Bubber.

II.

Morning found Kossweiller sitting in the conference room, staring at the wall. He was the first to have arrived. He had been more or less persuaded to try Bubber's *Raggedy Ann* book—what did he have to lose?—but then late the night before he'd started to read West's *En Masse* again. It seemed even better this time, and reading it made him feel very ashamed. How could he pass on it in favor of a coffee-table book?

People had begun to trickle in, editors and marketers and assistants from all over Entwinkle House. Soon everybody was there except for Cinchy.

"Did you hear about MacMaster & Bates?" Justice Turko was saying to an assistant next to her. "The author dump?"

"The author dump?" asked Kossweiller.

"Dropped over half their authors in a single afternoon," said Ted Billner, drawing a finger across his throat. "Yesterday. Ought to be done here."

"Orders straight from the top," said Turko. "Maybe it will be."

"Maybe it will be what?" asked Kossweiller.

"Done here."

"Here's an idea," said Helen Harman, the pseudo-attractive unnatural-blond marketing director who went by H. H. She swept her hand in front of her face in a wipe. "HarperCollins," she said, "and Tom Collins together at last. Free books with cocktails and vice versa."

"Good one, H. H.," said Turko.

"Why haven't they thought of it yet?" asked Billner.

Kossweiller just stared.

"Finally here," said Cinchy, striding in. "Just been on the phone with somebody big, can't say who, couldn't be ignored. Treat the stars like the stars they are. Got to, got to." He sat down. "All right, then," he said. "Go, go, go."

They started at his right, working their way around the table. Paul Musswen had on the docket a book by a conservative and inflammatory U.S. Congressman about how his transvestite brother was dying of AIDS because he had gone against the will of God. Cinchy looked at H. H. and when she nodded, he nodded. Turko had four nearly identical memoirs of public figures whose fathers had "incested" them but who had not only "survived" but "conquered." Again the nod passed from the marketing director to the boss of the people, like a tic. John Barnum Gotta had a photohistory of dresses belonging to J. Edgar Hoover and John Wayne ("Great!" yelled Cinchy. "Great!"). Duff McQuaid had persuaded the country's best-known professor of African American Studies to compile a cultural dictionary called *Afro-Americana!* "And the best part," said Duffy, "is his students are doing the work for college credit, so nobody has to pay them." H. H.'s nod was long in coming, but it finally came, and Cinchy's soon followed. Belva Adair had purchased three memoirs, one in which a female rock musician spoke out about her decision not to have children, another in which a woman poet spoke about her decision not to have children, another in which a woman novelist spoke about her decision, at age forty-five, to have a child (H. H. actually deigned to speak for this one: "Good coverage!" she said). Ted Billner just said, "Three different fetishes, three simple words, three simple titles: *Rubber, Leather, Silk.*

"Super!" said Cinchy. "Crackerjack!"

He turned to Kossweiller, who felt his throat go dry and tight as if he were in grade school again. Kossweiller opened his mouth.

"I've got a novel," he said quickly. "One of the best I've ever read. Albert West. *En Masse*. It's worthy of Faulkner or Joyce. I really think we should go with this one, sir."

An expression of mild hatred was on Cinchy's face. "Not *sir*," he said. "Cinchy."

"Cinchy."

Cinchy stared at him quietly. "Karsewelder," he said. "Karsewelder, I thought we had a talk. You should be ashamed."

Ashamed? Kossweiller wondered.

"What am I going to do with you?" Cinchy asked, half to himself.

H. H., Kossweiller noticed, was raising her hand. Eventually Cinchy noticed as well.

"Yes, H. H.?" he asked.

"Perhaps Koss has a marketing plan, Cinchy? Perhaps it isn't as hopeless as it looks?"

Cinchy brightened just a little. "That right, Karse? Do you mind if I call you Karse?"

Koss shook his head. "It's actually—" he started to say, but then, catching Tal Anders's eye, stopped. "No, sir," he said. "I mean, no, Cinchy. I don't mind at all."

"So let's hear it," said Cinchy. "What do you have up your sleeve, Karse?"

"Up my sleeve?"

"What's your strategy for making *En Masse* a blockbuster?"

"Change the title for starters," said H. H.

"So you'd change the title," said Cinchy to him. "And what else?"

"It's very good," said Kossweiller. "It's really a good book."

"But who's your target audience?" said Cinchy.

"My target audience?"

There was a long silence.

"Incoherent marketing strategy," H. H. finally said. "I can't work with it, Cinchy." She turned to him. "I'm sorry, Koss. Don't take it personally."

"That's it, then," said Cinchy. "You heard her, Karse. It won't work. No go. Strike one. Two more and you're out. What else you got?"

"What else?"

"You mean you don't have anything else?" asked Cinchy, his voice rising. "I thought we had a talk. Did we or did we not have a talk?"

Kossweiller shifted uncomfortably in his chair. "Well," he said. "There was one other thing."

Cinchy leered at him. "Something literary?" he said. "It better not be something literary, I swear to God."

"It isn't," said Kossweiller. "Picture this," he said, trying his best to imitate H. H.'s wipe. *The History of Raggedy Ann.* For the coffee table."

He was prepared to go on. He had for this one at least the rudiments of a marketing strategy. Who doesn't like dolls? It probably wasn't the best idea of the day, but certainly it wasn't the worst. It could go through. Which was why he was surprised, when he looked up, to find Cinchy red-faced and shaking.

"Who put you up to this, Kossweiller?" he asked, apparently forgetting, in his anger, to call him by the wrong name.

"I," said Koss. "But I—"

"The doll incident," whispered Anders, from beside him. "Don't you know about the doll incident?"

"No dolls," said Cinchy. "Never any dolls. Because of the incident."

"What was the incident?" asked Koss, but Anders was already interrupting him— "You don't ask about the incident," Anders was saying.

"You don't ask about the incident," said Cinchy, who seemed to be calming down now. "You just accept it. Ten years of therapy. No dolls. Never any dolls."

"I didn't know," said Koss.

"Dolls are creepy," said Cinchy. "Horrible things. You're fired."

The room was silent. Kossweiller felt stunned. Nobody would meet his eye. He looked at his pad in front of him a moment, then, gathering the pad and pencil, stood up to go.

"Perhaps he really didn't know," said H. H.

"I know Koss," said Anders. "He doesn't have a malicious bone anywhere in his body. He didn't mean anything by it, Cinchy."

"Maybe not," said Cinchy.

"A boss of the people might give someone a second chance," said Anders.

Cinchy scrutinized Kossweiller carefully. "All right," he said. "The boss of the people unfires you. Strike two. You get one more. But I swear to you, Karse, screw this one up, I'll not only fire you, I'll make you miserable. Ninety over ninety, I swear to God. And you," he said, turning and pointing at Anders, "you help him. You make sure he doesn't waste my time again. I want the two of you in my office in two days with something that nails all three b's right through the fucking skull."

•

It was Anders, knocking on his office door as he came in. "Dolls, Koss?" he was saying. "Whose idea was that?"

"I didn't know about the doll incident," said Kossweiller. "I swear to God."

"That was a close one. You should thank God Cinchy's a boss of the people."

"It was Bubber. He recommended it to me."

"Bubber? The agent? He hates Cinchy. Koss, you should know that."

"I didn't know that."

"He and Cinchy worked together at MacMaster & Bates until Cinchy fired him. Don't you know anything? I'm amazed you've managed to survive in this business as long as you have."

"What was the doll incident?" asked Kossweiller. He opened his center desk drawer, looked in. He closed it, opened a left-hand drawer, kept opening and closing drawers.

"How do I know, Koss? *Ten years of therapy, no dolls, never any dolls*, that's all I know. That's all anyone knows. It's some deeply Freudian, fucked-up thing." Anders sat on the edge of Kossweiller's desk. "It'd probably make a good book," he said thoughtfully, "and a small-scale indie movie. Maybe Bubber knows. What are you doing?"

"Trying to figure out how long it'll take me to pack."

Anders stood up. "Oh no, you don't," he said. "You can't expect the editor of such bestsellers as *The Secret Lives of Housewives* and *Darned but Not Forgotten* to let you give up now, can you? You're an editor, Koss, that's your so-called métier. Go home and think of something, and we'll hash it out tomorrow. I have faith in you. Besides, you heard Cinchy: my fate's wrapped up in your own now. I can't let you quit."

"I just can't do it, Tal. It's not me."

"What's 'me' mean? There's no *me* to be found in *team*. Well, actually there is a *me* in team if you rearrange the letters, but you get my point. Ninety over ninety, Koss. He won't let you quit. He'll make your life hell."

"Ninety over ninety. What does that even mean?"

"If I were you," said Anders. "I would do every goddamn thing I could not to find out."

•

Early the next morning, a few minutes after Kossweiller was in, Anders sent an intern by with a note. *Coffee in ten, keep the ideas flowing*. Eight minutes later, Anders was knocking on his door, tie carefully knotted, looking impeccable.

"Ready, Koss?" he asked. "Thinking blockbuster?"

They took the elevator down to the ground floor, walked out of the building and down the street one building farther, ducked into Sal's.

"Drinks, gentlemen?" the waiter asked.

"Water," said Kossweiller.

"Don't listen to him," said Anders. "It's almost ten, Koss," he said. "Nothing wrong with a drink this late in the day. Gets the creative juices flowing."

"It's only twenty-five of nine," said Kossweiller.

"Right," said Anders. "Ten if you round up."

"Coffee, then," said Kossweiller.

"Irish coffee for him," said Anders, pointing. "Whiskey for me."

"But—"

"But nothing," said Anders. "Without a few drinks, we won't get anywhere. We've tried it your way and you see where that got us. Now we try it my way."

Three Irish coffees in and Kossweiller found himself comfortably warm, loosened up enough to allow Anders to switch him over to vodka. *A pure drink*, as Anders had described it.

"So," asked Anders. "What you got?"

"I got nothing," said Kossweiller.

"Not good, Koss, not good." He looked at Kossweiller's glass. "The problem with you," he said, "is that you think your glass is half-empty when it's really half-full."

"It looks completely full to me," said Kossweiller. "I only had a little sip."

"Not that glass, Koss," said Anders. "The glass in your head."

"What glass in my head?"

"Metaphor. Focus, Koss. Give me a ghost of an idea, just one, something to work with."

Kossweiller leaned forward, stared into his glass. "Well," he said, "not dolls."

"Never any dolls."

"Never any dolls."

"What about something about history? Something historical."

"History? There were a half-dozen books on Lincoln this season alone. Queer Lincoln has already been done. Communist Washington has already been done. Battles of World War II have all been done to death. Only the real buffs give a shit about anything outside of the big wars and the founding fathers. You don't know the first thing about history and neither do I, and we wouldn't know who to turn to. It sells, some of it, but those guys work on books for years at a time. They're gluttons for punishment, and they're months late for deadlines. History's out."

"No history, no dolls."

Anders nodded.

Kossweiller stared into his drink, thought. He looked at his watch. "It's only quarter after ten," he said, "and I'm already drunk."

"Right," said Anders. "Let's go with that, but spin it. How about 'It's already tea time in Edinburgh and I'm only just getting drunk'?"

"That's an idea for a book?"

"Just a general attitude adjustment, Koss. Just a new way of seeing the world. Though it could be the first line for a book. Something a little Irvine Welsh-y, if you changed getting drunk to shooting up."

"But I'm not in Edinburgh."

Anders took a long sip, raised his glass to the light. "Ah, Edinburgh," he said, and took another sip.

"But —"

"—give in to it, Koss," said Anders.

Kossweiller, shaking his head, took a drink.

"Maybe a minority writer?"

"Who, you?" asked Anders.

"Sure," said Kossweiller. "Why not?"

"Koss, you don't know the first thing about publishing a multicultural writer."

"I don't? But I've published minorities," Kossweiller said, and began to tick off a list.

"Yeah," said Anders. "And some of your best friends are black, I bet. For starters, you can stop calling them minorities and call them multicultural. Maybe that's out now, too. Koss, you approach the problem that way and you'll just end up publishing another literary book and pissing Cinchy off." He moved his glass around on its coaster.

"Well, what then?"

"H. H. just came in," said Anders, looking toward the register. "Let's ask her."

"Is that a good idea?"

"I'll ask her, then," said Anders. "You stay here. Just wave when we look over, and look sexy. H. H. likes you."

"What do you mean H. H. likes me?"

"She gave you another chance, didn't she? The world's like grade school, Koss, nothing but crushes. You may have to sleep with her before this is all over. Are you straight, Koss? I've never asked and one can't always tell."

"But—"

But Anders was already up. He had taken H. H. softly by the shoulder, was speaking smoothly into her ear. After a moment, he pointed over to the booth, and H. H. looked over. Kossweiller waved half-heartedly. She waved back, smiled.

After a few minutes, she went off to join a friend. Anders slid back into the booth.

"Well?" said Kossweiller.

"You're having dinner with her," said Anders. "Vaguely. I didn't set anything specific up, but you probably shouldn't wait more than a week."

"Anders . . . ," said Koss.

"Mysteries," said Anders.

"Mysteries?"

"A mystery series. A brand-new name she can pump money and publicity into. H. H. has been wanting a new mystery series to play with for a while, she says. She thinks it'll be fun. If the books are even passable, she can make it work. She's pleased, ergo the boss of the people will be pleased. Mysteries."

"But I don't read mysteries," said Koss. "Did you actually say *ergo?*"

"Doesn't matter, Koss. We're doing this high-concept. We're not going to go looking in the slush pile, we're not putting out a call for manuscripts. We're building this baby from the ground up. Like the Monkees. Except mysteries. Let's order some lunch."

"But it's not even eleven."

"Brunch, then," said Anders. "Waiter!"

By the time they'd worked through the dizzying combination of blintzes and burgers that Anders insisted on calling brunch, it was mostly figured out. *We need a snappy title,* Anders had begun with, *something that sticks in the head and keeps coming back.*

"Foodstuffs have been done," he said. "Cooking's been done. 'The Cat Who' has been done, days of the week have been done to death. Seven deadly sins."

"Subway stops."

"Maybe," said Anders. "But probably not snappy enough for H. H. You can't woo a girl with subway stops, Koss."

"I'm not trying to woo anybody," said Kossweiller.

"Maybe start with a name. Something foreign but without too many consonants packed together. Nothing Eastern European or Finnish. Those goddamn Finns. Swedish?"

"All right," said Kossweiller. "Why not?"

"Bjorn?" said Anders. "Like the tennis player? Last name has to end in *son*. *Son* says *Swede* better than anything."

"Swenson?"

"Too common, too American. Verenson. Bjorn Verenson. I like it."

"Is Verenson even a legitimate Swedish name?"

"Doesn't matter," said Anders. "Nobody cares about that."

"I care about that."

"You got to stop caring, then. Remember: the three b's. So, a Swedish detective, phlegmatic but friendly, someone people can relate to and at the same time laugh at. A slight but pleasant accent. Now titles," said Anders. He looked up at the ceiling. "Swedes."

"Swedes?"

"Sure," said Anders. "Titles like *Swede Eater*."

"*Swede Eater?* What the hell does that even mean?"

"Like *weed eater*, but with *Swede* in it. It's clever. But maybe that one's too clever. We'll leave that one for late in the series. How about *Blue Swede Shoes?*"

"You've got to be kidding."

"Have you looked at mystery titles lately? *Blue Swede Shoes* is good for at least fifteen thousand sales. With good marketing, a lot more. *Now and Sven.*"

Kossweiller groaned.

"*First Bjorn Child.* Now they're really solid, Koss. *Rebjorn.* No, make that *Bjorn Again.* And how about *Bjorn Free?* Detective's named Bjorn too, maybe even pass it off as Bjorn Verenson's own experiences: 'Based on a True Story.' I see a TV movie, movies plural. *Not Bjorn Yesterday. Bjorn Under a Wandering Star. Stillbjorn.* Maybe a travel one called *Bjorneo.* They're coming a mile a minute," said Anders. "Are you writing these down?"

"You have to stop."

Anders took out his pen, scribbled on the back of a coaster. "Now we hire some hack out of New Jersey, give him the titles and have him write the fuckers."

"Some Swedish guy?"

Anders shrugged. "Doesn't make any difference. Your job is saved, Koss," he said, "and all it cost you was brunch. I'm a genius. Get the bill."

III.

It was a process that, once begun, Kossweiller didn't know how to stop. Suddenly he was the editor of a fake Swedish mystery series. He and Anders met with Cinchy and H. H., who were instantly very excited. There was even talk of doing graphic-novelizations under the moniker "A Bjornographic Book." Anders came to this meeting with the name of the person who would write them, a sixty-eight-year-old Jewish lady living in Jersey City whom he'd used in the past—for *The Secret Life of Housewives*, among other things. Cinchy, boss of the people, shook Koss's hand.

"I didn't think you could pull it off, Karse," said Cinchy. "But you did. You've turned over a new leaf. You must be very proud."

Kossweiller, as quickly as he decently could, took his hand back and left the room.

Anders had been right. The first Verenson book (*First Bjorn Child*) was a hit, and the second (*Bjorn Again*), published six months later, was even bigger. The most disturbing thing, Kossweiller felt, was that two men could sit down over drinks and in a few moments create a best-selling series. It didn't matter who wrote it, it didn't really matter how good it was; all that mattered was concept. Or maybe it did matter that it wasn't too good. And he could tell from the calls he got from editors at other houses that any of them would have been happy to have Bjorn Verenson on their list, even the editors he had considered literary. It was depressing to think about.

True, it wouldn't have been possible without H. H. and Cinchy to pump money into the books, but they got back a lot more than they had pumped in.

There was the matter, too, of H. H. Anders kept coming by to remind him he had promised her dinner.

"Actually, it was you that promised her dinner," said Kossweiller.

"But on your behalf, Koss. It was all for you. You don't want to go?"

"It just seems awkward," he said.

"Ah," said Anders. "It'll be fine."

But it was not fine. When he finally went, Kossweiller felt that they had nothing to say to each other. Or rather *he* had nothing to say to *her*. She spent more than an hour talking about book packaging, Kossweiller nodding and making brief noncommittal sounds. And then, suddenly, at the end of the date she managed somehow to coax him out of the car and up to her door and then pinned him between the door and her torso. It was all he could do to extricate himself, and it was clear the next day that listening to herself talk about packaging was her idea of a wonderful time, that she wanted to see him again as soon as possible.

I hate my life, he thought.

Before, editing had been his life. He had had his small Chelsea apartment to go home to, alone. A few friends he saw, sometimes sexually, and occasional distractions. It had been enough. Now, editing had become a problem, and, in addition, he had no life.

The sixty-eight-year-old Jerseyite writing the Verenson books liked to call him on the telephone and talk in a deep voice with a fake Swedish accent. She wasn't very good at it. It drove him crazy. The third Verenson book, *Bjorn Free*, he could barely stand to read, let alone edit. It was published and was a tremendous success. *I have no soul*, he kept thinking.

With the fourth Verenson book, he went to Cinchy, asking him if he could do something literary for a change.

"Literary?" asked Cinchy. "Why would you want to do something like that?"

He tried to explain in a way that Cinchy would accept. It was not that he didn't want to do the Bjorn books, just that now that he had the cake he wanted to put the icing on it.

"What cake?" said Cinchy. "What icing? What are you talking about?"

"But," said Kossweiller, "that's what you said, the icing, literature."

"Karse," he said. "Why can't you be happy with what you have? Why are you always trying to ruin yourself?" He took him by the shoulders, led him to the door. "I can't have my best mystery editor slumming in lit now, can I?"

He was on his way home when it started to rain. At first it wasn't bad, a light drizzle, but soon he was the only one still walking on the street, everyone else huddling under awnings. Soon he was freezing cold. *Perfect*, he thought. He left the street, went into the first coffee shop he saw.

He shook off in the entryway, then ordered a large coffee at the counter. He held it with both hands to warm them. Looking around for a place to sit, he spied Ralph Bubber. The man was staring at him but immediately looked away when he saw Kossweiller had noticed.

Kossweiller went over to his table, stood above him.

"Bubber," he said.

"Kossweiller," said Bubber. "What a pleasure to see you."

"I have a bone to pick with you," said Kossweiller, and sat down. He shrugged his coat off his shoulders. He took a drink of his coffee. Bubber watched him apprehensively, saying nothing. "Dolls?" Kossweiller finally said. "Why me?"

"I guess I do owe you an apology," said Bubber.

"Why did you do it?" asked Kossweiller.

"You'd never bought anything from me before," he said, "never treated me with anything but contempt, and suddenly you expect me to do you a favor?" Bubber shrugged. "That, and I hate Darba. Mostly that, actually. Besides, it doesn't seem to have worked out too badly for you."

"My life is hell. Why do you hate Darba?"

"Ninety over ninety," said Bubber. "He threatened me with that after the doll incident."

"He threatened me with that too," said Kossweiller. "What does it mean?"

"You don't want to find out," said Bubber. "It's different for everybody. That's the way Darba thinks, a very specific torture. I don't know what it would mean for you. For me, I was told that to keep my job I had to eat ninety eggs over the course of ninety minutes and hold them all down. I hate eggs. He knew I hated eggs. Nobody can eat ninety eggs in ninety minutes. Cool Hand Luke could only do fifty. He fired me, but I managed to work it to get him fired as well. And there was the doll incident." He gave a big, peeling smile. "Look at me now. All that did something to me. That was at MacMaster & Bates. I was his first ninety over ninety. No, second: Daniel Sherman, remember him?"

"Think so."

"Mine was easy and quick. Darba told Danny he had to accept ninety books over a ninety-day period. Danny took it seriously, read like a madman, got the best work he could get, thinking his job depended on not only doing it but doing it right. He did it, too, came to Darba on day ninety with ninety drawn contracts ready for his signature. Darba tore up every one of those contracts, one by one, in front of him. You know what that can do to a man?"

"What happened to Sherman?"

"Dead now. Won't go into that."

"What about the doll incident?"

Bubber looked at him hard, then reached out and took his arm. Kossweiller flinched. "You still haven't bought anything from me," he said. "Not one fucking book. You don't really like me. You're not my friend. I told you my ninety over ninety, I don't owe you anything. I don't talk about my ninety over ninety with anyone. And besides, the doll incident would sound trivial to you. The only person it's not trivial to is Darba."

"He's called Cinchy now," said Kossweiller.

Bubber nodded. "Boss of the people. I hate him. If I could get away with killing him, I would."

"Ninety over ninety?"

"Ninety over fucking ninety. Goddamn right."

An article was published on the Verenson phenomenon; foreign rights were sold, even back to Sweden, where, apparently, English was common enough that it wasn't a shock that a Swedish writer might actually choose that language to write in. Kossweiller could hardly stand to see Anders in the hall, though he knew Anders was simply as he was, perhaps not unreasonably so, and was not to be blamed. The problem was with him, Kossweiller.

After a few more nervous impasses at H. H.'s door, the end of one of them leading to Kossweiller's waking in H. H.'s apartment at three in the morning and trying to put on his clothes without awakening her, he stopped returning her calls. She seemed to take this in stride, had perhaps never expected more of him, though she would still sometimes corral him in his office, leaning one hip against his door while she explained a further development in the marketing of prepublication copies.

"You have to market prepublication copies?"

"That's the most important marketing you can do," she claimed, and kept on.

By the appearance of the fifth Verenson book, the amnesic *Not Bjorn Yesterday*, Kossweiller had had enough. The title didn't even make sense: if Bjorn had lost his memory, he *would* be Bjorn yesterday, just not Bjorn today. The joke had overwhelmed any sense of meaning the title might have. He wanted out.

•

He showed up in Cinchy's office to find the man staring at a box on his desk.

"Karse," he said, not taking his eyes off the box. "Who do you think this is from?"

"I don't know, sir," said Kossweiller. "Cinchy, I mean."

"Cinchy's right," he said. "Boss of the people. Read the return address for me, K-man."

K-man? He swiveled his head, looked at the box. "There's no return address," he said.

"That's what I thought too," said Cinchy. "A bad sign, no? Koss?"

"Yes?"

"I want you to do me a favor," he said, turning to face the wall. "I want you to open the box and see what's inside it. If there's a doll inside, I don't want to know. No dolls."

Kossweiller carefully opened the box, peered in. There was indeed a doll inside, a cloth doll, handmade. It had button eyes, its lips drawn with Magic Marker. Its hair was made of yellow yarn. Its fingers were not fully articulated, simply indicated by sewn strands of black thread. The words "Love from B" were written on a card pinned to its chest.

"Is there a doll?" asked Cinchy.

"Um," said Kossweiller.

"Don't tell me," said Cinchy. "If there's a doll, I don't want to know." He waited for a long moment. "Is there a doll?" he finally asked again.

"No?" said Kossweiller, closing the box.

"Good," said Cinchy. He turned around, very slowly. "Right answer. No dolls. Never any dolls. Take that empty box away and burn it, Karsewelder."

"I have something I need to say," said Kossweiller.

"Not yet," said Cinchy, looking nervously at the box. "Take the box and hold it outside the door."

Kossweiller went to the doorway, stood with his hand outside of it.

"Farther," said Cinchy, "farther," until Kossweiller had only his face inside Cinchy's office. "Good," Cinchy finally said. "What is it?"

"I'm quitting," said Kossweiller.

"Quitting?" said Cinchy. "You can't quit."

"I'm not happy."

"What's happy?" said Cinchy. "You're not allowed to quit. You're running one of the most popular mystery series going and you want to quit? You're not trying to take Verenson to another house, are you?"

"I want to do literary books," said Kossweiller. "*En Masse*. I want to do *En Masse*."

"No literary books," said Cinchy. "No *en* fucking *masse*. We know how you get once you start doing literary books, don't we? And no quitting. You're not a quitter, Koss. I won't let you quit."

"But—"

Cinchy raised his hand. "I don't want to hear it, Koss. You'll work for me or you won't work. And no literature. It's bad for you. It rots the teeth and then you don't eat the rest of your meal."

Kossweiller stared at him.

"No arguments," said Cinchy. "I may be the boss of the people but I'm still the boss."

Not knowing what else to do, Kossweiller brought the box back into the room. Cinchy, he saw, immediately began to sweat.

"What are you doing, Koss?" he said.

"I quit," said Kossweiller.

"You can't quit," said Cinchy. "And don't threaten me with that empty box."

Kossweiller began to open the box, giving Cinchy a glimpse of the doll's hand. Cinchy let out a terrified shout, his features shivering like water, and then crouched behind the desk. It was a horrible thing to watch. Kossweiller quickly tucked the hand away.

"Is it gone?" Cinchy asked.

"It's gone," said Kossweiller.

"Is it outside?"

Kossweiller turned around and put the box outside the door. "It's outside," he said.

"All right," said Cinchy. He stood up, smoothing his shirt with his hands. "I'll let you go. You can find yourself another house and I won't do anything to interfere. But first you have to do two things for me, Koss. Otherwise I'll ruin you. You'll never work in publishing again."

"What things?"

"First, take that box out and burn it."

"All right," said Kossweiller.

"Second," said Cinchy—and here he seemed to regain his usual bearings—"ninety over ninety. Do that and you're free to go."

IV.

All right, he had said, *ninety over ninety*. How bad could it be? He would steel himself and do it, prepared for anything to happen. If he was steeled, how bad could it be?

But it quickly became clear how bad it could be. Kossweiller's ninety over ninety was to put together an anthology of work by ninety people over the age of ninety, and to continue with the Verenson project and other things in the meantime. Literary quality didn't matter, Cinchy said. All that mattered is that the contributors were all over ninety and that there were ninety of them. "And I want proof," said Cinchy. "Driver's licenses, nursing-home records, birth certificates."

"This is crazy," said Kossweiller.

"It's your price," said Cinchy. "Your ninety over ninety, if you ever want to work in publishing again."

So he set out. He started with assisted-living facilities, found very few people over ninety, then went to nursing homes and hospices. When he was allowed in, he occasionally found someone ninety or above who was still, loosely speaking, coherent and who could give him something: a dirty joke, a recipe, a story from an episode of their life. Some of them even had poems. The poems were awful, things that made him wince, but what did it matter, what did he care? It was the price of his freedom.

By the time he finished with the nursing homes close to Manhattan, more than a month had passed. He had only twenty-three entries, not a literary moment among them. He scanned newspapers for notices of birthdays, spent a week in Boston, trying nursing homes there, gained a few more names.

Back in New York, people in the office, realizing he was on his way out, stopped talking to him. Even Anders offered him only a scattered and occasional word. H. H. refused to have anything to do with him face-to-face, sending him designs and marketing information for the next Verenson book by interoffice courier. He responded in kind. Only Cinchy went out of his way to talk to him, needling him about the progress of his ninety over ninety.

He went door-to-door in the older neighborhoods. Out of the smattering of the eligible geezers he finally met, only a small fraction could do him any good. He took sick leave and flew to the retirement communities in Florida, was dismayed to find that while nearly everyone was over sixty, very few were over ninety. Here and there, he gained a few more names. One woman actually died while she was talking to him, suddenly fluttering her eyes and stopping speaking. He wrote the rest of her entry—on a rural Nebraskan childhood—himself, culling heavily from Willa Cather.

Four months in, he was nearing seventy-five entries. He was exhausted, ready to be through with his ninety over ninety and free of Cinchy for good. He was going door-to-door in an old neighborhood in Queens, no longer looking for nonagenarians so much as trying to buy driver's licenses of deceased relatives who, if they had still been alive, would have been over ninety. It had been a good evening; he managed to get two for around twenty dollars each. He would photocopy them and then write up an entry or two himself on their behalf, if he could bear it.

He knocked on a door and when it opened was surprised to see Bubber. The man was looking as run-down as ever, still fat, still pale. His hair, greased back earlier in the day, was still plastered down in places, beginning to sprout up in others. He was wearing a worn plaid robe over an under-shirt and a paint-spattered set of trousers, a pair of filthy terry-cloth slippers.

"Kossweiller," he said. "I wondered when I'd see you again. Won't you come in?"

He turned around and shuffled back into the house, leaving the door ajar, as if there were no question but that Kossweiller would accept.

Kossweiller followed him through his living room and to a rickety table in the kitchen. They both sat down. Bubber pushed the cup in front of him across to Kossweiller, filled it with tea, reached another cup off the counter beside for himself.

"You're still with Darbo?" asked Bubber.

"Not exactly," said Kossweiller.

"Not exactly?" asked Bubber, his eyes lighting up slightly. "What do you mean by that?"

"Ninety over ninety," he said, and explained.

"Did it say 'Love from B'? That's my doll," said Bubber, smiling. "I send him one from time to time, just to keep him on his toes. It's good to know this one actually was put to good use. What's your ninety over ninety?"

Kossweiller explained. "Four months already," he said. "Two dozen names, then I'm free."

Bubber let go of his arm. "You won't be free," he said. "I know Darbo. He'll twist the knife. He'll figure some way to make it hurt more than you think."

"It hurts plenty this way," said Kossweiller, and felt very depressed.

"It'll hurt more," said Bubber.

Bubber, he knew, was right: Cinchy, boss of the people, was endowed with an almost unabatable reservoir of sadism. Cinchy would let him go, perhaps would let him quit, but he would never be free.

"What do I do?" Kossweiller asked.

"There's nothing to do, Koss," Bubber said. "Just survive it best you can."

They sat for a moment mulling this over, Kossweiller moving his teacup around slightly so that the liquid swished in the cup. "I should go," he finally said.

"There's something you should see first," said Bubber.

He took both teacups and shambled to the sink. He dumped and rinsed them, turned them upside down on the counter. He opened a cookie jar and removed from it a key on the end of a string. Taking Kossweiller by the arm, he led him down the hall, past a bedroom to a padlocked door.

"My workroom," said Bubber, as, one-handed, he worked the padlock open.

The room inside was windowless, dark. Bubber drew him in, still keeping hold of his arm. "Ready?" he said, and flicked on the lights.

Before them, on a makeshift shelf running the whole length of the wall, were a series of handmade dolls, just like the one Kossweiler had seen in Cinchy's office, except in this case, they were stacked in twos, one doll affixed to another doll's shoulders.

"Ninety over ninety," said Kossweiller.

"Actually right now just eighty-five over eighty-five, but nearly there. Maybe that's some consolation. Cinchy won't know what hit him."

"It may kill him."

"We can always hope," said Bubber.

A month later, by cutting a few corners, Kossweiller had hit his own ninety over ninety. He had several hundred manuscript pages, all of them terrible—even the recipes led to practically inedible food—but it was there. Setting his teeth, he took the typescript to Cinchy.

"Karswelder," Cinchy said. "Back so soon? Can your servitude be over? All there?" Cinchy said. "All ninety of them, and all of them over age ninety?"

"Yes," said Kossweiller. "It's done."

"Seems as though you've done it," said Cinchy. "Seems you're free to go."

Kossweiller headed toward the door, then stopped. "That's it?" he said. "That's the end?"

"What else would there be?"

"You're not going to double-check?"

"Why should I double-check, Karse? I trust you."

"You're not going to burn the manuscript or humiliate me in some other way?"

"Karse, Karse," said Cinchy. "Trust me. The last thing I want to do is get rid of all the hard work you did. Just the opposite, my friend."

Kossweiller nodded. He left Cinchy's office and started down the hall to his own office. Halfway there, he stopped, turned back.

"What do you mean 'just the opposite'?" he asked from Cinchy's door.

"Hmmm? You again, Koss?" said Cinchy, looking up from his desk. "Just what it sounded like. I'm going to publish the fucker."

"Really?"

"Of course. And to show my appreciation, I'll make sure that 'Edited by Philip Kossweiller' appears on both cover and spine. In fact, I wouldn't be surprised if your name wasn't in larger print than anything else. Back copy something like 'Esteemed literary editor Philip Kossweiller's personal choices for what's best in literature for the older set,' along with talk of a 'personal quest,' and whatnot. I'll make sure that it gets reviewed everywhere. And I'll save it for release until just the right moment."

"You wouldn't," said Kossweiller.

"I would," said Cinchy. "No dolls, Kossweiller!" he said, shouting now. "Never dolls! You should have remembered that."

Dazed, Kossweiller retreated. It was true, he thought. Cinchy had twisted the knife, and what was worse was it was a knife Kossweiller himself had given him.

He slowly made his way back to his office. Anders was there outside, fiddling with the change in his pockets.

"I hear you're leaving us, Koss," he said. "Sorry to see you go."

"You know already?"

"Word gets around," he said. "That and Cinchy called to give me the Verenson series. That doesn't upset you, does it?"

"No," said Kossweiller, "you're welcome to it."

Anders, perhaps feeling sentimental, perhaps trying only to put on a good front, attempted and bungled a hug, then left. Kossweiller found a box, began to pack up his desk. Cinchy, he knew, would wait until the worst possible moment to release the book, probably timing it to coincide with *En Masse*, if Kossweiller could ever find somewhere to publish it.

But, he thought, there was something he could do in the meantime.

He opened the bottom drawer and took out the doll. True, he had promised to burn the box, but Cinchy hadn't said anything about the doll. Technically, he had kept his promise.

He unpinned the note, "Love from B," and wrote on the doll's chest with permanent marker, *90/90*. Then, hiding the doll in a #6 envelope, he carried it down the hall and knocked on Cinchy's door.

The door was open but Cinchy had stepped out. *Am I the kind of person who does this?* he wondered. And then thought, *I have become the kind of person who does this.* In a way, he told himself, it was a kindness, a first shock before Bubber's larger, grimmer surprise, a warning to get ready. But he knew that this was not why he was doing it.

He set the doll up on the desk against a paperweight. It sat there limply, staring blindly at the door.

His desk was completely packed and he was already on the way to the elevator when he heard the scream. Despite himself, despite considering himself a literary man, he could not help but take great pleasure in the sound.

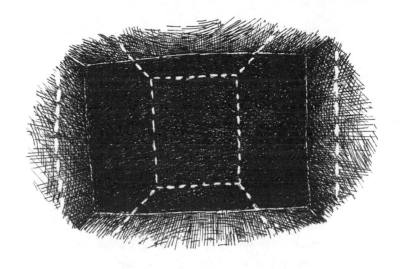

Invisible Box

In retrospect, it was easy for her to see it had been a mistake to have sex with a mime. At the time, though, she had been drunk enough that it seemed like a good idea. Sure, she had been a little surprised, once she had coaxed him upstairs, when he refused to speak, and even more surprised by his refusal to wipe off his face paint or shuck his beret, but, whatever, so what: it would give her a story to tell at parties.

But, ever since, she'd had trouble sleeping. She could manage a fitful hour but then woke up, imagining him there again above her, naked save for his face paint and beret and white gloves. She watched as, straddling her, he carefully felt out an invisible box around them. He kept making gestures to remind her about the box, feeling it out again, steadying her as she approached one imaginary edge, running his flattened palms along the box's ceiling just before penetrating her. It was a hell of a thing, at once funny and deeply disturbing, and distracting as hell.

When he was coming, pretending to cry out silently, she suddenly realized this was not a story she could bring herself to tell at parties. Mostly passed out, she lazily watched him lift the imaginary box off of them, get up and get dressed, then lift the box back in place, over her. She drifted off feeling it there around her, edges softly gleaming, holding her in.

She woke up early the next morning to find herself smeared with white face paint, as well as a few loops of black, like bruises, from his lips. She got up and brewed some coffee, had some toast, vomited. Her head felt wrapped in batting. The mime had not even been good in bed, though he had mimed being good in bed when she had picked him up. No, she thought, he had been more interested in his imaginary box than in her.

So she had slept with a mime, so what? In any case, it was over now, over and done.

But it wasn't over, nor was it done. True, she didn't think about the mime for the rest of the day, but later, that night, just as she was lying down to sleep, she felt something. There was the box, rising up around her. She closed her eyes and tried to sleep but kept seeing the box, its edges burning in flashes on the insides of her eyelids. It was hard to sleep feeling it was there, and when she finally did sleep, it was fitfully, dreaming of the mime moving inside of her, shoulders hunching to avoid the ceiling of the imaginary box, white face floating like a buoy in the darkness.

She brushed her hand through the box, but it remained undisturbed. She threw back the covers and got a drink and climbed back into bed, beside the box this time, but no, somehow the box was still over her, holding her in. No matter where she went on the bed, it was there. *This is ridiculous*, she thought, and tried to sleep, but instead sat there, staring at the inside of the nonexistent box, wondering how to get rid of it.

She got up and wandered the apartment, read a little in an armchair, made herself some warm milk, drank it. She began to feel a little sleepy. She nodded in and out in the chair, finally got up and went into the bedroom, climbed back into bed. An instant later, she was wide awake, staring again at the inside of the box.

Most of the night was like that, with her oppressed by the box that wasn't even there. She slept a little in the chair, on the floor, but never for long, mostly lying in the bed, in the nonexistent box, wide awake, feeling absurd. *I should kill that fucking mime*, she thought, around four in the morning. A little after five she wondered if there were support groups for women who had slept with mimes. Five minutes later, she started to wonder if the mime had worn a real or an imaginary condom. She kept picturing his exaggerated motions as he put it on. If she had a baby, would it be wearing a beret and white gloves? *Goddamn it*, she thought at 5:23 a.m., her eyes puffy, *what's wrong with me?*

She must have fallen asleep for a few minutes anyway, for by the time she awoke light was streaming through the window and the box was gone.

Relieved, she called her office and left a message saying she'd be late. She slept a few hours. The rest of the day was a little hazy, her responses slower than normal, and there was a point in a meeting where she completely blanked out, and came to herself seconds later to find the client staring at her strangely. She recouped as best she could, waded through the rest of the day, left right at five.

I'll sleep well tonight, she told herself on the drive home. She collapsed onto the bed before dinner, with the last of the sun coming in through the window, and fell asleep in her clothes.

She woke up an hour later in the dark, mouth dry, blouse rucked up around her breasts. In the dark she could feel the box there around her. Suddenly she was wide awake. She could not get back to sleep. She wanted to weep. Instead, she lay there feeling the box, trying to ignore it, trying to pretend it wasn't there. *But no*, she thought, *I'm not pretending. It's an imaginary box; it* isn't *there*. But thinking this didn't seem to help.

It was one night among many, each of them shading into each other, each essentially coming down to the same thing: her lying in bed, staring through a nonexistent box at the ceiling. In the days that followed, she tried everything she could think of. She slept naked, she slept clothed, sober, drunk, half-naked, half-clothed, half-sober, half-drunk. She took sleeping pills, which seemed to work for a few hours but didn't make her feel any less tired once she woke up. She changed the sheets; the box was still there. *I should kill that fucking mime*, she thought. She turned the mattress over; the box was still there. She tried to sleep on the couch, but even though the box wasn't over her, she could feel it in the next room, gently shimmering. She tried to sleep at a friend's house but somehow could still feel the box even from there, blocks away, waiting for her.

She started seeing a psychiatrist, who tried to give her *strategies for coping. Maybe*, he suggested after five or six sessions, *you need to give in to your inner mime, so to speak.* My inner mime? she wondered. She listlessly attended two or three more sessions, and then stopped.

Which left her where, exactly? In bed, beneath the box, having difficulty sleeping, eyes redder, mind more and more distracted, wishing every night, as she tried to close her eyes and found they wouldn't close, that she were dead. I'll try anything, she kept telling herself, I'll do anything. Just as long as I can get some sleep.

Which is what led her, one night, at three or perhaps twenty past three or perhaps somewhat closer to four—hard to say, since there had been so many nights since in which she had done the same thing—to begin thinking with two different parts of her head at once. One part of her head was thinking, as it had thought at least once per night, that she should kill that fucking mime, but the other part was thinking that, no, perhaps not kill but fuck him again and this time, after he came, get him to take his fucking box away with him. One part of her head was walking into the kitchen and taking a knife from the block and sliding it into her purse, but the other part was thinking what it would say to get the mime to go home with her again, how she would first find him and then fuck him, or, no, stab him dead, back and forth, until, when she came to herself again and was thinking with only one part of her head, there she was, alone, in the dead of night, in the street, searching for her mime, not knowing whether she would have sex with him or kill him or perhaps both. It was useless, she knew, to look for him so late, but there she was, walking, half-dressed, walking, and now the same thing seemed to happen almost every night, almost without her knowing it, that strange moment when her thinking split into either side of her head and she seemed to fall into the gap between, and by the time she had managed to clamber out, she was out alone on the streets, looking for a mime, only a mime would do.

And perhaps it is best to leave her here, half-asleep and wandering, grasping at straws that don't exist, for what good can possibly come of any of this? At best, she will soon have butchered a mime in her bed or will end up dead herself. At worst, she will soon find herself enclosed by not just one imaginary box, but two. That she might actually work her way free, that she might actually, for once, sleep through the night, ever again, seems the least likely possibility of all, even to her. So, let's leave her, let's tuck the covers up around her neck and take a step or two backwards. Let's turn out the light and—despite the soft gleam of her open eyes in the darkness, despite the sounds of her tossing and turning within her box, despite, as night deepens, her little groans of frustration—let's smile and, lying, tell ourselves yes, everything is all right, yes, shhh, yes, she's finally asleep.

The Third Factor

Clearly the method of elucidation I employed in my report did not satisfy the administration, and thus I am at a loss as to know how to proceed. I beg to be forgiven here for stretching regulations, for deviating slightly but, I hope, productively from the standard report. Since I have already tendered my resignation, I will also say frankly that I see a supplemental report as superfluous. Or, rather, I would see it as such were I not aware that failure to answer the administration's request might well result in my being subjected to a sustained process of observation—observation of the sort which I myself have been obliged to carry out in the past. Obviously I am assuming—hardly a safe assumption—that I am not already under observation.

Had I a copy of it, you would find appended to this notebook a completed copy of what I believe is grievance form 026/a, "Formal grievance, superiors, non-immediate, at hands of." I would have shaded the box marked "Request, redundancy" and would have, as per requirements, bolstered the form with the requisite material: my initial report, my letter of resignation, and the administration's latest request. Perhaps whichever administrator receives my materials will argue that, since I previously tendered my resignation, I am no longer considered an employee and thus not authorized to file a grievance. My inability, despite my best efforts, to obtain said form suggests as much. Yet if I do not *de facto* possess employee status, why am I being asked to supplement my original report?

•

The gestation of my current state of mind—a state of mind which led to my resignation—took place during my first assignment. I had been asked to note the movements of a silvery-haired gentleman who habitually sported a soiled trench coat. These movements consisted generally of a slow round from park bench to park bench. I had been noting his movements in a battered but sturdy notebook that fit snugly into the palm of my admittedly meaty hand. I wrote in a notational code devised by myself and my immediate supervisor—a code of such efficiency and concision that I needed less than a single page per day.

This assignment lasted for the better part of a year. The subject was of regular habits and there was only slight variance in his movements. I arrived early in the morning to take the place of the night observer. I left in the early evening, when I was replaced by the same man. At the end of each day I walked to a designated street corner, there to find an older make of car, nondescript save for the heavily tinted glass of its windows. It was a different car each day but always had the same license plate. My instructions were to try the passenger-side door. If it was unlocked, I was to open said door and climb inside, delivering my report aloud to my immediate superior. If it was locked, I tore the day's page free from the notebook and left it pinioned and fluttering between the windshield wiper and the windshield itself.

This first assignment, it should be evident, was a simple one. The subject under observation made no effort to avoid me. Indeed, he seemed consistently unaware of my presence. As this attitude persisted for the full course of the observation, I became lulled into complacency. For this reason I was surprised and unprepared when the subject, between benches, removed a small-bore revolver from his pocket and shot himself in the belly.

As my supervisor and I had developed no notational code for this behavior, I wasted valuable time rendering in longhand what I had seen. For the first time, I used more than a page, a fact which filled me with not inconsiderable distress. Once the event was recorded, it took me some time to decide what to do. In the end, thinking I might compromise my position were I to intervene directly, I called anonymously for an ambulance from a yellow call box enthicketed deep within the park. By the time this ambulance arrived, the subject had bled to death.

The paramedics covered him with a sheet and loaded him into the ambulance, two facts I also recorded longhand in my notebook. After a failed attempt to pursue the ambulance on foot, I returned to the designated street corner to report. My subject had chosen to shoot himself well before the conclusion of my day's observation; thus, no car was present, only a pair of orange cones banded with reflective tape.

Returning to the park, I waited out the end of my observation period. I was not replaced at dusk by the night observer. After waiting for some time, I made my way back to the designated street corner and there found a car waiting. The passenger-side door was open. I climbed in.

My supervisor sat silent while I began to read aloud from my report, his gloved hands resting delicately atop the steering wheel. When I reached my longhand description of the shooting, he lifted one hand slightly. I stopped speaking.

"You did not employ our code," he said.

"The experience unfortunately was not such as to render itself into a coding with which I was familiar," I said, somewhat uneasily.

In a few instants he explained how one might elegantly extrapolate a relevant coding of the event in a way that was logical and immediately comprehensible. Why I had not seen it before, I couldn't say.

In letting his hand fall back to the steering wheel, he signaled for me to continue. He stopped me yet again when I explained my telephone call.

"This," he said, "constitutes a description not of his movements but of your own."

He raised similar objections to my failure to follow the ambulance.

"These are hours," he stated, "that shall remain forever outside of observation."

But, I explained, by this time the subject was dead.

But by what authority, he wanted to know, had I determined that my observation should end with the subject's death?

For two days I stood outside a mortuary, at the end of which I was made to attend the graveside services and note the subject's movements. These, as one might expect, were minimal at best. I watched his coffin being lowered into the open grave and listened impassively as a friend of the family spoke of an *unknown assailant*—obviously not realizing the subject had shot himself—and of the *Good Samaritan who had called for the ambulance, which had come, alas, too late.* He was followed by a parade of friends and relations eager to grieve, whose words rapidly reduced the man's life to a half-smiling and impotent shambles. It disconcerted me to discover the ordinary banality of the fellow's life, though I cannot say why.

When I returned to the designated street corner after the funeral, I discovered a piece of paper fluttering between the windshield and the windshield wiper of the car in question, a paper which made clear that I was to report to another city, to another contact, to accept my second assignment.

My new assignment was slightly more complicated than my previous one, which initially seemed to suggest that the administration had been pleased with how I had performed on my previous assignment—though I was at a loss to understand how exactly I might have pleased them. I was given a photograph and an address, told that I was to observe the individual in question and follow him, report on his movements, his associates. I was to keep a record but to meet with my supervisor only if I noted anything unusual.

When I asked what exactly constituted *unusual*, my administrator, sitting beside me in the flickering half-light of the movie theater, made a vague gesture, hard to see in the dark. I was not, I was told, to wonder what I was looking for; when something was unusual, he assured me, I would know. Before I could inquire further, he softly squeezed my knee and stood, pushing past me and out of the theater.

I went to the address I had been given, establishing a locus of observation among the branches of an oak tree in a park across the street from it. The house was small, the lot cut into the side of a hill. I watched people come and go, and compared each face to the picture I held in my hand. None of them were the subject. In the late afternoon I was discovered by a park employee, whom at first I ignored but who subsequently prodded me with a stick until I was forced to climb down. Shortly thereafter, he forced me to leave the park.

In the three days that followed, I did my best to keep the house under observation, despite the continued harcelations of the park employee. I was tempted to kill him for the sake of the observation, and surely would have, had I not felt that his death was as likely to complicate my ability to use the park for observation as it was to facilitate it. I developed an elaborate series of maneuvers to avoid the fellow, quickly mastering the possible variants of his rounds and learning to anticipate his movements. He saw me at a distance once or twice, but by the time he came nearer, I had vanished.

Despite these setbacks, my observation was rigorous. I could state with certainty that the man in the photograph did not enter the house, nor did he leave it.

Perhaps, I thought, I have a bad likeness. But even considering the photograph a bad likeness, I still could not imagine that it represented anyone I had seen enter the house.

Or perhaps, I thought, I had been given this assignment as a punishment.

On the fourth day, not knowing what else to do, I approached the house and rapped on the door. A young woman—early twenties, baby slung on one hip, no resemblance to the man in the photograph—opened the door. I showed her the photograph, claiming I had found it fluttering on her front lawn. Had she or someone in her household dropped it? Did she recognize it? No, she said, it wasn't hers. Did she recognize the man in the picture? Perhaps it was a neighbor of hers? I would, I claimed, gladly return the photograph to the rightful owner if only . . .

She looked long and hard. No, she said, she was sorry, but she did not recognize the man.

I attempted to make contact with my supervisor by returning to the movie theater. I arrived early in the morning and waited outside until it opened. I went to the row where we had conversed before, and installed myself. There I remained until the theater closed, my sole encounter being not with my supervisor but with an elderly and uncircumcised man—the accuracy of this latter adjective made manifest to me through the fact that the fellow felt compelled to display for me his foreskin. I had neither encouraged nor discouraged him, simply remained staring straight ahead at the flickering images on the screen, waiting for my supervisor to arrive.

I had, in my first meeting with my supervisor, paid no attention to the film. Indeed, all my energy had been focused on gathering the particulars of the job itself. Thus, I had no way of knowing if that particular film and the film I was now regarding on this, my second visit, were in fact the same. I can speak only to the particulars of the film I saw on this second visit and hope they cast some light on the film of the first visit. Or, rather, what I mean to say is that what I say about the film might have some significance to my understanding the purposes of the administration or it might not, might reveal only something about myself and my subsequent actions. And perhaps not even that.

I was surprised to discover that I could make no sense of what I was seeing on the screen. There was occasionally an image that might have been a face, but it was so sunk within a general morass of light and sound that I could never fully apprehend it. There was a flux of what might have been bodies, but so abstracted as to have been equally likely scratches in an overexposed film stock. The images, if images they were, first entranced and then slowly unsettled me. At the moment when my distress had reached its height, the film flickered out and the houselights rose. The old man who had been beside me was gone; he had been kind enough to leave behind no sign of his presence. The few theatergoers—all men, curiously enough—filed out, save for me. A clubfooted employee armed with dustpan and broom swept the aisles and gathered garbage and then disappeared. A few minutes later the lights dimmed, a few dim men filed in, and the film began again.

Or perhaps I should say, merely, *a film began.* I was unable to tell if I was watching the same film or a different one. I experienced the same deep play of color and light that at once threatened to dissolve into abstraction and cohere into discrete images without ever quite doing either one. But there was no particular moment I recognized. I had the odd sensation of both seeing something for the first time and seeing it again. This exhilarated me and then unsettled me. I watched the remaining showings without ever quite being at ease.

Imagine me, then, seated, awaiting my superior, until the final showing of the evening came to an end and I was forced to leave the theater. I returned to the theater every day for a week, becoming more and more engrossed in the film or films, still unable to make sense of them. I kept to the same seat. My contact never appeared, though the uncircumcised man or someone not unlike him made several repeated forays down my aisle. On the eighth day, I found myself confronted not by the sort of film I had grown accustomed to but by a blaring and heaving image of a nude or nearly nude woman. Startled, I left.

I searched my mind: was there something I was forgetting, some method of contacting my superior that I had neglected? No, I thought, there was not.

•

What followed was a slow and lost movement through the city as I considered what, if anything, I should do. I kept my eyes open for the man in the photograph, to no avail. I shuffled in and out of movie theaters throughout the city without finding anyone who resembled my superior. Having no subject whose movements I might record, I began to record my own movements, slowly developing my own notational code, a code, I will acknowledge, derived from that of my previous supervisor.

I slept in the streets, plastered in newspapers. I became tattered, ungainly. I was awash, adrift, unadministrated.

How long this period lasted, it is difficult to say. Perhaps several months, perhaps more than a year. There are whole months of which I have only the vaguest memories. Even in my notebooks, pages in which each of a day's movements is carefully notated are followed by bursts of blank pages. I remember the act of notating certain days in the notebook but no longer recall the movements themselves: even as I was writing them, it was as if I were recording not my own movements but the movements of someone else.

In a moment of lucidity, it came to me that it might be possible to regain contact with the administration through my previous administrator. I boarded the first bus. After a journey involving little or no sleep and the changing of buses on four or five separate occasions, I found myself back in the city in which I had fulfilled my first assignment. After a brief sleep within a green metal dumpster behind the bus station, I set off. I pursued a trajectory straight through the city along the main street until the surroundings began to strike me as familiar, at which point I began to wriggle my way about on side streets. By such means I stumbled onto a park not unlike the park in which my first subject of observation had shot himself. I discovered a house seemingly identical to the house he had occupied. I made my way through the park and down a side street, turned right, turned right once more, but at what should have been the designated corner I found no car.

I sat on the curb and considered. Was it or was it not the designated corner? The name of the street was familiar, but for what reason it was impossible to say: perhaps it was merely a street I had often passed, or it bore the name of another street in another city. My notebooks, carefully coded, were of no help on this score—the relevant pages had all been long ago torn out and pinioned to windshields. What remained of my notebooks concerned only my abortive second assignment (also in a house near a park, but in a different city) and my period of self-observation. *Is this or is this not the place?* I wrote, and then held the pen poised above the paper to see what words might come next.

Nothing came next.

I am unable to say how much time had passed. At one moment, I was there on the curb, feet in the gutter, watching water swirling past the worn heels of my boots. The next, I was somehow in a park, conscious only of the fact that I had just heard, somewhere behind me, a voice.

The voice spoke again, uttering, perhaps somewhat tentatively, a name. I removed my notebook and made a notation in it, a notation meant to represent the name that had just been uttered: *B.*

I will be the first to admit that notation is not always enough. How much wiser it would have been had I recorded the name in full. But, having been scolded previously by my supervisor for moving from notation to long-hand, I felt I had no choice.

A hand touched my shoulder. "Is that you, B?" a voice asked, and uttered the name again. *No*, I said, *not me*, and tried to continue on my way. But the man attached to the voice kept tight hold of my shoulder and slowly turned me about until he was looking me in the face.

"Ah," he said. "It *is* you."

But no, let me state, for the record, that it wasn't me. Or, rather, wasn't him. B. Or I wasn't him, I mean. I tried to state as much, but without real success. As I tried again to disengage myself, the man tightened his hold, speaking excitedly and quickly. I was to come with him, he told me. I *must* come with him. I began to feel very afraid, though even now I am hard-pressed to say why. I struck him once, hard, and turned and ran.

I spent two days wandering the side streets, at night sequestering myself within a green metal dumpster. By the third day, I had convinced myself that I must flee the city. Perhaps, I told myself, if I returned to my second assignment, I would now understand what to do.

I had seated myself in the proper bus when it was boarded by the man whom I had encountered in the park, accompanied by a policeman. There was nowhere for me to go. As I watched them come down the aisle toward me, I discreetly recorded their movements in my notebook.

They stopped beside me, the man uttering the name again, like a greeting. I ignored him. *This the man?*, the policeman asked, and when the other man responded in the affirmative, he asked me, *You him?* I did not answer. Both addressed me again, both were ignored. Eventually the policeman took my arm and tried to coax me from my seat, which caused me to wholeheartedly embrace the seat in front of me—much to the surprise and consternation of the man sitting in it. What followed, not necessarily in this order, were shouts, a rush and a sway, a torn shirt pocket, hands prying at fingers, a billy club, a terrified face. All of which culminated in my expulsion from the bus and my temporary sequestration within a police station. I had, I was told, a lot of explaining to do.

I was asked for a name. As per administrative regulations, I did not surrender it. I was asked if I was not one B. No, I claimed, not he. Then what was my name? I chose not to answer. Did I know who I was? I remained mum. The other man, I was told, was my relation. I shrugged.

The other man displayed a number of photographs—photographs of a man who, I was forced to admit, resembled me to no uncommon degree. Even his frozen gestures, at least as they were captured in the photographs, seemed to have been modeled after my own.

I will insist again, as I did in my first report, that I was not for a moment convinced. I was not, and never had been, this B, was certain of that even though I have some small difficulty in assembling the details of my life prior to my employment by the administration. Yet, as my questioning continued, it became clear to me that the choice was not between acknowledging this ersatz relation and being released on my own recognizance; it was between acknowledging him and becoming a ward of the state. I could produce no fixed address, not having one, and I was unwilling to speak of my name or my admittedly obscure past. All of these things marked me as a danger and suggested I must be restrained. When this became clear to me, I reconsidered my strategies.

Thus, I slowly began to acknowledge a connection to my ersatz relation, in bits and pieces at first, but slowly with more and more force. I claimed to hope that these assertions would pass as long-denied memories slowly bubbling to the surface. I was asked questions about my ersatz relative, which I answered to the best of my ability, my answers largely gleaned from what I had heard him say to me over the previous few hours. When I had to make guesses—names of other family members, specifics regarding various family successes and tragedies—I turned out to be unaccountably lucky.

I used this same phrase, *unaccountably lucky*, in my first report. I expect it is one of the aspects of that report that the administration expects me to elucidate further in this, my second report. Unfortunately, I cannot elucidate it further. I want to emphasize again that I never for a moment believed in the charade I was performing. I simply guessed correctly. I cannot explain it myself, and this, above all, is something that continues to trouble me.

In short, I performed well enough to be released into the custody of my ersatz relation. He promised to take me to his home, wash me, clothe me, feed me, care for me. I would, I thought, stay with him for a few days and then, once his suspicions were lulled, make my escape.

What followed was a static period as far as my administrative responsibilities were concerned. True, I remained with my ersatz relation not for the two or three days I had intended, but for several months. This can be partly blamed on me: it had been some time since I had slept in a soft bed or eaten a decent meal. These pleasures I was reluctant to surrender. It also had something to do with the pleasure that my presence gave my ersatz relation.

Yet neither of these would have been enough in and of itself to keep me there. Had it not been for the presence of a third factor, I wouldn't have hesitated to leave.

The third factor: my ersatz relation occupied a house identical to the house in which the subject of my first observation had lived. At first, I wrote this off as mere coincidence, as an odd feeling of déjà vu, but as I continued to inhabit the house, the feeling grew rather than diminished. The proximity of the house to a nearby park was the same as well, and the park itself offered the same round of benches. It had to be the same house. But how was this possible?

I asked my ersatz relation how long he had lived in the house. Ever patient with my gaps of memory, he explained that the house had been in the family for nearly twenty years. I asked him if he had had a relation shot and killed in the adjacent park. True, he claimed, a man had been shot and killed in the park several years ago—a slow and painful death due to a bullet in the belly—but it had not been anyone he knew. And, he claimed, I—or B, rather—had disappeared shortly after this incident.

Troubled, I stayed on. I did not understand what this could mean. It exhilarated me and unsettled me. By day, I took a slow stroll through the park, moving from bench to bench, observing those around me. Was I myself, I wondered, being observed? By night I lay in my room with the lights extinguished, peering out from between the slats of the blinds.

What, I wondered, was the administration's role in any of this?
   I couldn't say.

I observed my ersatz relation, looking for any sign that he was more, or less, than he seemed. But he seemed neither more nor less, only himself. I began to record his movements in a notebook to see if any pattern developed. No pattern developed.

Where would it all lead?, I wondered, as I followed my slow round from bench to bench. Was this the administration's way of punishing me for some failure *in re* my task as an observer? Would I, too, eventually shoot myself in the belly with a low-caliber handgun? What did the administration hope to gain by torturing me, if in fact they were behind whatever there was to be behind?

The days that followed were nervous ones, involving a slow acceleration of doubt and fear. I made the circuit of the park benches faster and faster. I stopped sleeping. I was increasingly less myself. My ersatz relation regarded me with concern. Or perhaps suspicion. Or perhaps his regard was tainted by some third factor.

This lasted until the day when, on my rounds through the park, I sat next to a man wearing a narrow tie and a pinstriped suit. He was eating a sandwich wrapped in brown paper. When he was done, he licked his fingers. He crumpled the paper up and placed it on the bench between us.
   As soon as he was gone, I picked up the paper and opened it. The mayonnaise, I saw, had leaked out to form a wavery line, hooked at the bottom like a shepherd's crook. I turned the paper in my hands and saw the mark for what it was: a message: a question mark.

•

I stayed for a long time regarding the paper, the message written on it. I smoothed it flat on the bench, folded it, and secured it in my pocket. Instead of continuing my round by drifting to the next bench, I cut across the park and walked several blocks to the designated street corner. There I found an older make of car, nondescript save for the heavily tinted glass of its windows, a familiar set of digits on its license plate. A torn piece of paper fluttered between windshield wiper and windshield. I tried the door. It was unlocked. I opened it and stepped inside:

The car smelled of new leather, beneath which a stale, musty smell was only partly buried. A man wearing a tan raincoat and faun driving gloves, fedora tugged down low to shade his eyes, was sitting at the wheel, staring out the front windshield. He pressed a button and the door locks snapped down. He pressed another button and the engine started. Only then did he turn to look at me. He was, I saw, missing an eye.

"Well?" he asked.

"Well, what?" I asked.

He nodded slightly. Turning away, he began to drive.

We drove for some hours. I slept briefly, flickering in and out of consciousness. The man beside me drove with great precision, slipping smoothly through the busy traffic. We pushed out of the city and onto the open road, and then in and out of another city, and then through a third.

At last we arrived at a city I recognized. We drove to the center of town, stopping before a dilapidated theater. He pressed a button. The door locks snapped open.

An elderly but not unattractive woman was in the box office. I attempted to buy a ticket, but, pushing my money back at me, she waved me in.

I waited for my eyes to adjust to the stuttering light. I could make out four other heads. I sat beside one and waited. When nothing happened, I stood and moved to sit beside another, who immediately moved. The third, however, turned slightly toward me, and I recognized on him the face of my second supervisor. He smiled slightly, just enough to show the brief and unexpected glint of a gold tooth.

I was given a photograph and an address. I was to find the individual in question and pursue him. I was to report on his movements, on his meetings with his associates, on anything I found unusual. I was to keep a record of everything.

A question was mounting in my throat. I tried to swallow it down.

Did I understand? my supervisor asked.

Yes, I understood.

Did I have any questions?

Only one: Where was I to find my supervisor when I needed him?

He seemed to stiffen in the dark.

"You didn't understand," he said. He was silent for a moment and then stood and left the theater.

I went to the address I had been given, only to discover it to be that of the house I had already observed. The picture too was the same picture I had previously been given. I tried to convince myself I was grateful for a second chance.

I climbed up into the fork of a tree and settled in to wait.

I watched people come and go from the house, comparing each new face to the face captured in the photograph. None of the people corresponded to the face in the photograph. When I saw the park employee, I moved higher into the tree and remained hidden until he had passed.

Near evening, I climbed down long enough to buy a bag of bread and several liters of water, then climbed back into the tree immediately after.

For the next six days I remained in the tree, observing.

The man in the photograph did not appear.

Doubts began to assail me. Perhaps this is a bad likeness, etc.

On the seventh day, I approached the house and kicked in the door. In the living room was a baby in a playpen who seemed not at all displeased to see me. The young woman in the kitchen, however, I was forced to strike once, very hard, to stop her from screaming. No one else was in the house, nor was there any sign that anyone else was living there. On the way out, I straightened the woman's body on the kitchen floor, checking to make sure that she was still breathing. I considered taking the jovial baby with me but could see no way of justifying this to the administration.

•

Inside the movie theater, I solicited man after man until I found my supervisor. I filed my report, having mentioned the actions of the baby in a favorable light and the nonpresence of the subject in an unfavorable light. After I finished, my supervisor asked me to clarify a few small matters. Then he informed me I was to continue my observation.

I told him there was no point in continuing the observation. The subject in question was not to be found at the address in question.

Without acknowledging my words, he repeated that I was to continue my observation.

At this juncture, I resigned.

It proved not to be easy to resign from the administration. I was told to return to the theater the next day, where I found, in my administrator's seat, a pile of forms. These I took with me to my tree in the park. I cautiously sorted through them, discarding those that seemed irrelevant to my case. The rest I filled out and left the following day on the same seat.

From that moment on, I considered my connection to the administration severed. I found myself alone and adrift. I wandered from park to park, avoiding human contact except for moments when, crouched on my knees, hands miming prayer, I sat on the sidewalk with my hat in front of me, begging whatever meager coins I could. As I begged, I wondered what would happen next. Would I return to my city of origin and again see my family, assuming I could discover them again after so long? Would I return to my ersatz relation and piece together a substitute, ersatz life? Or would I simply continue forward, writing in notebooks not for the administration's pleasure but for my own?

I might have continued thus forever, drifting, slowly pondering the array of possibilities always open before me without ever definitively choosing one, had it not been for the appearance, two days past in my hat, among the worn, discarded coins of strangers, of a crumpled scrap of brown paper. Having been hurriedly balled up, it slowly expanded as I watched it. On it was traced in grease a notational siglum indicating, I realized, that the administration was not satisfied with my report, with my resignation.

What more can I say? This second, supplemental report I hope will answer whatever questions remain. When I have finished it, I will once again find the theater. I will leave this, the last of my notebooks, on what seems to me the proper seat, and will flee. Where I will go, I don't know, nor can I say what will become of me.

I have, if I am to be honest with myself, felt myself observed for some time. Nothing I can place my finger on, just a deep, uneasy feeling: a ghost of movement, a flicker. Perhaps over time this will fade. Perhaps not.

Anything can happen: anything. Or nothing. Who can say? The world, monstrous, is made that way, and in the end consumes us all. Who am I, administrated or no, to have the audacity to survive it?

Bauer in the Tyrol

I.

Late in the year, during a trip to the Tyrol, the sky so gray throughout the day that he felt himself to be living in a perpetual twilight, Bauer lost confidence in his ability to work with plaster. Stuck a dozen kilometers outside of Imst, his wife ill and watching him from her bed in the mountain inn, he spread newspapers over the parquet floor between the bed and the wall. Sitting on the bed, his back turned to her, his knees nearly touching the wall, he began mixing the plaster in a bucket stolen from behind the inn, bending the armature wire into slender standing figures which he set upon the windowsill. He could feel his wife's eyes on his back, never for a moment did not feel them, and perhaps it was this, he told himself at first, which was causing him to lose confidence. He could feel her eyes and hear her cough, and could hear as well, when she was not coughing and even sometimes hidden within the cough itself, the way the air caught in her throat as she breathed. Through the window, past the stiff wire figures, he could see a sky as dull as a pewter plate, fog, scraggled pine swags. If he opened the window, he could hear the awful torrent of the river and the screeching of unfamiliar birds—sounds that dampened out, at least for an instant, the air catching in his wife's throat. But sounds that proved in the end at least as irritating. He would reach into the bucket and scoop up plaster in his hand, smearing and clomping it onto first one armature and then another until there was an array of lumpy figures glistening on the sill. They were, at that moment, not bad, even bearable—standing figures, barely human, each no taller than a pencil and nearly as thin, as if seen from a great distance, hands to sides—but nothing special either, nothing he had not done before, no progress, a standstill. He would sit watching them as long as he could bear, a sheen condensing on the surface of the wet plaster—the air is wrong here, he told himself, it is not me, but a problem with the air. But soon, he took each figure up again, prodded it with his fingers or his pocketknife or a wire, gouged it down to nothing or pushed more plaster onto it until he had thoroughly ruined it. Then, stripping each figure down to bare armature, he would begin again, working from the gray of the morning sky to the gray of the evening sky without success, until plaster made his fingers too thick, until plaster was daubed all over the curtains and on the sill and on his legs too, the wire figures destroyed and cast aside.

Lighting the wick, he lay on the bed beside his wife, trying not to touch her. He lay there regarding the ceiling, listening to the air catch in his wife's throat. The quality of the air, he told himself again, was wrong, thus the failure of his figures in plaster, thus the way said air caught in his wife's throat. She wanted nothing, would eat nothing. If he brought her food, she softly refused to eat it; water she sipped at once or twice and then pushed the tumbler away. Once or twice in the evenings, in the first evenings of their unexpected and sudden residence in the mountain inn, she would stop breathing for a moment, just long enough to gather her breath and open her mouth to speak. He should go out, she would suggest, he was not needed, he should get some fresh air. He hardly bothered to answer, just lay on the bed beside her, tightening his jaw slightly. Soon she stopped talking altogether, and when he looked over, her eyes were closed, her breath still catching in her throat in that terrible way that made him wish she were dead.

He lay there until the candle guttered and went out, and some nights he kept lying there still, in the dark, his eyes open. One night, he stuffed bits of paper into his ears and covered them over with semihard plaster from the bucket. Then, he could not hear her, but he could still feel her beside him, the fevered heat steaming off her, her body turning there and there, and he could hear the sound of his own blood too loud in his ears, and that was as bad to him as his wife's breathing, perhaps worse. The bed, too, he felt was too narrow, and to keep from touching his wife, her damp flesh, he found himself at the very edge of it, one shoulder hanging off. He would stay there and after a time either fall into a terrible, fitful state adjacent to sleep or lie there until he was certain he could not sleep, then get up, leave the room, go down the hall to the common bathroom, where he would sit all night, carving at a cake of soap with his pocketknife. The soap, too, frittered away, growing slowly smaller and smaller until he was working with a brittle splinter of it hardly bigger than his thumbnail, a tiny, vanishing human figure, hardly human at all. And soon he would cut once too deeply and it would crumble to nothing in his hands.

The air, he had been told, was invigorating. When he and his wife had arranged to make this trip to the Tyrol, they had been perpetually told, by everyone they met, that Tyrolean air was invigorating. He had not found it so, had found precisely the contrary: that the air was *exvigorating*, if such a thing could be said, there was something wrong with the air, a problem with the air. He would breathe it in, but each time he breathed out, it would take something from him. He would breathe sitting against the bathtub, his knife still in his hands, crumbs of soap over his hands and legs. He would breathe and then each time he exhaled he would think, *there a little something, there a little something,* and feel himself to be less and less. But, he would tell himself, *it has not yet reached the point where there is little enough of me that that little something catches in my throat when it goes.* He would close his eyes, thinking, *there a little something, there a little something,* and then for a few hours, on the bathroom floor, he would fitfully sleep.

II.

In the mornings, particularly, it was clear to him that his wife was dying, and each day it was clearer still. He knew he was waiting in this inn for her to be dead, that in the bed beside her he was waiting, knowing that each time he climbed into bed beside her again, a little more of her was dead. One day the breath would catch in her throat and stay caught, and then she would be dead for good. There was, he argued with himself in the morning, looking at his wife sprawled in the bed, no real moment between dead and not dead for the body, for the body was changing, always changing, but even as he said it he wondered if it were not a lie.

And then, as the day progressed: plaster again, his back to his wife, the windowsill. No cough now, cough gone a few days back, a lessening, only the sound of air catching in her throat, and the body no longer so moist, harder to sense now with his back to it, closer in its dryness to bone. The catch in her throat still hard to hear, but in a different way now, like a clock. As he worked, as he destroyed the slender plaster figures one after the other, then built them up again, then destroyed them again, he found himself turning to look at her, her closed eyes, her face. The structure of her face seemed to have changed, he thought, the skin wrinkling differently, and it was hard to think of her in the same way, as the same woman, which made him, above all, a little less disgusted, a little more curious.

There was plaster on his hands and on the sheets, on the curtains and on his trousers and shirt. Each morning, when the maid came, she would, shaking her head, rub at the curtains with a damp cloth and change the sheets. As the day wore on, as night came, while glancing at his wife, while mangling the plaster figures, he continued to think of her, the maid, rubbing at the curtains, shaking her head. In the bed, he stared at the ceiling and waited for morning, and listened to his wife's breath catch, and thought about the maid, rubbing and shaking, shaking and rubbing, and, suddenly, somehow, he was asleep, decently for the first time in many nights. He knew it only because just as suddenly he was awake and light was pouring into the room and the maid was shaking him, trying to shake him out of the bed so as to help her change the sheets. He had been awake, then awake again, with nothing in between, and no memory of anything, almost as if dead, he thought, and then thought, no, and then thought simply that there was no way to know, no *as if* when it came to being dead. The maid untucked the sheet and pushed it to the center of the bed and then put the new sheet on the half of the bed that was now bare, his half. The maid's face, he saw, was the same as it had been yesterday, same as it had been the day before. Only his wife's face was changing. Unless his own face were changing too. He had no mirror, not in the room; there was a mirror in the bathroom, but it was affixed to the wall, screwed into place, and what he needed was to see his face here, in the room, beside his wife. He put his hands under his wife and rolled her onto one shoulder and then over onto her stomach and then over onto the other shoulder, and then held her there while the maid got the old sheet all the way off and tugged the new sheet on. His wife's breathing was fainter now. She hadn't reacted to being rolled about on the bed. Bauer wondered if she would react if he kept rolling her, rolled her off the bed and around the room, perhaps even out into the hall and into the bathroom, where the mirror was, where he could look in the mirror. But no, that was a crazy thought, and he tried not to think it again as he went about rolling his wife back into her usual place.

III.

The air was wrong, he was still certain the air was wrong, but he was no longer certain it mattered. He mixed the plaster without scraping out the bucket first, and there were, as a result, in the plaster, hard clumps and bits of crust. He stared at his wife. Her face, he thought, was different than it had been a day prior, more settled. The fragile beauty of the skull, the tongs of the jawbones, the grooves of the teeth: all almost seemed to show through the skin, and he felt he should be somehow terrified, but he was not. There was a calm to the room, he realized, as he continued idly to mix the plaster with his hands, but he could not have said why. As he continued to feel it, the sense of calm, he wondered *Have I changed? Am I wearing a different face? No*, he thought, *I have always had the same face.* But did it finally really matter? Even if he had the same face, he had entered a new space, he thought: being with this woman who was dying had put him up against life in a different way, but perhaps muffled him, or perhaps simply revealed that what he had always seen as sharp and clear—what the eye saw—was hardly clear at all. It was, he told himself, the inauguration of a new aesthetic moment, a sign perhaps that his ability to work with plaster had returned. Yet when he began to work with the armature, the plaster went on clomped and crusted and would do no more for him than it had done before, and he knew that he would get no further, and he wondered if he would ever get any further. And it was in thinking these thoughts that he realized, with a start, that what he was hearing—or rather *not* hearing—was his wife's breath no longer catching in her throat.

Uneasy, he turned away from the sill and put his hand on her neck. But no, he could still feel blood torpidly pulsing, and when he slid his hand between the sheet and her chest, he could feel that her heart, too, was beating as well.

He sat watching her. Did he love her?, he wondered. The question seemed somehow irrelevant, for it was now a question not of love but of both of them being in the same room together, the air bad, one of them with a face that was changing and continuing to change from instant to instant, the other with a face that changed not at all. It was the only relevant connection, if it was a connection at all. On her neck he could see the white daubs left by the plaster on his fingers, his white fingerprints like strangulation marks, and there were daubs of plaster on his clothing and on the drapes and on the sheets, too, and perhaps all over the room, and for a moment he thought that now what he should do was to spread plaster over her face and preserve it, not a death mask but a dying mask, but he knew that by the time the plaster hardened there would be an altogether different face underneath. He started for a moment to see if he could model the face in plaster, but he had lost his ability to work with plaster, plaster wouldn't do, it was the wrong medium, and in the end he went down the hall and washed his hands in the bathroom sink. And when he came back, he took up pencil and paper and began to draw.

IV.

In an instant, almost immediately, he had captured her profile, almost too easily somehow, yet when he looked at her again he saw it was not the same face and he drew it again, on top of the first profile. He kept drawing, adding to the profile the rest of her and the bed, and he kept drawing, the lines multiplying. He watched the head of his wife being transformed, the nose becoming sharper, the cheeks growing more and more gaunt, the open, almost immobile mouth seeming to breathe less and less. He kept drawing. He had never really seen his wife, he realized, and he realized further something that unsettled him, that he wasn't seeing her now. But there was nothing for it but to keep drawing. Toward evening, he was seized by a sudden panic in the face of her oncoming death, and looking down at the paper he realized, through the haze of lines, that every image was being destroyed but in that destruction something was arising unlike anything he had ever seen. A bed, a harrow of lines, the many ghosts of his wife, and all of them somehow, in their erasures and obscurements, beginning to add up to his wife herself. He kept drawing, trying to bring her out. But she was dead; there was no longer anything to bring out. He hesitated, trying not to look at her, looking instead at his own solitary and solid hand, afraid to let go of his pencil, wondering what line he could possibly bear to draw next.

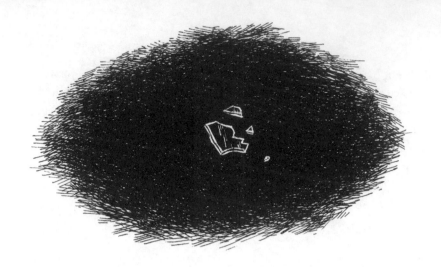

Helpful

It was a freak accident, a wire snapping off the load and whipping back to slash across his face, breaking his nose, tearing open both his eyes. They took him jouncing in the back of a pickup truck to the hospital, where a doctor packed the nose with cotton and straightened it while another doctor removed first the right eye, then the left. Two days later, his wife came to get him and helped him out to the car, and drove him home.

Is there anything I can do? his wife kept asking him.

No, he would say each time, no.

His face ached. The nose that had been reset and packed with cotton ached. Every eight hours his wife came and removed the cotton by tugging it out with her fingernails and then packed the nose again. After a while the bleeding stopped entirely. The outer rim of each orbit ached, despite the sedative, and he imagined if it weren't covered in bandages and he still could see, he would see the flesh beside them bruised black.

Do you need anything, honey? his wife asked.

No, he said.

His eyelids felt strange to him with his eyeballs removed: deflated. With the bandages covering them, he could not tell if he was opening and closing them or trying and failing.

Honey? his wife said. Anything?

No, he said. No.

•

After a week, he climbed out of bed. His room, reduced only to touch, had gone strange around him; a dresser that he would have guessed was four steps from the bed was in fact two. When he was certain he was at the door leading out of the room, he was in fact at the closet door, so that as he passed into what he thought was the hall, he found himself suddenly muffled on both sides by what it took him a moment to figure out were coats.

Honey, his wife said, anything the problem?

No, he said, and felt his way out of the closet, carefully shutting the door behind him.

But after a few more days, the place congealed for him, and a few days later became fully solid. He could walk from the bedroom to the bathroom, from the bathroom to the hall, from the hall to the living room and back again, without difficulty. He was beginning to sense things. He was becoming a different person.

He still seemed to see flashes of things, little crackling glimpses, as if the nerves in his sockets hadn't yet realized his eyes were missing. Half-seen things, ephemerae, ghosts darting through a dark space. His wife, too, he could hear creeping about, a little like a ghost as well, staying out of his way but often waiting in abeyance, ready to ask what she could do, how she could help. It was a habit of speech she had gotten into and couldn't seem to get out of.

Anything I can do?

How can I help?

What do you need, darling?

No, he would say. Can't. Nothing.

They were living in the same house, but for him it was no longer the same house anymore. It was as if they were living in two different houses that overlapped the same space, himself and his wife knocking slightly against each other as they passed through two different places. She lived in a world made of the images of things. He lived in a subtler world where he could hear a whispering noise and know it was the sound of her thumb rubbing against her finger. How could anyone who was still human hear that? It was as if he and his wife weren't even the same species anymore.

Sweetheart? she said. Anything I—

—no, he said.

He heard her suck in her breath. He waited for her to speak, but she did not, just stood there, silent. He wondered what sort of silence it was. Brooding? Hurt? Angry? Indifferent? If he could see her face, what would it look like? Would her lip be quivering? Her neck blotching? He started to turn his head toward where she was but halfway there he realized that, no, he wasn't interested in giving her the impression he was looking at her; he wanted only to hear her perfectly. So he stayed there, halfway facing her and halfway not. He wondered what she must think of it.

When she finally did speak, it startled him. He flinched.

Why are you cutting me off? she asked.

I'm not, he said.

You're ruining our relationship, she said. You're closing yourself in.

I'm doing nothing of the kind.

Open up to me, she said. Come back into the world.

And then he heard sounds that he sensed were her moving, sliding toward him, lifting her arms. He started to raise his own arms and suddenly found himself in her embrace. He let her hold on to him, patted her softly on the back. It struck him as artificial. How could he feel anything but distance from her when they were both in the same space but living in that space differently, occupying different worlds? At least he could see that. She couldn't even see it. Still, he should make an effort. He should let her be helpful to him. He kept patting her back.

But why, part of him wondered, do we have to have a relationship in your world? Why not in mine?

Three or four months later, when the relationship had improved not at all, when she was still asking him if she could help, what she could do, what he needed, wasn't there anything, how could she be of service, could she lend him a hand, lend him her eyes or her arm, he decided it was time to take matters into his own hands.

When she went to work, he called a taxi, asked to be driven to the grocery store. The driver spoke with an accent he could not place, and smelled slightly of sweat. The driver seemed nervous to have a blind man in his cab and chattered at him nervously, aimlessly.

Once there, he had the taxi driver guide him inside, told him to wait for him. A clerk let him take her arm. She led him where he wanted to go.

Garbage bags and duct tape? she asked. That's really all you want?

He nodded. They're black bags, right? I need black.

Yes, she said. Black. But why do you care? You're blind.

They're not for me, he explained.

The clerk didn't ask any more questions. He paid and then she helped him make his way out the door. He stood alone waiting just in front of the store, wondering if the taxi was still there somewhere. He was just about to go back in when he heard soft footsteps, a slight hint of stale sweat, felt a clammy hand on his arm.

I did not see you first, the driver said, and led him to the car.

In front of his house the driver named a sum. He handed the driver his wallet. Go ahead, he said.

How do you know I won't take much?

More? he said. I don't, he said.

What is to stop me?

Who knows? said the man. Try it and see.

He could hear the driver take some money out, sigh. There is some trick, the driver said, handing back the wallet. Some hiding camera. No, you will not fool me.

At last the driver was gone and he was alone in the house. How long would it be before his wife came home from work? He wasn't certain. There was no certain way, blind, for him to tell.

He felt along the wall until he found a window. With his hand he carefully traced its outline. He took one garbage bag out of the pack and unfolded it, then took the duct tape, began to tape the garbage bag over the window. When he was done, he ran his fingers along the edges to make sure there were no gaps, then moved on to the next window frame.

When all the windows in the house were sealed, he took a chair from the kitchen and stood on it in what he thought was the center of each room, groping up above him until he found each light fixture. He unscrewed the lightbulbs and then carefully placed them on the floor a few steps from each doorway.

Then he sat on the couch and waited.

Eventually he heard his wife's car turn in to the driveway. Rising from the couch, he made his way down the hall, deeper into the house.

He heard her open the door and then flick the light switch on and off.

Hello? she said. Anybody there?

He didn't answer.

Honey? she said, her voice a little tremulous. What's going on? What happened to the windows?

He heard her take a few steps, heard the sound of a lightbulb crushing beneath her shoe. She cried out.

Honey? she said, louder now. Where are you?

Down the hall, he waited without moving for her to approach. He would wait until she was near him, very near, and then would speak.

Do you need anything, honey? he would say, his voice just louder than a whisper. Is there anything I can do?

And then, suddenly, tables turned, she would understand, she would empathize, and they would embrace, talk about how foolish they had been and figure out how to be close again.

It would be an understatement to say that her reaction was not precisely what he had anticipated.

Life Without Father

I.

Life without father began some few weeks before he actually died, at the moment when he started encasing his head in orange plastic mesh held shut with twine. He did this because, so he claimed, it helped him. Helped him what or how, Elise never knew. It was, her father proclaimed that first day from within the mesh, the beginning of the most lucid period of his life. Yet whatever it was helping or helping with, it apparently didn't help for long, for soon her father had replaced the mesh with a bag made of wire netting cut from a window screen. He threaded it closed around his neck, the screen's raw stubble leaving a red band along his clavicle. *Correction*, the father stated. The orange plastic mesh had helped but not helped enough. The wire screen was in fact the real beginning of the only truly lucid period of his thought. He had not felt so good since before the mother had left, he told Elise, and probably not even then.

Elise wondered what, if anything, she should do. Early on, she suggested to her father that he should remove the netting from around his head, a suggestion that made him distraught. No, he said, didn't she see? It was a great help to him. She tried to see, and though she could not understand why, she began to hope that, yes, it did seem to help him, maybe, somehow. Her father had not been exactly himself since the mother's disappearance. He had been, at best, approximately himself and, at worst, not himself at all. With the wire encasing his head he was not exactly himself, either, but he was closer, and more stable in whatever he now was. So she decided that, yes, she was willing to go along with it. In any case, she apparently had no choice.

Yet, *correction*. This period too ground to a stop, the father's stability wearing away again, to be followed by the last and shortest stage: a long weekend that was for her the worst to remember, involving a plastic shopping bag. He held the bag gathered at his neck, the force of his breathing making it swell and collapse around his features until it was he who collapsed. While he lay there, Elise loosened the bag enough to let a little fresh air in. He was, he told her each time he came conscious, finally truly lucid, this time he was certain. His voice, bag-muffled, buzzed against the plastic. Soon he was staggering about again, holding the bag tight and closed at his throat. When he fell again, Elise was again there to save him.

During the course of the single long weekend, she loosened the bag around his head eighty-four times. She kept track, even after she grew tired. At one point when she thought she might lose count, she opened her fifth-grade math book and kept track inside its back cover with a series of hash marks. She made four straight vertical marks and one diagonal mark through them and then moved slightly down the page. When not making marks, she was waiting patiently for her father to collapse again. When she closed her eyes to rest, all she could see was the bag swelling and deflating, her father's features coming clear an instant then wavering away. When she opened her eyes, all she could see was her father lying on the floor, motionless save for his hands, which slowly curled or tightened as she loosened the bag. Until finally she closed her eyes and saw the bag swell and deflate in her head, and by the time she opened her eyes again, her father was dead.

II.

It took her some while to realize her father was dead. Indeed, just as before, she loosened the bag until she could see his square chin, the gash of his lips, the blunt tip of his nose. She got up and made another hash mark in her math book, and then she closed her eyes and slept again. When she woke up, he was still lying there where she had left him, bag still loose, so she closed her eyes and slept further. She could not remember there being a moment when she realized he was dead: when she had gone back to sleep, she didn't know, but when she awoke again, she knew already, there was no shock to it—in her sleep she had figured it out.

She wondered if she should erase the last hash mark in the math book, but in the end let it stand. Then she tallied them up by fives and came up with eighty and then added the last four strokes onto that. She had saved her father eighty-four times; how could she be blamed for failing on the eighty-fifth?

He was still lying there. All she could see of him were his hands, his chin, his lips, his nose, his clothes. She was not sure if clothes should count as part of someone. She wondered if she should take the bag off his head, and then decided no: on TV, they would leave it on until the police arrived. I will go back to sleep, she thought, and then I will call the police.

When she woke up, flies were turning circles on her father's face. The color of the face had started to turn, the skin lying differently on what she could see of his chin and lower face. The lips seemed stretched, and had drawn back to reveal the tips of his teeth. A fly slid in and out of his mouth.

She went to get the telephone from the kitchen, brought it back with her so she could keep an eye on her father as she dialed 911.

"What's your emergency?" asked a woman's voice.

Emergency? she thought. It wasn't exactly an emergency, since her father was already dead; there was nothing they could do except come get him.

"My father," she started to say, and then stopped, not knowing what to say next.

The line stayed silent for a moment, then: "What about your father?," the woman asked, her voice slightly queer. "What has he been doing to you?"

Doing to me? No, thought Elise, she doesn't understand.

"Darling," said the woman's voice. "Don't be afraid to tell me."

"I'm sorry, I have to go now," said Elise, and hung up the telephone.

The police came anyway, two officers who rang the doorbell and then stood on the porch, looking bored. She watched them through the peephole. One had a thin mustache and had lost most of his hair. The other was behind him and harder to see. She waited as they rang again and then knocked. It wasn't until the mustached one started talking into the transmitter affixed to the shoulder of his jacket that she opened the door a little.

The mustached one kept talking and listening to his shoulder, turning away from her slightly to look at the doorframe. Then the one behind came forward and she saw he had a mustache too.

"Hello," he said. "What's your name?"

"Elise," she said, watching him from around the edge of the door.

"Are your parents here?"

Elise thought about that a moment. "Sort of," she finally said.

"Sort of?" said the officer. "What do you mean?"

The problem, Elise realized, staring at him, was knowing what to say. You could say what you thought was right, what would make sense to you, and nobody else really understood it. It was as if they were living in a different world than you, or as if you were speaking under water.

The policeman was still standing, waiting.

"Would you like to come in?" asked Elise.

She pulled the door wide. He took a step forward, smiling, and then through the doorway he caught a glimpse of her father lying on the floor. He stopped smiling and his hand felt back behind him, searching for his partner.

III.

The two officers in uniform made her sit on the couch and stay there. Other people, not wearing uniforms, came and took pictures. She waited patiently, her feet crossed at the ankles. At one point a man wearing a brown jacket approached her, sat in the armchair across from her.

"Where's your mother?" he asked.

"I don't know," she said.

"When do you expect her home?"

When? she wondered. Her father had thought she might come home at any time, any day. In the days before he started to wrap his head up, he had said each morning, *She might come home today*, but she never had.

"She might come home today," Elise said.

"What do you mean, might?" asked the man. "That also means might not." They would have to arrange something, he was saying to a uniformed officer, somewhere for her to stay. Did she have any relatives nearby, anyone she could stay with?

"My aunt," she said.

"Your aunt," he said, and nodded. He went away and made some phone calls and then talked to the men who were loading the body into a zippered bag.

"Now," said the man, coming back. "Are you o.k.? How do you feel?"

She didn't know how to answer, so didn't. It didn't seem to matter.

"Can you talk?" he asked. Do you feel well enough to help us work through this?"

She nodded.

"It's like this," he said. "We need to know if your father did this to himself or if someone else did it to him. Can you tell me which?"

Did her father do this to himself? she wondered. Yes, he had put the bag on his head, but had he meant to die? No, she didn't think so, he hadn't been aware that he would die, didn't seem to want to die. Had she done it to him? Yes, in a manner of speaking, by not loosening the bag the eighty-fifth time. But it wasn't what she had done to him, but simply what she had not, finally, managed to do.

"He died," she said.

"Yes," said the man patiently, "but what did you see? Murder or suicide?"

It wasn't exactly either, she thought, but a third thing she didn't quite have a word for. She sat staring at her hands folded in her lap.

"Come on," the man said, "either you know something or you don't. You're old enough to understand. Which is it?"

"He died," she tried again.

The man shook his head. "We know he died," he said. "We just want to know more about it. Are you afraid to tell me?"

"No," she said immediately.

"There's no reason to be afraid," he said. "No harm will come to you."

Harm? she thought, and only then did she begin to consider that some harm could possibly come. Was she to blame? Would they punish her?

"Were you in the house when he died?" he asked.

"Yes," she said.

"What did you see?" he asked.

"I saw," she said, and then stopped. Was she to blame? She did not feel that she was to blame, hoped she wasn't. Was her father to blame? She didn't feel that he was, either.

"What did you see?"

"It just," she said. "I mean, he just . . ."

"Calm down," said the man. "No need to get excited." But she wasn't getting excited, was she? "I'm your friend. Can't you see I'm your friend?"

She looked at him, his eyes glittering like the eyes of a doll. If he lay down, they would click back up into his head.

He put his hands, clasped together, on the coffee table between them, and leaned forward. It was an awkward position for him. His hands seemed huge and made of plaster.

"Let's try another way," he said.

"O.K.," she said.

"Let's just," he said, then stopped. "Listen, did your mother have anything to do with this?"

"My mother?" she said.

He nodded.

Did she? Elise wondered. Her mother had left, her father was always talking about her. The mesh, the wire, the bag had all been, so he said, attempts to make him feel good again, as he had before the mother left. He always said that: *before your mother left*. Without the mother's leaving them, none of it would have happened.

She nodded slightly.

"Yes?"

She nodded again.

"There," he said, taking his hands off the table and settling them on his thighs. "Now we're getting somewhere."

IV.

And thus began the period that Elise, had she been her own father, might have called the only truly lucid period of her life—though Elise, being only Elise and not her own dead father, did not know what *lucid* meant. It was a word she had heard only from the father, only three times, each time as an inauguration of what he saw as a new period of his existence, a step closer to his own death. Perhaps *lucid* had something to do with that.

Elise moved in with the aunt, her father's sister, a large-boned and yeasty woman with a very red face. Elise liked her: she was a little like her father, but only in the best ways.

Each day the aunt drove her across town and to her school. Sometimes, instead of going straight into the school, she would instead hide just inside the doors and then go back out again. She would walk through the playground and the parking lot and down the street beyond until she reached her house, her father's house. There was no one living there now. There was a yellow-plastic tape line over the door—*Police Line Do Not Cross*—and a plastic ball encasing the door handle. She would go up and stare in through the tall window next to the door, and then walk back to the school, go to class.

Her aunt fed her and took her places. They watched movies together. They went to the library and checked out books. Her aunt told her that she had always wanted a daughter and maybe if Elise's mother didn't come back she could adopt her? How would Elise like that?

Elise didn't know what to say.

"But," said her aunt, "even if she does come back she probably won't get you after what she did to my brother. They'll lock her away for it," she said, nodding.

"For what?" asked Elise.

"You know," said her aunt. "After all, it was you who told them."

Me? thought Elise. What had she said? When she had said her mother had something to do with it, she hadn't known they would be upset about it. She had meant something else, nothing specific, just something in general. They didn't understand, nobody understood, it was better to keep quiet. They had phrased it all wrong, if they had asked her the right questions or if it had been someone else asking, then maybe, she thought. Someone like her aunt, she thought.

"They'd lock her up for leaving?" she asked.

"No, silly," said the aunt. "For killing him."

For killing him? "But she didn't kill him," Elise said.

The aunt came toward her, put her arm around her. "I've upset you," she said. "Darling. I'm sorry. I can understand how you feel. She's your mother, after all, but don't forget about your father."

"But," said Elise.

"If it hadn't been for your mother, darling," said her aunt, "your father would still be alive today."

She thought about it later, at night. Her aunt was right, she thought, but not exactly right. She shouldn't have said anything to the detective, Elise felt, he hadn't understood, nobody ever understood, her aunt didn't understand either. Then she fell asleep.

In the morning she woke up and had oatmeal for breakfast. Her aunt drove her to her school and she went right in. All day long it was a good day and it wasn't until late in the day, near the end of school, that she opened her math book and saw the hash marks inside the back cover and realized she had gone the whole day without once thinking of her father. In a manner of speaking, life without father was just beginning.

•

Ten days later, the man in the brown jacket was waiting at her aunt's door when they arrived home from school. The aunt ushered him in, offered him a cup of coffee. Elise went up to her room to play.

While at her aunt's house, she had learned to play at wild ponies. The aunt had two such ponies, both made of hard plastic but molded in such a way that you could see the muscles on their flanks, the twists and curves of their manes. They had belonged to the aunt when she was a girl, and sometimes the aunt would play at them with her. She and the aunt liked to gallop them across the carpet, which was green and like grass, and the ponies would talk and sometimes go places together. Elise thought it was a game she was too young to be playing, but since the aunt played it, she was willing to play too.

The wild ponies had just galloped off across the sward, as her aunt called it, and were standing, blowing and nickering, on the edge of a stream, trying to decide whether to swim across it or stay put, when the door opened and her aunt came in.

"Honey," the aunt said. "I don't know if you'll think it's good news or bad. They found your mother."

She just kept playing with the ponies.

Her aunt crawled beside her and ran her hand up and down Elise's back.

"The man downstairs," she said, "he wants to speak to you."

Elise shook her head.

"Now, darling," said the aunt, "don't be like that. He's not going to hurt you."

Elise realized that one of the ponies was restless, swaying and nickering, and didn't understand why, and then realized that she was holding it too tightly. She let her hand loosen up and the pony stopped. Then she felt someone else in the room and looked up and saw the man in the brown jacket.

"Elise?" he said. "Can I talk to you?"

Elise shook her head.

"She's not usually like this," said the aunt. "Not usually so stubborn."

"No?" said the man. "Elise," he said, "your mother is in custody. You're safe now."

Safe? thought Elise. Safe from what?

"I need," said the man, leaning down and toward her, "I need you to tell me everything that you saw."

Elise didn't answer.

"Elise," said the man, his voice stern. "This is important."

"I want to see her," said Elise.

"Now, Elise," said her aunt. "Don't you think—"

"I want to see my mother," she said.

"All right," said the man. "I can foresee that as an eventuality. But first, a few questions."

"No," said Elise. "Now."

V.

But by the time they were on the way to the jail, she felt drained, as if she had worked herself up by so thoroughly insisting on seeing her mother. The urgency to see her mother had left her. For once, they had listened and understood, but now that they had understood, she didn't know if it was what she wanted anymore.

They got out of the car and went in through a door with an alarm bell on top of it, the alarm going off as they pushed through. They went down a white hall and into a room with a mirror the whole length of one wall. She sat down at a table and the man in the brown jacket sat next to her. The aunt had to wait outside.

Elise waited patiently, her hands in her lap, her head slightly bowed. How long had it been since she had seen her mother? She didn't know. Would she recognize her mother? Yes, of course. But would her mother recognize her?

After a while the door opened and her mother was led in. She was wearing orange and had her hands in front of her in handcuffs. She was being punished, Elise realized. She smiled nervously at her daughter.

"Darling," she said, "please, tell them I had nothing to do with it."

There was something wrong, Elise suddenly realized, something truly wrong. It was as if her mother had been coached on what to say, as if she had practiced saying it. She couldn't quite put her finger on it, but she was sure it was a trap.

And with that, Elise entered into what she felt at the time, and even for some years after, was the only truly lucid period of her life. *Correction*, she heard a part of her mind state. *Do nothing*, she thought. *Say nothing*. Watching her mother across the table, she closed her mouth and kept it closed. She steeled herself, at once terrified and elated over where it all was likely to lead.

Alfons Kuylers

On the night of 12 October, I was compelled for reasons I still find quite difficult to explain to kill one Alfons Kuylers, esteemed dealer in imported goods of a specialty nature, my mentor, my master in the art of philosophical paradox, my tutor in all things theological. I gained nothing from this crime save for a ring he had offered me many times before, and a long letter he had apparently intended to give me, in which he urged me to leave the country immediately. This was the final piece of advice I would have from him, and also one of the few which, perhaps impulsively, perhaps sentimentally, I ever followed.

It was well past midnight by the time I left Kuylers's apartment. The night was gusty and dismal; with the curfew still in effect, I had to take great care in journeying through the streets. I had burnt Kuylers' letter after reading it, believing as I did that it would be better, if I were questioned, not to have it on my person. Other than his ring, I carried nothing of real value—a few loose coins, the clothing I wore, an overcoat with a crumpled handkerchief in the pocket, and the lacquered walking stick I had used first to knock Alfons Kuylers off his feet and then deliver the fatal blow. This object, stained with blood and brains, was rapidly washed clean in the rain.

By way of alleys and backstreets I progressed toward the waterfront. There was, traveling always with me, sometimes closer and sometimes farther, the memory, surprisingly vivid, of Kuylers's face changing as he realized what was going to happen to him. Until I saw it in his face, I did not know that I would kill him, but from that moment forward it felt as if the matter were entirely out of my hands. My steps were at first confident and unhurried, but as this memory continued to plague me, the sounds of my own footsteps seemed to my own ears increasingly erratic. Soon I heard at a little distance the sound of a scuffle, followed quickly by a shot and an anguished cry, after which my composure abandoned me altogether, so that by the time I arrived at the docks I was harried and utterly out of breath.

Not utterly out of breath, I thought at the docks, smoothing back my hair, trying again to calm myself. For I had seen earlier that evening a man who was, being dead, utterly out of breath: one Alfons Kuylers. No, the problem, I realized, was—as Alfons Kuylers had said in so many of our philosophical sessions together—*the opposite and the inverse,* not that I was too out of breath, but that I was, as it were, too alive, living too many lives at once, as if I were *breathing for many men.* In retrospect, this realization seems far from cogent, simply another layer of ontological mystification, but at the time it seemed akin to revelation.

It was in such a state, slightly feverish perhaps from the rain or from the fatal events that had transpired earlier, that I began my search. At this hour most vessels were inaccessible, gangplanks raised, ramps blocked off. I moved from ship to ship, trying to find one that would grant me a berth. I hailed several from the docks without receiving a reply. The one reply I did finally have suggested that surely nothing was to be done in the dead of night, particularly considering the unrest in the city: I should return in the morning.

But morning, I feared, would be too late for me. I persisted, moving slowly from ship to ship, crying out, trying my luck with vessels large and small, albeit with little hope. *It would be better,* I counseled myself, *to turn yourself in, for your crime was pointless and worthy only of regret.* And yet I kept on, calling out, asking for passage, proclaiming that, though a scholar rather than a sailor, I was eager and willing to learn.

Near the end of the wharf, I came upon a small freighter, manged with rust, older than the other vessels, but seaworthy nonetheless. A light on its deck shone uncomfortably into my eyes. I thought this light at first to be stationary, until it swung slowly away and I saw it held by a human hand.

"Who is it?" a voice asked.

I explained again my plight. I said I asked for no favors, only the privilege of working for my passage. I was, I said, willing to learn.

"Do you not care where we are bound?"

It was, I claimed, a matter of complete indifference to me. I wanted only to leave. I cited the unrest in the city, and wanderlust, saying nothing to hint at the fatal events that had taken place earlier.

"Shall we have your name then?" the sailor asked.

"My name?" I said, and, not caring to give myself away, said, "My name is Alfons Kuylers."

"Ah," the sailor said. "We've been expecting you, Kuylers. Come aboard."

I should have gathered something from this odd reply and indeed might have, had I not been so rattled, and so pleased to have gained a berth. At the time, I simply forced the words from my mind—or rather pushed them below the surface, where they would remain in the murk, before slowly, like a corpse, rising again. Later, when I was unable to dismiss the sailor's words so easily, I turned them over and over in my head. I had misheard, I told myself, my guilt substituting an impossibility for what had actually been said. When this ceased to satisfy, I began to think that perhaps Kuylers had meant to depart with me, that he had in fact forewarned the captain of the freighter of our joint arrival. This made me fear that I had killed my mentor for no reason.

But in the instant, such thoughts had been quickly pressed down unexamined and had long to wait before bloating and slowly surfacing again. For the moment, I simply placed one foot before the other, ascended the gangplank, and came aboard. When, on deck, I approached the lantern, looking for the sailor who had hailed me, I found that he had hung his lantern on the loop of a guideline and had disappeared. Thus when I moved toward what I thought to be him, I found no one at all.

Almost immediately, the vessel started to sway and move. I had seen no other figures on the deck, but perhaps they had been there all along, near their posts, veiled in darkness, only awaiting the arrival of one Alfons Kuylers. I caught myself on the rail and steadied myself, and then, as an afterthought, turned and looked back at the city. I was not sorry to see it go. I thought how, had I not been forewarned by Alfons Kuylers, the city might well have become my grave.

And it was in that moment, thinking of my mentor with a certain melancholy fondness but with something akin to hysteria and hatred bubbling just beneath, that I thought I saw, on the pier, motionless, a figure possessed of the same stooped posture as Kuylers. He stood there, unmoving. I watched him, and was unable to look away, until he faded into the darkness and, along with the pier he stood upon, was lost.

I felt my way forward until my fingers found the wall of the deckhouse, and then I followed the wall of the deckhouse to a small stooped entrance, which I passed through, and then found myself on a narrow set of stairs that I descended into darkness. I felt my way down a dark passage and came finally, after three locked doors, to a fourth door, which was cracked open slightly, a faint glow seeping through the crack. I pushed my way in, found myself in a narrow cabin, two berths on either side, one above the other. In between, a candle glimmered on a cask that had been turned on one end to serve as a makeshift table.

I had begun to crawl into a berth before realizing it contained another man, his skin, which I touched in my fumbling, oddly chill.

"Kuylers?" he asked.

I assented.

"Your berth is above," he said. "But blow out the candle first."

I apologized and, after blowing out the candle, clambered up and into the upper berth. The room was still a shade away from sheer darkness, lit now by the lesser dark of the night shining through the porthole. My eyes, already accustomed to the dim candle, quickly adjusted.

Even so, only once I'd been there for some time did I start to realize that the sailor below me was not the only other man in the room, that the other bunks were occupied as well. Why I had not seen this before in the light of the candle, I couldn't say, but I saw the men now—first the faint gleam of their eyes, turned as I could tell toward me, and then, after more time, just a slight variance from the shadow of the berth itself, the hint of their large bodies.

"Hello," I said.

There were vague rumblings in reply, the gleams of the eyes shifting or disappearing.

"My name is Kuylers," I said. "Can you tell me yours?" I asked.

One of the men chuckled, but none offered their names.

"What is the name of this ship?" I persisted. "And what is our cargo?"

At this they all laughed. "Ah, Kuylers," one of the men said, "go to sleep."

Such responses being curious enough, I was reluctant to inquire further. I lay in the bunk wondering what I had got myself into, but exhaustion quickly caught up with me. Before I knew it, I was asleep.

•

I was awoken by sunlight streaming through the porthole. My companions, I saw, were already up and departed, bunks neatly made. I clambered down and arranged my own bunk as well, then made my way slowly out and onto the deck, the clean, cold salt air sharp in my lungs. I looked around for my cabinmates, but the deck itself seemed deserted, the deckhouse as well, and the ship itself stood still, as if becalmed. I made my way from stem to stern and back again, but found nobody there.

Once belowdecks, I found my own cabin just as I had left it, the three doors I had previously examined still locked. Following the passage back farther, I found it to lead past two other doors, also locked. An iron stairwell descended to the hold and to the engine room, both of which seemed deserted. I went on deck and found another stairway, at the bottom of which was another series of locked doors. The final door at the passage's end, according to a bronze plaque, was the captain's cabin. I opened this and found it deserted as well, bunk neatly made.

Not knowing what else to do, I knocked on each of the locked doors in turn, but had no reply. Uncertain of what to think of this, I spent the day wandering the vessel, examining it, doing what I could to occupy myself. In the captain's cabin I found several books, including one on knots and their uses, and I spent the last part of my day trying to replicate the knots therein described, growing hungrier all the time.

I searched the ship for food, but could find nothing. Perhaps the galley was behind one of the locked doors where the crew, for reasons that were beyond me, had chosen to sequester themselves away from me.

It was like that throughout the day, the vessel motionless, becalmed, my hunger growing. In the captain's cabin I found a hook and a coil of fishing line, but there was nothing with which to bait the hook. Still, I let the hook dangle over the side in hopes of catching something, coiling it in from time to time and regarding the empty, dripping curve of metal at its end before paying it out again.

Near evening, leaning over the side, a twist of fishing line around one wrist, I thought I saw something at a little distance. At first I took it for another vessel, but as it drew closer it seemed too small to be a boat. As it came closer still, it proved too animate to be anything not alive. I squinted against the fading light, becoming more and more convinced that the figure in the water was human.

Where had the fellow appeared from? How long had he been swimming? It was growing too dark to see clearly. I looked about for a line that I could cast to him, but he was still too far away for that. Perhaps, I thought, he would make it to the ladder on his own. But he was swimming awkwardly now, as if on the verge of exhaustion, as if ready to go under.

And then suddenly with a lurch the ship began to move, slowly at first and then with increasing speed. I watched the swimming man stop midstroke, staring after us, and then he sank below the waves and was gone.

I rushed about the ship, crying out until I found the captain again, standing just where he had stood before, on the night I had first met him, holding the same lantern.

"Ah, Kuylers," he said. "Relishing the journey so far?"

I explained, shielding my eyes from the glare of the lantern, what I had seen, the man swimming, making doggedly for us, then stopping and sinking beneath the waves.

"A shame," said the captain.

"But we must go back," I said.

The captain shook his head. "If he is to catch up with us, he'll catch up with us tomorrow. If not, it's not meant to be."

"He won't be alive tomorrow," I said.

"He'll travel all the faster then," said the captain. "Besides, who's to go, Kuylers? We have a full ship: who is to go?"

I told him he was callous. There was room aboard, I said, plenty of it. *What kind of men have I thrown my lot in with?* I wondered aloud. He just laughed, turned away.

I spent my early evening wandering the deck, finding as I could crew members who, busy though they were with their various tasks, deigned to listen to me as they worked. It was a matter of a human life, I told them, we must go back. Most listened in silence. They paused just a moment as I concluded and then shook their heads and went on with their tasks. One asked me, in a soft, whispering voice, what the captain himself had had to say about it, and when I explained what the captain had said, the fellow nodded and declared the captain to be quite right.

"But what does he mean, 'Who's to go?'" I asked. "Surely we can take a man as far as the next port."

The man shook his head. "The captain's right," he said, and would say no more.

•

Soon my hunger, forgotten in the excitement due the swimmer, returned and I made another circuit of the deck, inquiring of my shipmates when I might expect a meal. They ogled me as if I were mad, and refused to respond. As I backed away from them, I found them whispering among themselves, their heads inclined toward one another against the lesser dark of the night sky. There was something wrong, I started to feel, with my having posed this question, some breach of etiquette, as if I had crossed a boundary of taste without knowing. I was not a sailor; perhaps there was something I should know but did not. And yet, could they not make allowances for my ignorance and let me know both how I had mistepped and also what I must do to be fed?

I withdrew, then sat alone up near the prow, watching the waves. I stayed there staring out into the darkness, the breeze chill against my flesh, trying to ignore the way my stomach pounded like an unbattened shutter in the wind. It had been a mistake, I told myself, to leave the city as precipitously as I had, a mistake, too, to kill Kuylers. All of it a mistake. And yet here I was, I reminded myself. I must make the best of it.

In the end, after hours of waiting, my stomach convinced me. Surely it could not hurt, it told me, to speak with the captain about food. He at the very least had to acknowledge me. If I were in fact breaking etiquette, I had breached it already, and the captain, who knew something of my circumstances coming aboard, of my lack of experience at sea, might at least prove sympathetic.

The captain was to be found where I had seen him before, lantern still in his hand.

"Yes?" he said gruffly. "What is it now?"

It was only, I said, that I had perhaps somehow missed the bells that called the crew to meals. Surely my fault but, you see, I hadn't had anything to eat since boarding the ship last night, and little, to be honest, to eat the day prior. If it wasn't too much trouble, a few scraps, just something to line my stomach with, the smallest thing—

"What?" he asked, as if amazed. "You want to eat?"

Well, yes, I said, just a few scraps . . .

He swung the lantern toward me. "Are you really who you claim to be?" he asked. "Are you Alfons Kuylers?"

"What does my being Kuylers have to do with it?" I asked. But when he kept regarding me without responding, I saw no choice but to repeat my lie. Yes, I claimed, I was Alfons Kuylers, hadn't I told him as much from the first?

With this, his brow relaxed slightly and he turned away, mumbling that perhaps there was still something in the hold, that I should help myself to anything I could find.

And indeed, after a good moment of scrabbling through the hold, I found, at the bottom of an overturned barrel, some old hardtack and, in a bottle rolling loose among the debris, a good measure of third-rate whiskey. *It will be enough*, I told myself, soaking the hardtack in whiskey so as to choke it down. *It will keep me until morning, when I can find out more about regular meals and learn where to get water.*

Yet in the morning I awoke alone again in my bunk, the ship no longer moving, the bunks around me neatly made as if never having been slept in. I made my own bunk in the same fashion, then made my way up abovedecks. I could see no anchor dropped and yet the ship remained as motionless as if it were encased in stone. The deck, too, as on the day before, was deserted, the deckhouse as well, and my investigations of the spaces belowdecks led to the same locked doors, the same absence of personnel. I pounded on these locked doors and demanded admittance, without response.

My throat, deprived of water for a day and a half now, was parched and dry. After much searching, I found in the corner of the hold, strewn with garbage, a few mouthfuls of brackish water that at first I gathered in my palm, and then, once it was nearly gone, I crouched to lap the rest up like a dog.

In the captain's cabin, in a small lacquered chest, I found a short crowbar, alongside a loaded pistol. I took both. The crowbar I used on one of the locked doors, knocking first and, when there was no response, slowly prying the lock out of the frame. Behind it was the galley, but the room itself was empty, no foodstuffs or staples of any kind. I managed to undo the pipe under the sink and drank the fusty water that had gathered in its angle. But there was nothing to eat.

I went from locked door to locked door, bellowing, and then, when I received no response, forcing my way in with the crowbar. I had, I realized, crossed over some sort of line that I was not likely to be able to cross back over again. With the opening of each new door and the revelation of yet another room, I felt a little more unhinged myself, a little madder, the lack of food, too, acting oddly upon me so that I felt as though my skin were being eaten by insects. *What were they playing at?* I wanted to know, increasingly furious, *Why would they hide from me?* When I found them, I told myself, I would hold a pistol to the captain's head and demand he tell me what was going on.

But what was I to do when, cracking open the last door, the door behind which the captain and crew by default had to be gathered, I found the room as impossibly empty as all the rest?

My memories of the next few hours are tenuous at best. I recall a kind of vague stumbling belowdecks, panic alternating with fury. I entered each room again to assure myself my shipmates were not there, then entered yet again. I held the pistol to my temple and tried to persuade myself to pull the trigger, but could not. With the crowbar, I broke what I could in the captain's cabin and then remained there among the wreckage, listless. At some point I lost the gun, abandoned it somewhere belowdecks, and when I ran out of things to break, I let the crowbar trail from one hand and scrape along the floor until that too slipped from my fingers and was gone.

In the end, unwilling and unable to understand where they might have gone, I made my slow way up onto the deck. It was late afternoon, almost evening, the sun starting to blister the horizon. The deck was unoccupied. It was impossible, they were nowhere; it was impossible. *I must leave the ship*, I couldn't help thinking, and once I'd thought it, the idea became intense and urgent, unavoidable. *I must leave the ship*, my mind kept telling me, *I must leave the ship*, and I might well have thrown myself overboard—for indeed I moved aft to do just that—had I not seen as I mounted the rail, at a little distance, a figure, human, swimming, slowly drawing closer to the boat.

I stayed leaning against the rail, fixed, watching the fellow come. He came only slowly, but still was almost upon us. The sun would soon set, I knew, and if our movement yesterday had been any indication, with the fading of the light the captain would weigh anchor and the boat would depart. Would the swimmer arrive before that?

And yet, I told myself, it was impossible, all of it. It was impossible that we had been pursued for the last two days by the same swimmer, impossible even if we had for his sake maintained a pace that would allow him to catch the ship. It was equally impossible for there to have been two different men in open ocean swimming after us on two successive days. What I was seeing, I told myself, was not in fact present; it was an absence, a nothingness, a trick of the light on the horizon, the movement of a blood vessel within my eye, a hallucination caused by lack of food and water.

But as the figure came closer, it became more and more difficult for me to maintain the idea of its nonexistence. It was impossible, it was a nothingness, but it was palpable, it was there. I could make out now the movement of the arms as the swimmer propelled himself forward. I caught sight of his head, a small bead, as it surged up for air and then returned to skim just below the surface again.

I watched him come, judging his speed, his distance, my apprehension growing. He would, I judged, reach the ship before the sun disappeared. I shouted for the crew but there was no response, the deck still deserted. I stayed, watching. He came on farther, and faster, and now I could see that he appeared fully dressed, his arms and back covered by what looked like a waterlogged overcoat. Why hadn't he wriggled his way out of it? How had he managed to keeping swimming despite it? *Another impossibility*, I thought, and my apprehension deepened.

He kept coming. And then, almost as if time had torn, he was suddenly arrived, just below me, his hands on the ladder far below. He stayed there an instant, floating, facedown in the water, resting, just holding to the ladder, and then pulled his body forward and looked up at me, revealing his face.

I took a step back, staggered, feeling the deck spin out from under me as I went down. For the face I saw was both the last face I had expected to see and the only face I knew I must see: the face of Alfons Kuylers.

When I regained consciousness, it was to find myself in a heap on the deck, my head aching, darkness gathered save for the glow of a few scattered lanterns. There, across the deck, was the crew, crowded now around a blanket-draped man whose gaze I could not bring myself to meet.

I gathered myself and tried, slowly, to make my way belowdecks, whether to retrieve the captain's pistol or simply to hide myself I wasn't sure. I gave a wide berth to the crowd of sailors and the man they surrounded, but before I had set my feet on the treads of the stairs, the captain hailed me.

I stopped, waited. He came forward slowly, his eternal lantern held before him.

"Kuylers," he said.

"Yes," I said.

"That man there," he said, flashing the light behind him, "claims you are not Kuylers after all."

"There is some mistake," I said.

"Yes," said the captain. "He insists that it is he who is Kuylers. But who, then, are you?"

"No," I said, not looking him in the face. "I am Kuylers."

"You insist you are Kuylers?" asked the captain.

"I am Kuylers," I said again, and turned to start down the stairs.

"So be it," said the captain. "As you wish."

I started to descend, but before I had wound even halfway down, I found myself roughly seized from above and below and dragged back up, a man on each arm and each leg. They hauled me despite my protests back onto the deck and from there across the deck, then dumped me into one of the lifeboats. When I tried to clamber out, I was struck on the side of the skull with a belaying pin. I fell back. I tried again, but after a second blow, this one striking my forearm in such manner as to render my whole arm numb, I desisted, lying instead along the curve of the bottom of the boat while the boat was slowly winched free of its cradle and swung out to hang over the waves. Slowly my descent began. From above shone the captain's lantern, light and shadow aswirl around me with each rock and sway of the lifeboat suspended in the air. Behind him was gathered the crew, faces dim behind the lantern's glare.

"Have pity!" I called to them.

But they merely continued to ratchet the lifeboat down toward the waves. I could see now, there beside the captain, the swimmer, still wrapped in his blanket, still resembling for good and all Alfons Kuylers, but his face behind the lantern oddly transformed. And then the release was sprung and the lifeboat crashed into the waves and I was swept back and forth and, finally, away.

How many hours I floated solitary and alone in that lifeboat I cannot say. I hid from the sun as I could, crouching low in the boat, drawing my coat up to shield my head. I watched from beneath my coat the shadows shiver about in the bottom of the boat as we shook and spun with the waves, and then the shadows thickened, and then the light would vanish entirely and I would be left only to that dizzy, rolling darkness of the waves, to a motion that never stopped. I had no food, no water. How many nights did I lie there huddled against the cold, counting each swell, waiting for morning to come until I could not even do that but lay dying along the bottom of the boat, unable to move? And then my former shipmates came to me and I could see their faces clearly for the first time, as gaunt and drawn as my own, and they gathered around me and spoke in quiet whispers as if waiting for me to die. And then, of a sudden, they were gone and Alfons Kuylers came alone, striding slowly over the weary waves like some dead, mad Christ and clambered into the boat and sat there beside me to continue my philosophical and theological instruction, as if death had whetted Kuylers's appetite for paradox rather than quelled it. And then, when he realized I was almost too weak to take in his words, he leaned in close over me and I could see the way his skull had been broken by the lacquered walking stick and the way the blood had spilled out to darken the side of his face, and he whispered, "Wasn't it sufficient to murder me? Did you have to steal my name as well?"

When I awoke, it was on a large vessel. Delirious at first, I thought myself back on the ship where I had begun, and had I the strength, I would have thrown myself overboard. But no, it was a ship like any other, bustling with men by day and night, and once they realized I was coherent they brought me a few thimblefuls of water and the smallest crust of bread. I must eat slowly, they told me, and not much; after my ordeal I must slowly and gradually learn to eat again.

They gave me a little more each day, and slowly I began to recover, to feel more and more human. Soon, I was told, I would be able to leave my bed. It was amazing, claimed the captain, a man without a lantern in his hand or even within reach, that I had survived, a man of my age. *Of my age?* I wondered, and then took the tin cup that the captain held out to me and drank it slowly dry. The captain, a man of ruddy complexion and questionable accent, stayed at my bedside, watching me.

"There is only one thing," he said, hesitantly.

"I am happy to pay for my passage," I said quickly, thinking of the ring I had had from killing Kuylers, the ring he would have gladly given me and had offered me many times before.

"No," he said, ducking his head, "a man adrift, he does not pay. It is not this."

"Then what?" I asked.

"This boat," he said. "Where did you find it?"

"The boat?"

"This lifeboat," he said. "This is registered to a ship that fell to the winds and went down many years past."

I opened my mouth and shut it again, not knowing how to respond. Nor did I know how to respond to the questions that followed, nor how to think about the ship I had found myself, under false pretenses, aboard for several days. And, as over the next few weeks the questions kept coming, I felt increasingly the necessity to leave them unanswered, to do what I could to avoid the yawning space they opened up before me.

But what I could not avoid came on my first day afoot, as I abandoned my bed and stumbled my way down the passage, razor in hand, to shave myself for the first time in many days, and found myself seeing, in the burnished zinc panel that served as a mirror, not my own reflection but that of Alfons Kuylers. Was it any surprise that seeing this I would opt to use the razor not to strip away the beard and thus reveal Kuylers all the more but rather instead to open Kuylers's wrists?

It is only now, still days from port, wrists bandaged, restrained in my bed, fighting madness, avoided by the crew, days after attempting what was not so much suicide as an attempt, responding to the look on his face, to kill Kuylers yet again, that I begin to understand what a fitting fate this is, how it springs naturally from the philosophico-religious discussions I shared with my mentor both while he was alive and, once in a lifeboat, after his death. What, I have asked myself again and again, remains for me if not to become Kuylers wholeheartedly, to return to my former city, to resume my trade in imported goods, to continue to read, to study? Until the day when a young student appears and begs me to serve as his mentor and I teach him slowly, preparing him carefully for the moment when he will see astonishment mingled with fear in my face and know he has been condemned to kill me. And by so doing he will enter into the trap that will strip him of his own name and leave him bereft and adrift. It is a fate neither of us can avoid.

But isn't this simply, Kuylers suggests later, trying to console me or provoke me, *the trap everyone falls into sooner or later? And understanding this, shouldn't we simply accept our fate?*

But I do not respond. Instead, I test yet again the strength of my restraints. Surely they cannot be strong enough to hold me forever.

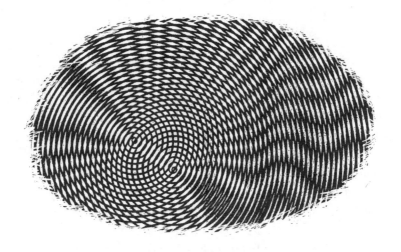

Fugue State

—for Arnaud and Claro

I.

I had, Bentham claimed, *fallen into a sort of fugue state, in which the world moved past me more and more rapidly, a kind of blur englobing me at every instant.* And yet he had never, so he confided to Arnaud, felt either disoriented or confused. Yes, admittedly, during this period he had no clear idea of his own name, yet despite this he felt he understood things clearly for the first time. He perceived the world in a different way, at a speed that allowed him to ignore the nonessential—such as names or, rather, such as his own name—and to perceive things he could never before have even imagined.

Arnaud listened carefully. *Fugue state,* he recorded, then removed his eyeglasses and placed them on the desk in front of him. He looked up, squinting.

"And do you remember your name now?" he asked.

At first, Bentham did not answer. Arnaud remained patient. He watched Bentham's blurred image glance about itself, searching for some clue.

"Yes," said Bentham finally. "Of course I do."

"Will you please tell it to me?" asked Arnaud.

"Why do you need to know?"

Arnaud rubbed his eyes. *Subject does not know own name,* he recorded.

"Will you please describe the room you're in?" he asked. Bentham instead tried to sit up, was prevented by the straps. *Subject unaware of surroundings*, Arnaud noted. "Will you describe your room, please?" asked Arnaud again.

"I don't see the point," said Bentham, his voice rising. "You're here. You're in it. You can see it just as well as I can."

Arnaud leaned forward until his lips were nearly touching the microphone. "But that's just it, Bentham," he said softly. "I'm not in the room with you at all."

It was shortly after this that Bentham began to bleed from the eyes. This was not a response Arnaud had been trained to expect. Indeed, at first, his glasses still on the desk before him, Arnaud was convinced it was a trick of the light, an oddly cast shadow. He polished his glasses against his shirtfront and hooked them back over his ears, and only then was he certain that each of Bentham's sockets was pooling with blood. Startled, he must have exclaimed, for Bentham turned his head slightly in the direction of the intercom speaker. The blood in one eye slopped against the bridge of his nose. The blood in the other spilled down his cheek, gathering in the whorl of his ear.

6:13, Arnaud wrote. *Subject has begun to bleed from eyes.*

"Bentham," Arnaud asked, "how do you feel?"

"Fine," said Bentham. "I feel fine. Why?"

6:14, Arnaud recorded. *Subject feels fine.* Then added, *Is bleeding from eyes.* Picking up the telephone, he depressed the call button.

"I need an outside line," said Arnaud when the operator picked up.

"You know the rules," said the operator. "No outside line during session with subject."

Blood, too, Arnaud noticed, had started to drip from Bentham's nose. Perhaps it was coming from his ears as well. Though with Bentham's visible ear already puddled with the blood from his eye, it was difficult to be certain.

"The subject appears to be dying," said Arnaud.

"Dying?" said the operator. "Of what?"

"Of bleeding," said Arnaud.

"I see," said the operator. "Please hold the line."

The operator exchanged himself with a low and staticky Muzak. Arnaud, holding the receiver against his ear, watched Bentham. It was a song he felt he should recognize but he could not quite grasp what it was. Bentham tried to sit up again, straining against the straps as if unaware of them, without any hint of panic. In general he seemed unaware of what was happening to him. A bloody flux was spilling out of his mouth now as well, Arnaud noticed. He groped for a pen to record this, but could not find one.

Bentham shook his head quickly as if to clear it, spattering blood onto the glass between them. Then he bared his teeth. This was, Arnaud felt, a terrible thing to watch.

The Muzak clicked off.

"Accounting," said a flat, implacable voice.

"Excuse me?" said Arnaud.

"Accounting division."

"I don't understand," said Arnaud. "The subject assigned to me is dying."

The man on the other end did not respond. Bentham, Arnaud saw through the glass, had stopped moving.

"I think he may have just died," said Arnaud.

"Not my jurisdiction, sir," said the voice, still flat, and the line went dead.

It was hard for him to be certain that Bentham was no longer alive. Several times, as Arnaud prepared to record a time of death, Bentham offered a weak movement that dissuaded him, the curling or uncurling of a finger, the parting of his lips. He was not certain whether these were actual movements or whether the corpse was simply ridding itself of its remaining vitality. For accuracy's sake, he felt, he should unlock the adjoining door between the two rooms and go through, to manually check Bentham's pulse with his fingers. Or, rather, to make certain there was no pulse to check. But the strangeness of Bentham's condition made him feel that it might be better to leave the adjoining door closed.

As to leaving his own room, he had no choice but to wait until the session had officially expired and a guard came to unlock the door. He waited, watching Bentham dead or dying. He watched the blood dry between them, on the window. When his ear began to ache, he realized he was still pushing the dead receiver against his face, and hung up.

He stood and looked under his desk until he found his pen, then wrote in his notebook: *6:26. Patient dead?*

The remainder of the session he spent, pen poised over the notebook, watching Bentham for any signs of life. He watched the skin on Bentham's face change character, losing its elasticity, seeming to settle more tightly around the bone. The nose became more and more accentuated, the cheeks growing hollow. The frightful perfection of the skull glowed dully through the skin. Even when the guard opened the door behind Arnaud, it was very hard for him to look away.

"Ready?" the guard asked. "Session's over."

"I think he's dead," said Arnaud.

"How's that?" said the guard. "Come again?"

The guard came and stood next to Arnaud, stared into Bentham's room. Arnaud looked too.

When he looked back up, he saw that the guard was looking at him with frightened eyes.

"What is it?" Arnaud asked.

But at first the guard did not answer, just kept looking at Arnaud. *Why?* Arnaud wondered, and waited.

"What," the guard finally asked, "exactly did you do to him?"

It was not until that moment that Arnaud realized how wrong things could go for him.

II.

The guard became businesslike and efficient, hustling Arnaud out of the observation room and down the hall.

"Where are we going?" Arnaud asked.

"Just down here," said the guard, keeping a firm grip on Arnaud's arm, pushing him forward.

They passed down one flight of stairs, and through another hall. They went down a short flight, Arnaud nearly tripping, and then immediately up three brief steps and through a door that read "Conference Rooms." The door opened onto a short hallway with three doors on either side and one at the end.

The guard walked him down to the final door, coaxed him inside. "Wait here," the guard said.

"For what?" Arnaud asked.

But the guard, already gone, did not answer.

Arnaud tried the door he had come through; it was locked. He tried the door at the far end of the room; this was locked as well.

He sat down at the table and stared at the wall.

After a while, he began to read from his notebook. *Fugue state*, he read. Had he done anything wrong? he wondered. Was he to blame? Was anything in fact his fault? *6:13*, he read. *Subject has begun to bleed from eyes.* Even if it were not his fault, would he somehow be held responsible? *Subject feels fine,* he read. *Is bleeding from eyes.*

Oh no, he thought.

He got up and tried both doors again.

He sat down again, but found it difficult to sit still. Perhaps he was in very serious trouble, he thought. He was not to blame for whatever had happened to Bentham. But someone had to be blamed, didn't they? And thus he was to blame.

Or was he? Perhaps he was becoming hysterical.

He opened the notebook again and began to read from it. The words were the same as they had been before. They seemed all right to him now, mostly. Perhaps the guard was simply following routine procedure in the case of an unusual death.

No, he began to worry a few moments later, something was wrong. Subjects did not customarily bleed from the eyes, for a start. He closed the notebook, leaving it facedown on the table.

On the far side of the room, affixed to the wall, he noticed a telephone. He stood up and went to it.

"Operator," a voice said.

"Outside line, please," he said.

"Right away, sir," the operator said. "What number?"

He gave the number. The dial tone changed to a thrumming, punctured by intervals of silence.

Nobody was answering.

After a time the thrumming stopped and a recorded voice came on, the tape so distorted he could barely make the words out. It was a man's voice. *Not the right number,* he thought, and started to hang up, and then thought, no, he might not have a chance to dial out again. *Hapler,* the distorted voice identified itself as, or perhaps *Handler,* or *Hapner.* Nobody he knew. But Handler or Hapler would have to do.

"Hello?" he said. "Mr. Hapner? Is that in fact the correct name? My name is Arnaud. I'm afraid I've been given your number in error."

He swallowed, then began choosing his words carefully.

"There's been a misunderstanding," he said. "I have every hope it will be quickly resolved, everyone's heart is in the right place. But, Mr. Hapner, could I trouble you to contact my wife? Would you ask her, assuming that I am not safe and sound by the time you reach her, to do what she can to find out what has become of me? It would mean a great deal to both of us." He stopped, thought. "She might," he finally added, "begin with Bentham."

Immediately after he hung up, the phone began to ring. Almost reflexively, he picked it up.

"Hello?" he said.

"Who is this?" a voice asked.

Arnaud hesitated. "Why," he asked slowly, "do you want to know?"

"Mr. Arnaud," said the voice. "Why are you answering the telephone?"

He didn't know what to say. He held the receiver, looked out the window.

"You made a call a few moments ago," the voice said. "What was the purpose of this call?"

"I don't know what you're talking about," said Arnaud.

"How are you acquainted with—" he heard a rustling through the receiver "—this Mr. Hapner?"

"I—" said Arnaud.

"—and what, in your opinion, is the nature of the so-called . . . misunderstanding."

Not knowing what else to say, Arnaud hung up the telephone.

By the time he was sitting down again, a guard had appeared in the room. A new guard, not the same one. He stood just inside one of the doors, watching Arnaud nervously.

"Hello," said Arnaud, just as nervously.

The guard nodded.

"What's this all about?" asked Arnaud.

"I'm not allowed to converse with you," the guard said.

"Why not?" asked Arnaud.

The guard did not answer.

Arnaud thumbed through his notebook again. His eyes for some reason were having a hard time focusing on his handwriting, which appeared furry, blurred. No, he thought, he had followed procedure. He was not to blame. Unless they blamed him for the phone call. But couldn't he explain that away? Nobody had told him he wasn't allowed to telephone. There was really nothing to worry about, he told himself. Bentham's death could not be attributed to his negligence.

The original guard came back in. The two guards stood together just inside the door, whispering, looking at him, one of them frequently scratching the skin behind his ear. Eventually the original guard went to the telephone and disconnected it from the wall. Telephone under his arm, he came over to Arnaud and took his notebook away. Then he went out again.

Arnaud swiveled his chair around to face the remaining guard. He spread his arms wide.

"What harm could it possibly do to talk to me?"

The guard pointed a finger at him, shook it. "You've been warned," he said.

He stood up and went to the window. Outside, past the doubled fence, dim shapes wandered about beneath a mottled sky.

He heard the door open. When he turned, both guards, edges blurring, were present again, conversing, watching him. They seemed to be speaking to each other very rapidly, in a steady drone. He had to concentrate to understand them.

"He's been standing there," one of them was saying, "just like that, hours now."

But no, he had been there for only a few moments, hadn't he? Something was wrong with them.

One of them suddenly darted over and stood next to him.

"Come with us," the guard said.

"No use resisting," the same guard said.

Arnaud nodded and stepped forward, and then felt himself suddenly swept forward. Each guard, he realized, had taken hold of one of his arms and was dragging him.

The conference room was replaced by a stretch of hall.

"Malingerer, eh?" said one of the guards, only the words didn't seem to correspond with the quivering movement of his lips, seemed instead to be coming at a distance, from the hall behind him.

No, Arnaud suddenly realized, amazed, something isn't wrong with them. Something is wrong with me.

They rushed him through the hall and into an observation booth. His observation booth, he realized, the one he had used to interview Bentham. Perhaps he was being allowed to return to work. Who would his next subject be? Bentham, he saw on the other side of the glass, was gone, though pinkish streaks of diluted blood were still visible on the glass.

He started toward his chair, but the guards were still holding him. Gently, he tried to free himself, but they wouldn't let go. Then he realized that he was being dragged toward the adjoining door, toward the subject chamber.

"No," he said, "but I, I'm not a subject."

"Of course not," a guard soothed, his face more a splotch of color than a face. "Who claimed you were?"

"But—" he said.

He grabbed hold of the doorframe on the way through. He held on. Something hard was pushing into his back, just below the blade of his shoulder. Something ground his fingers against the metal of the doorframe, his hand growing numb. Then his grip gave and he was through the door, being strapped to Bentham's bed. A fourth person in the room, a technician, was snapping on latex gloves.

"I'm not a subject," Arnaud claimed again.

The technician just smiled. Arnaud watched the smile smear across her face, consume it. Something was wrong with his vision. He could no longer see the technician clearly, she was just a blur, but from having watched subjects through the glass he could derive what she surely must be doing: an ampoule, a hypodermic, the body of the first emptying, the chamber of the second filling.

The blur shifted, was shot through with light.

"This may sting just a little," the technician said. But Arnaud felt nothing. What's wrong? he wondered. "Not so bad, is it?" the technician asked, coming briefly into focus again. And then she stepped away and was swallowed up by the wall.

"Hello?" Arnaud said.

Nobody answered.

"Is anybody there?" he asked.

Where had they gone? How much time had passed? He looked about him but couldn't make sense of what he saw. Everything seemed reduced to two dimensions, shadow and light becoming replacements for objects rather than something in which they bathed. He lifted his head and looked down at his body but could not recognize it, could not even perceive it as a body, despite being almost certain it was there.

Fugue state, he thought, idly. And then thought, *Oh, God. I've caught it, too.*

•

"Hello?" said a voice. It was smooth, quiet. It struck him as familiar. "Arnaud?" it said.

168

He turned, saw no one, just a flat, black square. *Speaker*, he thought. Then he remembered the observation booth, turned instead to where, though he couldn't quite make it out, he thought it must be.

"Yes?" he said. "Hello?"

"How do you feel?"

"I feel fine," he claimed.

He heard a vague rustling, was not certain if it was coming from somewhere in his room or from the observation booth.

"Hello?" he said.

"Yes?" said the voice. "What's wrong, please?"

Arnaud waited, listened. There it was again, a rustling. He swiveled his ear toward it.

"I apologize for these precautions," said the voice, "but we had to assure ourselves that you were not a . . . liability, didn't we? For your own . . . safety as well as ours."

Arnaud did not answer.

"Arnaud, did you understand what I said?"

"Yes," said Arnaud. He tried to get up, and thought he had, but then realized he was still lying down. What was happening, exactly?

"Good," said the voice. "Shall we move straight to the point? Did you murder Bentham?"

Bentham? he wondered. Who was Bentham again? He blinked, tried to focus. "No," he said.

"What happened to Bentham?"

"I don't know," said Arnaud.

"Arnaud, seven days ago, you interviewed Bentham. During that session he died."

"Yes," said Arnaud, remembering. "He died. But it wasn't seven days ago. It was just a few hours ago."

"Are you sure, Arnaud? Are you certain?"

"Yes," said Arnaud. "I'm certain."

The rustling seemed gone now. He found that if he tilted his head and squinted he could make the plane of glass between his room and the observation booth rise from the flat surface of the wall, hovering like a ghost just above it. The glass was flat as well, depthless. Bentham's blood, the dull, nearly faded swathes of it, drifted like another flattened ghost on its surface. But somehow he could not see through blood or glass to the other side.

"Who is Mr. Hapner?" the voice asked.

Arnaud hesitated. "I don't know," he said, perplexed.

"You don't know," the voice said. "And yet after Bentham's death you placed a telephone call to a Mr. Hapner. How do you explain this?"

"I'm afraid I have no explanation," said Arnaud. "I don't even remember doing it."

He closed his eyes. When he opened them again, the room seemed to have shifted, flattening out like a piece of paper. It was still a room, he tried to convince himself, only less so.

For an instant, the room grew clearer.

"—case," the voice was saying. "How did he die?"

He tried to remember. "He began to bleed," he said. "From the eyes," he said.

"Yes," said the voice. "So you wrote. What made this happen, do you think?"

"I don't know," said Arnaud. "How should I know?"

"Think carefully. Did it have anything to do with you?"

He kept looking at the plane of glass, trying to worm his vision through. The voice kept at him, asking him the same questions in slightly different ways, repeating, following procedure. Arnaud kept answering as best he could.

"About this record of your interview," said the voice. "Is it, to the best of your knowledge, accurate?"

"Of course," claimed Arnaud. And then, "What record?"

The voice started to speak, fell silent. Arnaud waited, listened. There it was again, a rustling.

"What does the word term *fugue state* mean to you?" asked the voice. But now it sounded harsher, less encouraging, almost like a different voice.

"It doesn't mean anything," said Arnaud.

"And yet you wrote it. What exactly did you mean?"

"I don't know," said Arnaud. "I just wrote it."

"Do you see, Arnaud? Right here? *Fugue state?*"

He turned his face toward the black square and then, remembering, toward the glass, saw nothing.

"Well?" said the voice.

"Well what?" asked Arnaud.

"And yet," said the voice.

But then it interrupted itself, argued with itself in two different tones and cadences about what question should be asked next.

But how could a single voice do this? Arnaud wondered.

"How many of the one of you are there?" he asked. "Two?"

He waited. The voice did not answer. Perhaps he had said it wrong. Perhaps he had not said what he meant. He was preparing to repeat the question when the voice answered, in its harsher tone.

"How many of us do there appear to you to be?"

He opened his mouth to respond, closed it. He must have said something wrong, he realized, but he was no longer sure what.

"Do you remember your name?" said a voice slowly.

"Yes," said Arnaud. "Of course I do." But then realized no, he did not.

"Will you please tell it to me?" the voice said.

Arnaud hesitated. What was it? It was there, almost on the tip of his tongue. "Why?" he asked. "Why exactly do you need to know?"

A voice said, changing, "Arnaud, what do you see?"

A voice said, changing, "Arnaud, what is happening to you?"

A voice said, changing, "Arnaud, how do you feel?"

"Fine," said Arnaud. "I feel fine."

He waited. "Why do you ask?" he finally said.

His face felt wet. Was he in the rain? No, he was indoors. There couldn't be rain. He could no longer see through his eyes.

He knew, from the tone of the voice, or voices, that someone thought something was wrong with him. But he couldn't, for the life of him, figure out what that could possibly be.

III.

There was a series of days he could not remember, how many days he was never certain, days in which, he temporarily deduced, he must have lain comatose and bleeding from the eyes on the floor of a kitchen, next to a woman he assumed, but no longer was certain, must be his wife. And all the days before those, which he could not remember either. By the time he managed to open his eyes and felt as though the world around him were moving at a rate his senses could comfortably apprehend, the woman, whoever she was, was dead. Thus his first memory, quickly coming apart, was of lying next to her, staring at her gaunt face, at the lips constricted back to show the tips of her canines.

Who is she? he wondered.

And myself, he wondered, who exactly am I?

Near his face was a puddle of water. He did not recognize the reflection that quivered along its surface. He rolled his head down into the water, lapped some up with his tongue.

After a while he worked up enough strength to crawl across the kitchen floor, tracing the water to its source, and to duck his head under a skirt below the sink. There, an overflowing metal bowl rested beneath the leaking elbow of a pipe.

The water in the bowl was filthy, covered with a thin layer of scum. He brushed this gently apart with his stubbled chin, then tried to lap up the cleaner water below.

It was musty, but helped. He lay still for a while, his cheek against the damp, rotting wood of the cabinet floor, one temple applied to the cold metal of the bowl.

Later he managed to pull himself up and stagger to a cabinet. Inside, he found some stale crackers and sucked on these, then sat in a kitchen chair, his mouth dry. His eyes hurt. So did his ears and the lining of his mouth.

He got up and ate some more crackers, then stared into the refrigerator. The food inside was rotting. He scavenged the heel of a loaf of bread, scraped off the mold and ate.

After the better part of the day had waned, he began to feel more human. He searched the pockets of the woman on the floor. They contained a few coins and a wallet stuffed with cards. Something, he discovered, was wrong with his eyes. He knew what the cards were by their shape and appearance—credit card, identification card, cash card, library pass—but was puzzled to find he could not read them. The characters on them, what he assumed were characters, meant nothing. He stared at them for some time and then slid them into his pocket. Later, he covered the woman's body with a sheet.

In the bathroom mirror, he did not recognize himself. The face staring back at him had blood crusted about its eyes, above its lips, and to either side of its chin, the center of the chin now covered with a diluted slurry of blood and water. His eyes were bloodshot, oddly scored and pitted. His vision, he realized, was dim, as if he were slowly going blind. Perhaps his pupils had always been that way.

He washed the face, scrubbing the blood from the wrinkles around the eyes with soap and with a toothbrush he had found in the cabinet above the sink. When he was done, he shaved carefully.

He regarded himself in the mirror. Who am I? he wondered. But that was not what he meant exactly. Only that he had no name to put with what he knew himself to be.

When he tried to open the door, he found it locked. He unlocked the deadbolt, tried to open it again, but the door still wouldn't open. He wandered from room to room. The windows were barred from the outside, the street lying far below. The sheet was still in the kitchen, the woman still dead under it. Yes, he thought, that's right, he remembered. It was in a way reassuring to know she had not been imagined, though in another way not reassuring at all.

What was her name? He didn't know. Nothing leaped to mind. Nothing sounded quite right. And what about him? Nothing sounded quite right, nor quite wrong, either.

In the back of one of the closets he found a small prybar and a hammer. He used them to knock the pins from the door hinges, then tried to pry the door open from its hinged side. It creaked, but still didn't come.

Using the prybar as a chisel, he slowly splintered a hole through the center of the door at eye level. There was, he discovered, something just beyond the door, made of plywood. He slowly broke a hole through this as well until, at last, he had a fist-sized opening that debouched onto an ordinary hall.

"Hello?" he called out. "Anyone there?"

When there was no answer, he went into the kitchen, stepping over the sheet. He started opening drawers. There was a drawer containing a series of utensils, stacked very carefully into slots, a drawer containing stray keys and books of stamps and a rubber-band ball, a drawer containing nested measuring cups and spatulas and turkey basters and pie shields. Then, above them, a shelf holding a jumble of pots and pans, a cabinet scattered with ascending stacks of dishes and nested hard-plastic drinking cups. He worked two of the rubber bands off the ball, then slid the rest of the drawers closed.

In the bathroom, he took a last look at himself and then struck the mirror with the prybar. Cracks shot through. The silvered glass tipped off in shards, which broke further on the floor.

His hand, he saw, was blood-soaked, a flap of skin hanging open and folded over on its back. He was surprised to find it didn't hurt.

He pushed the flap back in place, found gauze in the cabinet, wrapped his hand in it.

He picked out a smaller, more regular square of glass. After scraping each of its edges against the tile floor to dull it, he used the rubber bands to fasten it to the hooked end of the prybar. At the door, he worked the mirror-end of the prybar through the hole he had made, then slid the prybar through as far as he could without letting go of it.

It was hard to see past his knuckles and past the bar itself, harder still to hold the bar steady enough at one end to make sense of what he was seeing in the shard on the other: a wavering square of light and color. But there it was, he slowly could make it out, despite the wavering image: a large panel of raw wood, plywood, larger, it seemed than his door, studded with black pocks at regular intervals around its edge. The same black pocks in two lines up the middle of the panel as well. Stretching from the bottom corners to top corners of the panel were two strips of yellow plastic tape, covered in black characters that he could not read.

But something must have been awry with his thinking. He remained slightly crouched, holding the prybar, trying to keep it steady, concentrating, looking past his knuckles into the reflection, and it was all he could do, really, just to see the flittered bits and pieces and make some cohesive image out of them in his head. It was too much to force that image into actually meaning something as well. Even after his difficulty in trying to open the door, even after seeing the image in the shaky shard of mirror, after seeing the black pocks around the edge of the plywood, it took him some moments of just staring and thinking to realize he had been deliberately boarded in.

But when he did realize, the shock came all at once. His fingers let go of the prybar, and, overbalanced, it started to slide out of the hole and away from him. He just caught it. He pulled it back through and, shaking, sat down with his back to the door.

Why? he wondered.

He couldn't say. Perhaps, he thought, they hadn't known he and his wife were there. Assuming, he corrected himself, that she was his wife. Perhaps they had thought the apartment unoccupied.

But who, he wondered, were *they*?

•

There was the phone, he thought after a while. He could telephone someone to come get him out.

But whom did he know? He couldn't remember having known anyone.

On the answering machine beside the phone a light was blinking. Why hadn't he noticed it before?

He got up and pressed the button beneath the light.

Hello? A voice said. *Mr. Hafner? Is that in fact the correct name? My name is Arnaud. I'm afraid I've been given your number in error.*

Hapner, he thought, *my name's Hapner. Probably. Or something close to that. Unless he's talking to somebody else.*

There's been a misunderstanding, the voice continued, Arnaud's voice continued. *What sort of misunderstanding?* Hapner wondered. He was, Hapner was, to contact Arnaud's wife. He was to ask her to do what she could to find out what had happened to Arnaud. He might, he was told, begin with Bentham. *What a strange message,* Arnaud thought. *Or wait,* the man thought, *I'm not Arnaud, that's not my name, my name is something else. What was it?*

After listening to the tape several dozen times, he was almost certain he could remember his name. *Hapner.* Every few minutes he brought the name to his lips, whispered it. It would, he hoped, stay with him, on his tongue if not in his brain. And now, he thought, I have something to do. *Bentham,* he thought, *Arnaud.*

With the hammer and the prybar he began to widen the hole, first cracking and splintering away his own door and then slowly hammering the flattened, flanged end of the prybar through the plywood.

He was weak; his arms quickly grew sore and tired and the light he had at first been able to see coming through the windows had long faded. The hall outside, however, remained brightly lit.

The plywood broke loose in odd, thatched fragments, splitting within the body of a layer of wood rather than between layers. In the end he had a splintery and furzed channel wide enough to squeeze through. He drank some more water, ate some more crackers, and then sat on a chair in the kitchen, gathering his strength. His gaze caught on the sheet on the floor and he stooped to uncover the woman's face. He regarded her closely, but no, he still did not recognize her.

Perhaps, he thought, I never knew her.

But then why, he wondered, was she here with me? Or, if you prefer, why was I here with her?

He went into the bedroom, looked through the closets. One was full of a woman's clothing, the other of clothing belonging to a man. He tried on a sport coat. It was too small, and musty.

He tried on some of the other clothes, all too small.

Puzzled, he returned to the kitchen, stared again into the dead woman's face.

It's her home, he thought, not mine. And somebody else's. I'm probably not even Hafner. Or Hapner.

He sat staring at her. The corpse was changing shape, becoming even less human. Soon it would start to smell. He couldn't stay there, whether he was Hafner or no. And if he wanted to be anyone, he had to be Hafner, at least for now.

IV.

Hapner rummaged a shoulder bag from a closet and dropped the hammer and the prybar into it. After unplugging the answering machine, he put it in as well, then pushed the bag through the door's hole.

It was tighter than he'd thought. He had to work one shoulder through and then turn sideways to get the other past. The ragged edges of the hole scraped raw the underflesh of one arm as well as the skin over his ribs. Halfway through, he thought he was stuck, and grew desperate and maddened, scratching and wriggling until he had worn the skin covering his hipbones bloody and until he fell on his neck and shoulders out onto the floor.

The other doors too had been sealed off, he saw. Along the length of the wall, where he would have expected doors to be, were sheets of plywood fastened to door and wall with ratchet-headed black screws.

He went down the hall and down the stairs. Doors on the floor below were sealed too, but not all of them, and he knocked on the three that weren't. Nobody answered any of them. He tried to open them but found them all locked.

The next floor down was the same, doors mostly boarded over, no one answering the few still unsealed. He chose one at random and worked at it with the prybar and the hammer until he cracked the latch out through the frame of the door and the door swung open.

The layout of the apartment was identical to that of the apartment he had been in, except reversed.

"Hello?" he called.

No answer came. The windows were slightly ajar. A thin layer of dust covered everything. Not quite dust, he realized: stickier. What exactly, he couldn't say. On the table a sheet of paper was held down by a burnished brass paperweight. There was something written on it, but he couldn't read it. He picked it up and folded it, slid it into his back pocket.

In the closet were two smeared, bloody handprints. Under one of the beds was what seemed to be a human ear. He sat on his knees a long time, squinting at it, wondering if he was really seeing what he thought he was seeing, but in the end left it where it was without touching it. In the oven he found the tightly curved body of a cat, long dead, dry as a plate. When he touched it, its hair crackled away.

He closed the oven door and hurriedly left.

Two floors down, he knocked on an unsealed door and heard behind it some transient living sound, cut off nearly as quickly as it had begun.

"Hello?" he called.

He knocked again, but heard nothing. He pressed his ear to the door, thought he could hear, vaguely, just barely, something pressed to the other side, breathing. Was that possible, to hear something breathing, through a door? Perhaps it was his own breathing, he thought, and this made him feel as if he were on both sides of the door at once, and made him wonder why he wouldn't open up for himself.

"I don't mean any harm," he said. No response. "I'm just a neighbor," he said. "I just want to talk." Still no response.

"Shall I break down the door?" he asked. "If I do that, anybody can get in."

He waited a few minutes, then got out his prybar and his hammer. Aligning the prybar in the gap between door and wall, he struck the end with the hammer, started to drive it in.

He was a little startled when the voice that rang out from behind the door was not his own.

"All right," it said. "All right."

He worked the prybar free of the crack, then stepped back. The dead-bolt clicked. The door handle shivered, and the door drew open.

Behind it was a small man, scarcely bigger than a child, wearing a moth-eaten sweater. Though not old, he seemed to be hairless, the skin hanging sallow on his face. His mouth and his nose were hidden behind a surgical mask that he had doubled over to make fit. He stood mostly hidden, hand and head visible, a pistol in the former.

"Well?" the small man said. "What is it?"

"I'm your neighbor," Hapner said.

"I suppose you want to borrow a cup of sugar."

"No," said Hapner. "To talk."

"All right," said the man. "You're here. Talk."

"Can't I come in?"

"Why do you need to come in?" the man asked, a little surprised. "There's no reason to come in. It's not safe."

Hapner shrugged.

The man looked at him for a long while. His eyes, protruding and damp, seemed slightly filmed. He opened the door farther, shifted the pistol to his other hand.

"What floor?"

Hapner counted in his head. "Five floors up," he said.

"Eighth floor," said the man. "Why didn't you just say eighth? I thought all the eighth was boarded off."

"Almost all," lied Hapner. "Every door but one."

The man's eyes narrowed. "You're not ill, are you?"

"Don't be ridiculous," said Hapner. With what? he wondered.

"O.K.," said the man. "O.K. Prove it. Tell me your name."

"My name?" said Hapner.

It started with a letter midway through the alphabet, he knew, one he could almost remember. It was there, nearly on the tip of his tongue, but what exactly was it?

"Well?" the man said. "Either you know your name or you don't."

"Mind if I use your bathroom?" asked Hapner.

"The bathroom?" said the man, surprised. "I, but I—"

"Thank you," said Hapner, and, hands raised above his head, eased his way carefully past the small man without touching the pistol, toward where he suspected the bathroom must be.

"Wait," the man said. But Hapner kept walking, slowly, as if under water. He gritted his teeth, waiting for the man to shoot him in the back, following each slow step with another slow step until he reached the bathroom. He opened the door and slipped quickly inside, locking it behind him.

What now? he wondered.

He regarded his face in the mirror, his frightened eyes, then opened his bag and removed the answering machine. Having unplugged the man's electric razor, he plugged his answering machine in and dialed the volume down. He held the machine pressed against his ear and depressed the button.

"Hello?" a voice said into his ear. "Mr. Hapner? Is that in fact the correct name?"

Is it? Hapner wondered. The voice kept on. There were other names mentioned, but Hapner struck him as the only viable one. Arnaud. He, Hapner, was looking for Arnaud, he discovered, and for Bentham as a way to reach Arnaud. The answering machine made it all perfectly clear. *Hapner*, he made his lips mime. He rewound the tape and listened to his name again, then again, until he was certain he could remember it. At least for a few minutes.

The small man was knocking on the bathroom door, urging him to come out or be killed.

"I'm coming," Hapner said. He quickly packed the answering machine away and opened the door. The small man was there, face red, pistol aimed at Hapner's waist.

"Hapner," he said. "My name's Hapner."

The pistol wavered slightly, a strange expression passing across the man's eyes. "I know a Hafner on the eighth floor," he said, "or ninth. Can't remember. But you're not him."

"No," said Hapner quickly. "I'm Hapner, not Hafner. Eighth floor as well. Strange coincidence, no?"

The man looked at him a long time, then took a few steps back, gun still poised. "Tell me what you want again?" he asked.

"That depends," said Hapner. "Are you Arnaud?"

"No," said the small man. "Who?"

"What about Bentham?"

"I'm Roeg."

"Do you know either an Arnaud or a Bentham?"

"Do they live in this building?"

"I don't know."

"I don't think so," said the small man. "These are strange questions to ask. If they do live here, I don't know them."

"Then I don't want anything," Hafner said, and started to go.

"I thought you wanted to talk," said Roeg.

Hapner turned, saw Roeg had let his body sag. The small man went and sat down on the couch. He sat there, eyes looking exhausted, finally motioning Hapner into the chair next to him. "It's been long time," he said. "Let's talk."

But it was not an *us* who talked, for Hapner spoke hardly at all. Roeg hadn't left the house in several weeks, he claimed, ever since the plague had begun. *Plague?* Hapner wondered, but just nodded. Roeg's wife had gone out and never come back. She was, Roeg figured, probably dead.

"But maybe she just left," said Roeg.

Roeg took the surgeon's mask off his face and laid it on the coffee table, smoothed it out with the palm of his hand. His mouth, Hapner saw, was delicately formed, the lips nearly translucent.

"Maybe," said Hapner. "I'm sorry."

Then, Roeg said, someone had arrived wearing protective suits. Each apartment had been opened. If anyone was found with indications, they were boarded in. No doubt it had been the same on Hapner's floor.

"No doubt," said Hapner.

"Eventually they stopped coming," said Roeg.

"Probably dead themselves," said Hapner.

"Probably," said Roeg, and lapsed into silence, staring at the tabletop.

"And what now?" asked Hapner.

"Now?" said Roeg. "How should I know?"

Almost as quickly as the information was given to him, Hapner felt it begin to slip away, the details wavering and eroding, only a large, vague sense of contagion remained. The knowledge itself was being simplified, made brutish within his head. He wondered how much of even this he would remember, and for how long?

There were other things Roeg was telling him, he realized, but even as the small man was saying them, Hapner felt them going. The authorities, he did remember Roeg saying, were silent. As for the silence, either Roeg didn't know its cause or Hapner had somehow missed it or was already forgetting it. Perhaps it was simply *ongoing silence, unexplained.*

As Roeg spoke on, Hapner became more and more confused. When he realized, from Roeg's puzzled look, that he must have asked a nearly identical question twice, he began to be concerned.

And then Roeg acquired a panicked look. "Why are you speaking so quickly?" he asked. "Slow down."

"I'm not speaking quickly," Hapner said.

As Roeg tried to continue, it became clear to Hapner that something was wrong. Roeg became prone to long, reptilian fits of silence and would stop speaking to peer nervously around him.

"Roeg?" said Hapner. "Roeg?" But the small man wasn't answering, wasn't paying attention. Filled with doubt, Hapner asked, "That's your name, no?"

"My name?" said Roeg, suspiciously. "Why do you want to know?"

And then Roeg groped his pistol off the couch cushion and began to jab it into the air. He pointed not at Hapner but at where Hapner had been a few moments before, for Hapner had stood and taken a few steps so as to get a closer look at Roeg.

"You had it?" Roeg shouted. "But why aren't you dead?"

Roeg fired the pistol into the couch across from him. He moved the pistol a little to the left, fired into the credenza, left again, into the wall—just behind the spot Hapner had been just a few seconds before. Reaching out, Hapner wrenched the gun out of Roeg's hand and dropped it to the floor. But it was as if Roeg didn't realize the gun was gone, for his curled hand was still aiming, his finger flexing, over and over, and he was, desperately, asking Hapner why he wouldn't die.

He spoke softly and carefully into Roeg's ear, stroking and rubbing the small man's hand until it loosened its grip on the absent gun. He persuaded him into lying down on the couch, then went into the kitchen and got a damp cloth, and carefully wiped away the blood already seeping up through the man's eye sockets.

"How do you feel, Roeg?" he asked.

"Fine," said Roeg. "I feel fine. Why do you ask?"

And indeed, thought Hapner, the fellow seemed to believe this, despite the blood.

"You shouldn't feel bad," said Hapner. "You might come out of it all right."

"Come out of what?"

Blood began to leak from the man's mouth and nose and ears. Slowly he lapsed into unconsciousness. Hapner was at a loss to know what else he could do.

He let his eyes drift about the room until they found the telephone, then the answering machine. He held the latter's button down until it beeped, and then began to speak.

"Your name is Roeg," he said into it. "You are a small man. This is your house. I'm very sorry for all that's happened to you. My name is—" and there he stopped. What was his name again? Could he remember? No.

He turned off the answering machine and left the apartment.

V.

There was a name he had been using, just on the tip of his tongue. He could almost remember it. But, he wondered, was it his name? Even once he remembered it, how would he know for certain it belonged to him?

He wouldn't know.

He made it to the end of the hall and started down the stairs to the next floor. What floor was it? He had kept track, had been keeping track, but was not quite certain. He would go down the stairs and then look for a door leading to the street. If there wasn't one, he would try to find another set of stairs and go down them.

What had the name been? He had been found, had found himself, he could still trouble himself to dimly remember, lying beside a corpse. A woman, he was almost certain. Who, alive, had she been to him? His wife, his lover, a relative, a colleague, a stranger? Who could say?

Before he reached the bottom of the stairs, he could see a man in the hallway, first only his feet and then, with each step down, a subsequent portion of his body, all the way up to a shaved head. The man was standing beside a door, a large crowbar ending in a fanlike flange in one meaty hand. Leaning against the wall behind him was a sheet of plywood, apparently prized off the door. A large duffel bag, empty or nearly so, was swung over the man's back. He had begun on the door itself, Hapner could see, the door's frame splintered and gouged.

Hapner stopped a little way down the hall. The man too had stopped working and was watching him.

"Hello," Hapner finally said.

"Hello," the man said.

"What exactly—"

"—this your house?" asked the man. "Your door, I mean? I'm not stepping into a delicate situation, am I?"

Hapner shook his head. "No," he said. "It's not my door. Are you breaking in?"

"Some neighbor's?" asked the thief. "Some friend's then? Anything to get touchy about?"

Hapner shook his head.

"Any objections then? No? Then I'll proceed."

The man turned partly away, still trying to keep track of Hapner out of the corner of his eye, which made his attempts at opening the door awkward, blunted. But the door was slowly giving way.

"Aren't you afraid?" asked Hapner.

"What?" said the thief. "Of catching it? Was at first but then everybody around me went under and I never did. I don't think I will. What's the word? *Invulnerable?*" He worked the flanged end of the prybar back in, and then one twist of his torso cracked the door open. "No," he said, *"immune."* And then added, "After a while you feel invincible too."

He pushed open the door, bights of a brass chain tightening at eye level inside the apartment. The man fed his crowbar into the gap, broke the chain's latch off the doorframe.

"Well," he said. "Coming?"

Hapner took a half-step forward, stopped.

"I don't think so," he said.

"Come on in," said the man. "Where's the problem? You didn't have any objections last I checked. Besides, I haven't had anyone to talk to for a while. They all keep dying on me. You're not going to die on me, are you?" The man started through the door. "I'll let you have some of whatever we find, maybe."

Hapner hesitated, followed him in.

"What about you?" said the man in front of him.

The apartment inside was windowless and extremely dark; it was difficult to see anything. The man grew gray and then was reduced to a series of fluttering movements. Then he vanished entirely. Hapner stepped after him.

"What about me?" Hapner asked.

"Aren't you afraid? You're in a quarantined apartment now. Doesn't it worry you?"

The man struck a match and Hapner saw his face spring from the darkness, in a kitchenette area. He was not where Hapner had thought he would be. He was holding the match in one hand, rapidly opening and closing cupboard and cabinet doors with the other.

The match guttered and went out and the room was swallowed in the darkness, save for the dull-red bead of the match head, and then this was gone too, replaced by the smell of the burnt-up match. A sharp scratch and another match fluttered alight. Hapner watched the man's hand reach into a drawer, come out with a curious silver cylinder that he manipulated, transformed into a flashlight.

"That's better," the man said, and shined the flashlight's beam into Hapner's face.

"Now," he said, his voice changing in a way Hapner didn't understand. "What did you say your name was?"

"I didn't say," said Hapner. "What's yours?"

"What's that in the bag?" the man asked.

"My bag?" said Hapner. "Not much," he said.

"Open it up," said the thief. "Let's have a look."

Hapner put the bag on the counter between them, unzipped it. He took out the answering machine, set it beside the bag, then the short prybar, the hammer.

"That's it?" asked the thief.

"That's it," said Hapner.

"You don't have much," said the thief.

"I'm not like you," said Hapner. "I'm not a thief."

"Then what are you doing?"

"Looking for someone," he said. "A . . . Mr. Arnaud, I think. Is that you?"

"What, you just have a name?" said the voice behind the flashbeam.

Hapner nodded.

The man was silent for a moment. "All right," he finally said, "you can go."

Hapner nodded to himself. He reached out, began to put his possessions back into the bag. The thief's crowbar cut through the flashbeam and struck the counter between his hands.

"Leave it," said the man. "It's mine now."

"But—"

"This is my building," the man said. "Whatever's here belongs to me."

"But there's nothing I have that's worth—"

"It's a matter of principle," the thief said, his voice rising. "Now get out."

He kept staring at the answering machine. *Arnaud*, he thought, *Bentham. Hapler.* Or no, that wasn't it exactly, he was already forgetting. He squinted into the light. Where was the flashlight exactly? How far away? He could make it out, mostly. He could see the man behind it, a dim form wavered at the edges.

He turned as if to leave and took half a step and then whirled and crouched, battered at where he thought the flashlight would be. The thief cried out, Hapner's hand striking the casing of the flashlight hard. His fingers were instantly numb, the flashlight flicking away end over end and going out.

The crowbar passed moaning over his head, ruffling his hair, then smashed into the wall. The thief cursed. Hapner groped about, touched the man's shirt but, unable to find the crowbar, dropped to his knees and crouched under the lip of the counter.

The crowbar crashed into the counter above him, rattling the walls.

"Where are you?" the man said.

Hapner said nothing.

"I'll find you eventually," said the thief. "You belong to me."

Hapner stayed still, listening to the dim birds of the man's feet, the scrape of the crowbar as it met floor or wall. He reached carefully up and touched the counter above him, his fingers feeling slowly along it.

There was a groove the crowbar had dug in the surface, the countertop splintered and cracked to either side of it. Hapner's hands felt past it until they found his hammer.

"But maybe I already killed you?" the thief said.

The voice was right there, almost beside him. In one motion he swung the hammer up and forward. It struck something firm but not as hard as the wall.

The thief screamed and swooned toward him, striking the counter, stumbling over Hapner's legs. Hapner struck him hard and repeatedly with the hammer. Something struck his shoulder and it suddenly became a numb, useless thing and he heard the crowbar splintering the wood behind him. He groped with his good hand for the dropped hammer. He heard the thief stutter-step and then, groaning, fall.

He moved toward the body, pounding along the floor in front of him until the hammer struck flesh. He fell on the other man and lost his hammer and felt the man's face into existence and then fumbled up the hammer again and then, as the man still struggled his way out of shock, struck at his skull again and again until it sounded like he was hitting a wet sack.

He felt around the floor one-handed until he found the flashlight. He stood up and flicked its switch but no light came from it, so he dropped it again.

On his way back to the counter, he stepped on what must have been the thief's hand and then, as he moved quickly off it, stepped into something damp and squishy, perhaps the thief's gore, perhaps his own, and almost fell. One arm ached badly and swung loose, battering against his side like the trussed body of a shot bird. Moving it created little flashes of light behind his eyes.

He fumbled around on the counter until he found the answering machine, picked it up. There was something wrong with it, he could tell: its surface was no longer smooth.

The room seemed with each moment less and less familiar to him.

He managed to stumble out of the dark and back into the hall. His arm, he saw, in the light, seemed mostly dead, oddly lumped and turning black in two places. He tried again to move it but could not.

The answering machine was shattered in the back, and the slatted casing covering the speaker was destroyed, the speaker itself and the transformer beside it mangled. Why had he wanted to keep it anyway? He couldn't remember.

He dropped the machine and, crouching beside it, worked the cassette free with one hand. One of its corners was crushed but the tape itself was still intact, could be listened to on another machine. Where had he seen one?

The hallway, he saw, was slowly going out around him, flattening out, the door he had come through now just an odd square of black, a vertical panel, two-dimensional, rather than an entrance. The whole world, he thought fleetingly, was like that for him, there was nothing he could hold on to but this hall and perhaps a few other halls above that and an answering machine he might or might not have seen, somewhere above him. But what did *above* mean? What's wrong with it? he wondered of the hall. It all struck him as vaguely familiar, as if he had lived through it before, in another life.

He turned and looked where he was almost certain stairs had been, and found that it too had gone strange, a flat black rectangle scored with lighter lines. He stumbled toward it and, closing his eyes, pushed into it. The pain in his shoulder, too, he realized, seemed to be fading, was all but gone. He hit against something and pulled himself up, kept moving forward, kept stumbling, and when he opened his eyes saw that the stairs were stairs again, more or less, and that he could navigate them. He pushed through the yellow wall at their end and found himself in a hall, or what seemed like a movie set for a hall, everything slightly false. He reached up to touch his face and, when his hand came away, saw it was not a hand exactly, though a reasonable facsimile. There, floating above it, was a strange crimson cloud, the color of blood.

An anxiety began rising in him that he had a hard time placing.

By strength of will he managed to transform a brown rectangle into a door and push his way through. Inside, the cardboard cutout of a tiny man, hardly bigger than a child, was lying prone on what stood in for a couch, a crimson cloud hovering over his face. He took a deep breath and tried to relax and there, momentarily, saw a real, flesh-and-blood man on an actual couch, his face stained from blood that had seeped from his eyes. He felt, almost, that he recognized him. But then, suddenly, he was only a child in a crimson cloud again.

There was a blinking light near him, not far away, very quick, not blinking so much as strobing. He moved toward it slowly and stood near it and in a little while began to imagine that it was an actual manmade object, an answering machine. He found a button and pressed it.

A voice came out, speaking too rapidly. It sounded familiar to him, perhaps a voice he had heard before, but where?

Your name is Roeg, the voice said. *You are a small man. This is your home. I'm very sorry for all that's happened to you. My name is—*

And then it stopped. *Roeg*, he thought. *Is that my name?*

What is my name? he wondered.

My name? he wondered. *Why do I want to know?*

There was, he managed to trouble himself to remember, something in his hand, something important, but why or what, he couldn't remember. He tried to raise his hand but it wouldn't move. What was wrong with it? The other hand he tried to move and it came, and there, clutched in it, he saw a small black rectangle that just for a moment he found himself mistaking for an open doorway. But no, it was not that, it was smaller than his hand and pierced through with two toothed circles: a cassette.

He shook his head to clear it. It did not clear. He managed, after some effort, to raise the lid of the answering machine and pop the cassette out and get his own cassette in. He pressed the play button and then stumbled away toward where he hoped a chair would find him.

There was a crackle and a beep and the voice began to speak.

Hello, it said. *Mr. Hapner? Is that in fact the correct name? My name is Arnaud . . .*

Did it all come flooding back to him? Not exactly, no. It went on from there but he was no longer listening. *Hapner*, his mind was saying, *Arnaud*. He tried to sit down, crashed to the floor. He lay there, staring at the ceiling, trying to hold on to the two names, to keep them at least. But they were already slipping away.

VI.

He awoke to find himself lying on a couch, prone. Across from him, collapsed on the floor, was an abnormally large man with his shirt and hands smeared with blood, blood crusted around his eyes as well. The man's arm was clearly broken, turned out from the body at a senseless angle, a pinkish lump of bone protruding just above the wrist.

He sat up, feeling weak. His mouth was dry. When he tried to stand, he grew weak and quickly sat down again. He sat there on the couch, gathering his breath, waiting, staring at the man on the floor.

Did he know him? Surely he must know him or why else would they both be there?

"Hello?" he said to the man.

The man didn't move, dead probably.

But where was here? he wondered. Was this his apartment? It didn't look familiar exactly, but he couldn't bring another apartment to mind either. But if this was his, why wouldn't he know it?

He stood, and stumbled across the room and toward the kitchen, passing the man on the way. Up close he could see the man was clearly dead, his face the color of scraped bone, a smell coming off him.

In the kitchen he looked into the fridge, found it empty. The pantry was full of cans. He couldn't read any of the labels. *What's wrong with me?* he wondered. He opened a can and drank the contents cold—some kind of soup, glassy with oil on the top. After a while, he felt a little better.

When he went back into the living room, he saw the blinking light. It took him a moment to figure out what it meant, what it belonged to.

He had to stand on a foot ladder to reach it. The casing of the machine, he saw, was streaked with blood. He depressed the button.

Hello, a voice said. *Mr. Hapner? Is that in fact the correct name?*

Hapner, he thought, the name sizzling vaguely in his head and then beginning to fade. Unless it was not his house, unless the name belonged to the man dead on the floor. But no, it must be his name, it sounded right enough, and the foot ladder, the dead man wouldn't have needed a foot ladder to step on. *Ergo,* his house. *Ergo,* Hapner. *If that is in fact the correct name?*

There had been, the voice told him, Mr. Arnaud told him, a misunderstanding. Everyone's heart was in the right place. But he, Hapner, was being asked to contact Arnaud's wife, to pass on information, to find out what had become of him.

I must be a private detective, thought the small man, thought Hapner.

He went into the bathroom and looked at his face. He too, like the dead man, was wearing a mask of blood, the blood thickest around his eyes. They shared that at least. The face—small, pudgy—was unfamiliar. *But it must be my own face*, he thought. Nevertheless he couldn't help but reach out and touch the mirror, assure himself that it was solid, flat glass.

In the bedroom, he changed his clothes. The new clothes fit. Thus, this was his house. *Ergo.* Thus, he was Bentham. Or not Bentham exactly, Bentham was whom he was looking for. What had the name been exactly? It started with an *h*, he thought, or some similar letter. Similar in what way? He went back into the living room, skirting a dead body—had he seen it before? yes, he had, but who was it?—and depressed the answering-machine button again. Ah, yes. Hapner. That was him. And it was Arnaud he was looking for, not Bentham.

He got out a pen and a piece of paper and wrote it down, but found he could make no sense of the marks on the paper. *What's wrong?* he wondered, *what's wrong?* He would, he supposed, somehow just have to remember.

He started out the door—*Arnaud*, he was saying in his head, *Hapner, I'm Hapner, I'm looking for Arnaud*—and stopped dead. The other doors around his own had been barricaded over with sheets of plywood. *But why?* he wondered, and then wondered, *Why not my door?*

He went down the stairs and then down a hall whose walls were smeared with blood, then down another set of stairs that opened onto a lobby, two shattered glass doors leading out into the street. He pushed one open, felt a pricking on his hands and looked to see them glittery with powdered glass, minute cuts all over them. He used his shoe to open the door the rest of the way, stepped out into the street.

The street was deserted, a car overturned and burnt to a husk a dozen feet from where he stood, another car in the middle of the street, both doors open, clumps of paper eddying about it, garbage, a fine rain of ash. The building across the street from him, a large complex of some sort, was surrounded by a chain-link fence topped with barbed wire, another similar fence a half-dozen feet inside it and parallel to it, the gates of both fences twisted off their hinges. The building was set off from the road, and between him and it were scores of abnormally large men in white protective suits, sprawled about, no marks on them, suits intact, all probably dead. *Good Christ*, he thought. For just an instant, the scene wavered, flattening out in front of him, everything fading away or coming all too close. But then he blinked, and blinked again, and it all seemed all right again, though somehow the sun had moved and the sky had gone darker.

He crossed the street and passed through the gate and approached one of the prone men. The glass shield over the man's face was obscured by blood. He looked at another. It was the same. He stopped looking.

What am I doing? he wondered. *What am I looking for?*

He couldn't remember exactly. He was looking for something or someone, it started with, he could almost remember, it was a letter that he . . . perhaps *r?* But what did that tell him? It didn't tell him anything at all.

He turned around and looked over his shoulder at the building across the street. It was an apartment complex, ten or twelve stories tall, its door shattered.

He stood staring at it for a long time. Something about it struck him as significant. Familiar? What, he wondered again, was he looking for, and who was he exactly, again? What was the name?

He kept staring, feeling a slow panic welling through him.

He took a step forward without looking, almost fell over one of the bodies. He kicked it softly, then stepped around it.

I am looking for something, he tried to tell himself, or someone. Probably, he tried to tell himself, I'll know it when I find it.

He looked back again at the building across the street, then turned toward it.

Probably as good a place to start as any, he thought. He crossed the street, opened the door to the building. *Who knows what I will find?* he thought.

Another instant and he was gone.

Traub in the City

I.

Toward evening, well before Traub expected it, came a notable transformation in the face. The nose became more and more accentuated, like a blade, the cheeks grew hollow, the skin began to tighten. Traub continued trying to draw the profile, but the face was changing with such rapidity that he could capture it, when he captured it at all, only at several removes. He had the distinct impression that he was observing not one but several faces, coming one after another, quicker and quicker until finally, moments before death, the rush of faces was so rapid that it made Traub feel dizzy, and he forgot the paper, the pencil, and just watched, and in the vast shuffle of humanity nearly caught sight of himself.

II.

Days later, back in the city, having left the mountain inn, the body buried and left behind, Traub found himself shaken. He began to see heads in the emptiness, in all the space that surrounded them, isolated and remote. On the platform in the metro, surrounded by hundreds of people, he saw nothing but a series of heads, each suspended in a vast emptiness, each face in the crowd part and parcel of a single face that was changing with a rapidity he could no longer comprehend—as if a progression in time had been instead smeared out over space, all the faces of the city a record of one man's death. No matter where he was, he had the distinct impression that there was only he, Traub, sitting beside a bed where a body was slowly giving way, through a desperate flurry of faces, to an implacable and faceless corpse.

III.

How many nights?, Traub wondered about himself, night after night, as in the darkness that one face broke into multitudes and spread all about the ceiling separating out until each face was surrounded by a terrifying silence. All around him in the light of the street, the light of the moon, the room was rendered harsh and was taking on at last its true character, its true face: no object, he realized, touched any other—the legs of the chair, weightless, no longer touching the floor; the table too, shimmering and discrete; the curtains not touching the window, but rather each panel riding remote and alone. Everything was its own solitary world, he realized; if he tried to touch something, he would touch nothing. He rode on his bed above a void, was suspended above a solitary world that was a bed in his own solitary world, all of it hanging in a void. He lay there, feeling faces tick across his flesh like a clock, slowly now, but a little faster every day. *And who shall draw my profiles?*, he wondered, no longer certain of who he was. *And who shall render all my faces as I die?*

The Adjudicator

—for Peter Straub

We have been for some time putting our community back into a semblance of body and shape, and longer still sifting the living from the dead. There are so many who seem as alive as you and I (if I may be so bold as to number you, with myself, among the living) but who already are all but dead. Much has been done that would not be done in better times, and I too in desperation have committed what I ought not have, and indeed may well do so again.

I have become too accustomed to the signs and tokens of death. I meet them both in the faces of the living and in the remnants I have encountered in my daily round: the blackened arm my plough turned up and which I just as quickly turned back under again; the bloody marks smeared deep into the grain of the wood of my door and which I have not the fortitude to scrub away; the man who lies dying in the ditch between my farm and my neighbor's, and who, long dying, somehow still is not altogether dead.

Shall I start at the beginning? No, the end. Here am I, waiting for this same beditched man to either die or lurch to his feet and return to claw again at my door. I have no crops, my entire harvest having been pilfered or razed because of all I have witnessed and done and refused to do. If I am to make it alive to the next harvest, I must carefully pace the consumption of my few remaining stores. I must catch and eat what maggots and voles and vermin I can, glean and forage a little, beg mercy of my neighbors if any are still wont to deliver mercy to the likes of me. And then, if I am lucky, I shall sit here and starve for months, but perhaps not enough to die.

No, let us have the beginning after all: the end is too much with me, its breath already warm and damp on the nape of my neck.

At first there are wars and rumors of wars, then comes a light so bright that it shines through flesh and bone. Then a conflagration, the landscape peeled off and away, and nearly everyone dies. Those who do not die directly find themselves subject to suddenly erupting into pustules and bleeding from every pore and then falling dead. Most of the remainder are subject to a slow madness, their brains softened so as to slosh within their skulls. All but dead, these set about killing those who remain alive.

The few who survive unscathed are those in shelters underground or swaddled deep within a strong house. Or, simply, those who, like myself, seem not to have been afflicted for reasons no one can explain. Everything slides into nothingness and collapse, and for several years we all live like animals or worse, and then slowly we find our footing again. Soon some of us, maybe a few dozen, have banded together into this new order despite the disorder still raging in all quarters. We appoint a leader, a man named Rasmus. We begin to grow our scraggled crops. We form a pact to defend one another unto death.

At times I was approached by those who, having heard that I had been left unscathed in the midst of conflagration, believed I might provide some dark help to them. Others were more wary, keeping their distance as if from one cursed. Most, however, felt neither one thing nor the other, but saw me merely as a member of their community, a comrade-in-arms.

This, then, the fluid state of the world when, of a sudden, everything changed for me in the form of a delegation of men approaching my house. From a distance, I watched them come. The severed arm, having surged up under the sharp prow of the plough, was lying there, its palm open in appeal. Uncertain how they would feel about it, I quickly worked to have it buried again before they arrived.

I watched them come. One of them hallooed me when he saw me watching, and I waved back, then simply stood watching them come. I had grown somberly philosophical by this time, and was not distant enough from the conflagration ever to feel at ease. I still in fact carried a hatchet with me everywhere I went, and even slept with it beside me on the pillow. And it was upon this hatchet that Rasmus's eyes first alighted once the delegation had approached close enough to form a half-circle about me, and upon the way my hand rested steady on the haft.

"No need for that," he said. "Today will not be the day you hack me to bits."

This remark, perhaps lighthearted enough, based no doubt on the rumors of my past and meaning nothing, or at least little, drew my thoughts to the arm buried beneath my feet. I was glad, indeed, that I had again inhumed it.

"Gentlemen," I said, "to what do I owe this pleasure?" and I opened my pouch to them and offered them of my tobacco.

For a moment we were all of us engaged in stuffing and lighting our pipes, and then sucking them slowly down to ash, Rasmus keeping one finger raised to hold my question in abeyance. When he finished, he knocked the pipe out against the heel of his boot and turned fully toward me.

"We have an assignment for you," he said.

"The hell you have," I said.

Or at least wanted to say.

I do not know how to tell a story, a real one, or at least tell it well. Reading back over these pages, I see I have done nothing to give a sense of how it felt to have these determined men looming over me, their eyes strangely steady. Nor of Rasmus, with his wispy beard and red-pocked face. Why did we choose him as a leader? Because he was little good for anything else?

So, a large man, ruddy, looming over me, stabbing the air between us with a thick finger, nail yellow and cracking. Minions to either side of him.

What I said was not *The hell you have*, but "And it takes six of you to tell me?" Perhaps not, in retrospect, the wisest utterance, and certainly not taken exceptionally well. Not, to be blunt, in the proper community spirit. But once I was started down this path, I had difficulty arresting my career.

He tightened his lips and drew himself up a little, stiff now.

"What," he asked, "was your profession?"

"I have always been a farmer," I said. "As you yourself know."

"No," he said. "Before the conflagration, I mean."

"You know very well what I was before the conflagration," I said.

"I want to hear you say it," he said.

But I would not say it. Instead, I filled my pipe again as they regarded me. Then lit and smoked it. And he, for whatever reason, did not push his point.

"There are rumors about you," he claimed. "Are they true?"

"For the purposes of this conversation," I said, not knowing what he was talking about, which rumors, "you should assume they are all true."

"Paper," he said, and one of the others came forward, held out a folded sheet of paper. I stared at it a long time, finally took it.

"We have an understanding then," said Rasmus, and, before I could answer, started off. Soon, he and his company were lost to me.

After they had gone, I dug the arm up again and examined it, trying to determine how long it had been rotting and whether I had been the one to lop it free. In the end, I found myself no closer to an answer than in the beginning. Finally I could think to do nothing but plough it back under again.

The matter of my former profession amounts to this: I had no former profession. I was dissolute, poisonous to myself in any and all ways. At a certain moment, I reached the point where I would have done anything at all to have what I wanted, and indeed I often did. Many of the particulars have faded or vanished from my memory or been pushed deeper down until they can no longer be felt. There was one person, someone I was, in my own way, deeply in love with, whom I betrayed. Someone else, of a different gender, whose self I stripped away nerve by nerve.

When the conflagration came, it was nearly sweet relief for me. And, to be honest, what I did to survive, largely with the hatchet I still carry, is little worse, and perhaps better, than what I had done beforehand.

But for Rasmus, before the conflagration I had been a jack-of-all-trades, someone with little enough regard to take on any business, no matter how raucous or how bloody.

How much easier, I think now, *had I just raised my hatchet then and there with Rasmus and his crew and started laying into them. And then simply sewed their bits wide about my field and ploughed them in deep.*

There are other things I should tell, and perhaps still others forgotten that I shall never work my way back to. There are the rumors he had mentioned, asking if they were true. I cannot say one way or the other what he thought they were. Some people, as I have said, believe me charmed because of my aboveground survival, others believe me cursed. I am, I probably should have said before, completely devoid of hair—the only long-term consequence I suffered from the conflagration—and as such look to some homuncular, although as though not fully formed. I also heal, I have found, much faster than most, and it is, fortunately, somewhat difficult to inflict permanent damage upon me. It could be this that Rasmus had been referring to, which has become a rumor that I cannot die: a rumor that may well be disproved this winter. Or perhaps it was something else, something involving the past I have just elucidated above, or something touching on my deadly skill with the hatchet with which I live affectionately, as if it were a spouse. Who can say? Certainly not I.

The piece of paper, once unfolded and spread flat, read as follows:

In two days' time a man will approach your door. You will invite him in and greet him. You will share with him of your tobacco. You will converse with him. And then, when he stands to leave, you will lay into him with your hatchet until he is dead. This is the wish of the community, and we call upon you as a man of the community and one who has often proved himself capable.

There was, as one would have expected, no signature. The words themselves were simple and blocky, anonymous. I screwed the note into a twist and then lit one end of it, used it to ignite my pipe, discarded it in the fire, watched it become its own incandescent ghost and then flinder and flake away into nothingness.

How much shall I tell you about myself? Do I have anything to fear from you? How much can I tell you before I lose hope of holding, by whatever tenuous grasp, your sympathy? Or have I already gone too far?

I have no strong moral objection to murder pure and simple, nor, for that matter, to anything else. Why this is so, I cannot say. And yet I derive no pleasure from murder, have no taste for it. I was as content— and perhaps more content—being a simple farmer as I had ever been in my earlier, dissolute life. I felt as if most of my old self had been slowly torn free of the rest of me, and I was not eager to have it pressed back against me again.

True, I had, on the occasions when our community had been afflicted by swarms of the dead or dying, done my part and done it well. After a particular effort, standing blood-spattered over the remains of one of the afflicted who had refused to stop moving, I had sometimes seen the fear in the eyes of those who had observed my deeds. But I did not like Rasmus's quick slide from witnessing my having dispatched the dead to his assuming I would do the same without reluctance to the living. Not, again, that I had any reservations about the act of murder, only that I did not care to be taken for granted. And I knew from my past that, having been asked once, I would be asked again and again.

Still, there are sacrifices to be made when one has the privilege of living in a community. I could see no way around making this particular one, even if I was not, technically speaking, the one being sacrificed.

I spent the rest of the day at work on my house, replacing the shingling of the room where the wood had grown gaunt and had been bleached by wind and sun. The next day it was back to the fields, with ploughing and plant-ing to finish and the ditch to be diverted until the near field was a soppy patch that glimmered in the sunset. A pipe at evening as always, and early the next morning a walk two farms away for some more tobacco, trading for it a few handfuls of dried corn from the dwindling stores of the previ-ous year's harvest. Then a careful survey of the property, the dark, loamy earth of the still damp fields.

He came late in the day, just before sunset. Had I not known he was com-ing, I might well have been reluctant to swing wide the door, or at least would have opened it with hatchet raised and cocked back for the swing. He was a large man in broad-brimmed hat and long coat, wearing what once would have been called driving gloves.

"I have been sent to you," he said. "They claimed perhaps you could help me."

And so I ushered him in. I gestured to a chair near the fire. I placed my tobacco pipe and pouch within easy reach. I invited him to remove his gloves, his coat, his hat.

To this point there had been a certain inexorability to the proceed-ings, each moment a tiny and inevitable step toward the time when I would, without either fear or rage, raise my hatchet and make an end of the fellow.

And yet, when he was freed of hat and coat and gloves and I saw the bare flesh of his hands, his arms, his face, I suddenly found everything grown complex. What I had seen as a simple deathbound progression now became a sequence of events whose ending I could not foresee, one in which, from instant to instant, I could not begin to divine what would happen next.

What was it that had thrown me into such uncertainty? Had I, as in the dead art of a dead past, glimpsed in the lines and the contours of his visage the face of a long-lost brother? A long-lost lover? No, nothing as simple or as clever as that. Rather, it was the fact that his hands and arms, his face and skull, had been completely epilated. Like me, he had lost all his hair. Had he been a brother or a lover, it would not have been enough to confuse me. But this, somehow, was.

He came in, he sat. His hat and coat I hung from a hook beside my door. His gloves he paired and smoothed and laid gently over his knee once he had sat. His name was Halber, he claimed.

"And who was it sent you?" I asked, though I knew the answer.

Your leader, he claimed. Who had said that I would adjudicate for him.

"Adjudicate?" I said.

Yes, he claimed, since that was my role in the community or so he had been told by Rasmus.

I nodded for him to go on.

The story he unraveled was one of the utmost wrongheadedness. He had once, it seemed, so he claimed, owned all of this property, but when the conflagration had come he had traveled quickly and hurriedly to try to throw his body in the path of his parents' death. He had of course misthrown himself; they had died despite him, his mother going mad so that in the end he had had to be the one to kill her, and his father simply having his skin slough off until the bone was showing. Upon which he thought to return, but the world being as it was, he had spent many months just keeping alive, and only now had he begun to manage.

What he wanted, he stated, was not to reclaim his land. He understood well enough the degree to which everything had transformed. All he wanted was to be given a small plot of land and be allowed to farm it, so he could be back in a place that he knew, and to be accepted into the community. He had said this to Rasmus and the council, and they had deliberated for three days as he awaited their decision. At last they had sent him to me, the adjudicator.

Adjudicator, I thought. *Well, that's one name for it.*

I thought, too, with sudden insight, *Normally they would kill him themselves, and perhaps have done so with others in times past. But because, like me, he is hairless, they have sent him to me. They are frightened.*

And this made me think, too, of what they must have thought of me, and why they had chosen to admit me into the community. And I could not but think it was out of fear or because I was already there, and perhaps it was only because there were those among them who believed I was charmed or cursed and could not die. And perhaps soon, once I had done away with Halber and proved that a man like myself could be killed, they would see no reason not to do away with me as well.

"Please tell them," I said, "that I have thought carefully and have adjudicated in your favor. You shall join us."

He stood and awkwardly embraced me, an operation I suffered only with great reluctance. And then after gathering his things he left, leaving me to ponder why I had done what I had done, and what would be its dark consequence.

I was not to wonder long. Late that night I heard shouts and, as I roused myself, a banging had begun at my door. "It's Halber!" a man was screaming, his screams enough to curdle the blood. "It's Halb! Let me in!"

And indeed I almost did. I might well have, had I not heard the other voices and sounds that followed, the grunts and indifferent, dull sounds of metal slipping into flesh, and heard the pounding suddenly stop. I climbed onto the bed and looked down through the high window. In the pale moonlight I saw him, dying and staring, being dragged away by the legs. Had it been only a pack of the dead and the dying, I would have perhaps opened the door and commenced to lay about me with my hatchet, as I had done in the past when the dead came for the living. But as it was, seeing that the faces were those of the living, Rasmus's face among them, I hesitated just long enough to feel that it was too late.

And perhaps it is there that the story should have ended. Perhaps, had I said nothing, done nothing, kept to my house, then my reputation, the myths surrounding me, would have been enough for Rasmus and his council to decide to let me be. Perhaps they would have grudgingly levied a fine, remembered my usefulness in other ways, and life would have gone much as usual, if anything can be described as usual in these days. But we both of us made mistakes that made this impossible.

The mistake I made was in not staying to my house for a few days, deciding instead to tend to my crops, to go about the business that needed to be attended to on my farm. This, under most circumstances, would not be considered a dire mistake. Or, to be frank, in most conditions, even a mistake at all.

Their mistakes were more severe. Tired of dragging the body, they abandoned it in a ditch halfway between my and my neighbor's farms. And instead of tearing the head free of the corpse and incinerating it, they left the hairless Halber lacerated but more or less intact.

With every disaster, I have come to believe for my own personal reasons, comes a compensation, a certain balancing of the accounts—not spread evenly about but clumped here and there, of benefit to very few. I heal, as I said, very quickly—or at least I do now; before the conflagration I did not. There are rumors I cannot die. Not having died, I can neither confirm nor deny these rumors, nor am I curious enough to uncover the truth that I feel compelled to slit my own throat. But from what I have seen of what is happening to Halber, I fear these rumors might well be true, and hardly in the way one would hope.

So, we have reached the day after Halber was hauled away, my door clawed and scratched on the outside, the bloody marks of his dying smeared there and on the threshold. I stare at the door a moment, checking to see whether my hatchet is with me. Outside, there are always things to attend to, things to do to keep the farm going. I do them, wondering all the while when, if ever, the little poultry and livestock remaining in the area will start to breed again and if I will ever be able to afford my own chickens. I irrigate my fields again, just enough, then sit on a stone near the border of the field, and smoke.

That is when I begin to hear it, a slow and distant whistle, a soft wind. At first I think nothing of it. But when it persists, I become afflicted with the disease of curiosity.

I stand, trying to ascertain where it is coming from. I follow it in one direction, then another. It slowly becomes louder, just a little louder, just a little louder, a moan now.

It is some time still before I make my way out to the road and follow it a little distance down and find him there, Halber, bloody in the ditch, grievously wounded—by all rights he should be dead.

What do I do? One look is enough to tell me he should be dead. I have dealt often enough with the living turned dead to be leery, but he struck me as something different, as a new thing.

He was in any case too hurt to be moved. I went back to the house, brought back a blanket and some water. I wrapped him in the former and dribbled the latter into his mouth. He was delirious and hardly conscious. He would, it seemed to me, soon be dead.

And so I stayed there beside him, waiting for him to die.

Only he did not die. His body seemed unable to let go but also unable to heal itself, and so he struggled there between life and death. I thought for a moment to kill him, but what if he did heal himself? I wondered. Was he not like me? Would he not eventually heal himself?

In the end I left him and went home to sleep.

That night I dreamt of him, lying there in his ditch, slowly dying but never dead, breathing in his shallow way but breathing despite everything, never stopping. And then, his breathing no less shallow, he managed over the course of long, painful moments to make it to his feet and shuffle forward, like the walking dead. I watched him coming. Later, much later in my head, I heard a knocking and a dim, inarticulate cry and knew him—suddenly and with, for once, a certain measure of terror—to be knocking on my door.

When I came back the next morning, I found my blanket was gone, stolen. Some creature had eaten most of one of his hands and the finer portion of his face. But he was still, somehow, alive. And so I slit his throat and watched the blood gurgle out, and then went back to get on with my work.

This seemed to me sufficient, and I must confess that I did not think about him through the course of my day. There were fences to be attended to, wood to be chopped, brush to be cleared. A corner of the field had become too soggy and I found myself cutting a makeshift drainage channel, thinking up its course as I went. By the end of the day I was mud-spattered, my bones and muscles aching.

And still, as the sun set, I found my thoughts returning to Halber. I could not stop myself from going to see him.

There are strange things that happen that I cannot explain, and this is one of them. He was as I had left him, but still alive. His throat, I saw, had filmed over, the veins not reconnecting exactly but blood moving there, pulsing back and forth within the film in a kind of delicate bag of blood and nascent tissue, pus-like. I watched it beat red, then beat pale, in the gap where his throat had been. At that sight I nearly severed his head from his shoulders, but I was too terrified of what would happen inside of me if I removed his head, and somehow, despite this, he still refused to die.

So instead I went home and sharpened my hatchet.

What can I say about the night that followed, when I chose to become the one who would judge who lived and who died? I have no apologies for what I did, nor any justification, either. I did it simply because I could think of nothing else to do. I am neither proud of my actions nor regretful.

I sharpened the hatchet until it had a fine and impossible edge, and then in the dark I set out. Perhaps if I had met some of the dying and the afflicted, some of those made vicious and deranged by the conflagration, I would have been satisfied. But the only one I met in my path was Halber, and I gave the fellow a wide berth.

What need is there to pursue in detail what followed next? I did unto Rasmus as might be expected. A single blow of the hatchet and I was through his door. I caught him on his way out of bed as he moved down the hall and went after his gun, the hatchet cutting through his back and ribs and puncturing one lung so that it hissed. He went down in a heap, groaning and breathing out a mist of blood, and I severed first one forearm, then the other, and, as his eyes rolled back, lopped off his head. His wife arose screaming from the bed and rushed to the window and tried to hurl herself through. I struck her on the back of the skull with the cronge of the handle, meaning only to silence her screams, but it was clear from the way she fell and the puddle of blood that soon spread from her head that perhaps I had struck too hard. Then I approached Rasmus again and very delicately, with the sharpest part of the blade, peeled off his face.

The other five who had earlier come with him to see me now suffered the same fate, though I killed them more swiftly, with a single blow, and did not disjoint or decorticate them as I had their leader. There is no need to say more than that, I suppose. In the end, I was sodden with blood and gore, and made my way back to my farmhouse, past the still dying Halber, and slept the sleep of the truly dead.

I awoke to the smell of burning, saw when I burst open the door that they had set my fences afire. My fields, too, had been trampled apart, then the ditch redirected and trenches dug to wash away the topsoil. Had my house not been stone, they would have burnt that, too. I stared at the flames a moment and then, not knowing what else to do, went back to bed.

•

It was a week before I could bring myself to leave the house. Finally I stripped off my gory clothing, the blood now gone black, and burnt it in the fireplace. Then I took water from the irrigation canal and washed in it and dressed myself in my town clothes and set off for my neighbor's farm.

I do not know what I expected. At the very least I expected, I suppose, for Halber to be dead. But he was still alive, still feebly dying in the ditch. I chose not to get close to him.

My neighbor was at his farm, his crops just starting to sprout. When he saw me coming, he rushed inside, came out with his rifle.

"Not another step," he said.

I stopped. "Do you think your gun can stop me?" I asked him.

"I don't know," he said, "but if you come any closer we shall find out."

"I have no grudge against you," I said. "I only want those who destroyed my crops."

"Then you want me," he said. "You want all of us, the community."

"But why?"

"Can you possibly ask?"

And I suppose in good conscience I could not, though I thought my neighbor had at least a right to know why I had done what I had done. So I sat on the ground and kept my hand far away from the hatchet and, rifle trained on me, recounted to him, just as I have recounted to you, all that had occurred.

When I was finished, he shook his head. "We have all been through much," he said, "and you have made us go through more. None of us are perfect men, but you are less perfect than most."

Then he gestured with his gun. "Come with me," he said.

He led me back to the road and toward my farm, to the place in the ditch where the dying man was to be found.

"Is this the man you meant?" he asked.

"Yes," I said. "Halber."

"But you can see for yourself that he has been long dead," he said. "And that when he was alive he was not hairless but in fact replete with hair. Please," he said, "go away and do not come back."

But I could not see it. Indeed, to me he still appeared as hairless as a baby and, though dying, still alive. I wondered to myself what my neighbor was trying to do to me. Had he not had his gun trained upon me, I would have turned upon him and laid into him with my hatchet. Instead, I simply turned away from him and returned to my house.

•

Where I have been ever since. I do not know if what is wrong is wrong with me or wrong with the world. Perhaps there is a little of both. I find it difficult to face the man dying in the ditch, and it is clear that my neighbors and I no longer live in altogether the same worlds.

It seems strange to think that after all this, after my years of dissolution and then the hard years after the conflagration, I might die here alone, might slowly starve to death. Assuming it is true that I can in fact die.

I will make do as long as I can and then when my straits are indeed dire I shall leave my house and beg mercy from my neighbors. Perhaps they will show mercy, even if only out of fear, or perhaps they will kill me. Either way, it cannot be but a relief.

As for now, though, I shall sit here and write and very slowly starve, waiting part in anticipation and part in fear for the moment when the dying man who so greatly resembles me shall drag himself to his feet and leave his ditch and come again to knock at my door.

This time I shall be ready for him. This time I shall know what to do.

COLOPHON

Fugue State was designed at Coffee House Press,
in the historic Grain Belt Brewery's Bottling House near downtown Minneapolis.
The text is set in Garamond.

FUNDER ACKNOWLEDGMENTS

Coffee House Press is an independent nonprofit literary publisher. Our books are made
possible through the generous support of grants and gifts from many foundations, corporate giving programs, state and federal support, and through donations from individuals who believe in the transformational power of literature. Coffee House receives major
general operating support from the McKnight Foundation, the Bush Foundation, from
Target, and from the Minnesota State Arts Board, through an appropriation by the
Minnesota State Legislature and from the National Endowment for the Arts. Coffee
House also receives support from: three anonymous donors; the Elmer L. and Eleanor J.
Andersen Foundation; Bill Berkson; the James L. and Nancy J. Bildner Foundation; the
Patrick and Aimee Butler Family Foundation; the Buuck Family Foundation; the law firm
of Fredrikson & Byron, PA.; Jennifer Haugh; Anselm Hollo and Jane Dalrymple-Hollo;
Jeffrey Hom; Stephen and Isabel Keating; Robert and Margaret Kinney; the Kenneth
Koch Literary Estate; Allan & Cinda Kornblum; Seymour Kornblum and Gerry Lauter;
the Lenfestey Family Foundation; Ethan J. Litman; Mary McDermid; Rebecca Rand;
the law firm of Schwegman, Lundberg, Woessner, PA.; Charles Steffey and Suzannah
Martin; John Sjoberg; Jeffrey Sugerman; Stu Wilson and Mel Barker; the Archie D. &
Bertha H. Walker Foundation; the Woessner Freeman Family Foundation; the Wood-Rill
Foundation; and many other generous individual donors.

NATIONAL
ENDOWMENT
FOR THE ARTS

*This activity is made possible
in part by a grant from the
Minnesota State Arts Board,
through an appropriation by the
Minnesota State Legislature
and a grant from the National
Endowment for the Arts.*

MINNESOTA
STATE ARTS BOARD

TARGET.

To you and our many readers across the country,
we send our thanks for your continuing support.

Good books are brewing at coffeehousepress.org

Praised by Peter Straub for going "furthest out on the sheerest, least sheltered narrative precipice," **BRIAN EVENSON** is the author of eight previous books of fiction, including *Last Days* and the Edgar and International Horror Guild Award-nominated novel *The Open Curtain*. He lives in Providence, Rhode Island where he directs Brown University's Literary Arts Program. Visit his web site at www.brianevenson.com.

ZAK SALLY is the author of the graphic novel *Recidivist,* nominated for two Eisner Awards and named one of SPIN magazine's "favorite things." He is also the author of the Fantagraphic Books *Sammy the Mouse* series, the former bassist of the band Low, and the publisher of La Mano press in Minneapolis.

Printed in the USA
CPSIA information can be obtained
at www.ICGtesting.com
JSHW022005270524
63875JS00004B/34